# Back Into Black

## THE GRAY WOLVES MC CASCADE OF LIES
### BOOK 3

**R. B. CARIAD**

# Connect With R. B. Cariad

Join R. B. Cariad and The Cascade of Lies by signing up for her
newsletter and giveaways at
Home – R. B. CARIAD author (rbcariadauthor.com)

Follow RB on Facebook
R. B. Cariad

Instagram
@rbcariadauthor

Tik-Tok
@rbcariadauthor

# Acknowledgments

To my beautiful family, thank you for the love and support.

To Trev, my biggest fan. Thanks for reading everything I threw at you.
When God made sisters, he gave me a best friend, too!

To Cain, who read my very first notes and encouraged me to pursuit
my dream and to Dav, and Bethan, thanks for supporting me and
keeping me stocked in Penderyn Whisky.

To my hometown, you will never know how much you changed my life
with your love, support, and encouragement. Thank you!

And to my ARC readers, Booktokkers and Bookstagrammers who love
to get lost in a world of dark and handsome bikers.
This one's for you!

# CHAPTER ONE
## On His Way

"Agent Reed, we've just had confirmation of a sixth body. Female, late thirties, blond hair, blue eyes. Same MO, beaten, tattoos removed, and a knife to the heart."

Frankie loosened his tie and pinched his nose. He'd not slept a wink since leaving Uskiville. Three months had passed since he last saw B: he missed her, but he knew her life depended on his mission to bring Jericho to justice.

Three months of tracking his best friend's killer was too much. Frankie was tired of discovering bodies left by the man who tormented his soul. The man who left messages on his victim's body for Frankie to find, letting him know he was coming for his family.

Jericho Walters had to be found and before he killed another of Frankie's best friends.

"Agent Reed…"

"I heard. Thank you. Location?"

"Pleasant Hill. Contra Costa. A twenty-year-old female discovered the body on her way to the train station at 05:30 hours. The whack job dumped the body at the station. Propped her up on a park bench."

Frankie shook his head. "Jeez! Security footage?"

"Yeah. He smiled and blew a kiss at the camera. He's taunting us, sir."

"Don't call me sir. You track him from the station?"

The junior agent shook his head as he fidgeted in the doorway. "He just vanished. We couldn't locate him after that."

"What the fuck do you mean, he just vanished? How is he doing this to us? Every fucking time," Frankie said, rising from his black leather office chair to stand at the window.

"I'm sorry. We haven't been able to establish that yet. We've scanned through every inch of the security footage, and we still know nothing."

"Then what *do* we know, agent?"

"Uh, he left another message."

Frankie spun around, raising an eyebrow to see the junior agent gulp. The fear in his eyes and clammy looking skin suggested he was more terrified of Frankie than he was of Jericho himself.

"Well?" Frankie raised his voice.

"It wasn't your name carved into the torso like the other five victims. This time he left this." The agent's shaking hand handed Frankie a photograph of the corpse.

Staring at the victim, Frankie swallowed hard. Nausea reared its ugly head as the color drained from his face. A single bead of sweat trickled down his temple. The likeness was uncanny, creating uneasiness within Frankie's already tormented soul. Jane Doe had a striking resemblance to B, just like Jericho's other victims, only *she* could have been B's doppelgänger. Her skin on her tattooed rib is missing; cut out and the chilling words carved into her defined abdominal muscles made Frankie's hair stand on end.

*You're next, Dragon!*

Frankie clutched his jaw, covering his mouth with his free hand. He knew Jericho would come for her after she extracted evidence from Blaze, naming Jericho as Rocky's murderer. He also believed one of Blaze's little spies contacted Jericho following his escape from the farmhouse that night. Local PD had picked him up after he made multiple phone calls and sent detailed messages to a series of burner phones. Frankie remained adamant one of those messages was a warning to Jericho.

With the burner phones untraceable, Frankie had grilled the little spy for days, only to find him dead in his cell prior to Frankie's final intended interrogation.

*No doubt Jericho tying up loose ends.*

Regaining his senses, he donned his FBI cap.

"I want every available agent on this case. We have a serial killer roaming the streets like he fucking owns them. Jericho is targeting women and has his eye on another innocent woman who aided our case. He has to be found."

The agent shuffled with nervousness toward Frankie. "Forgive me, Agent Reed. I thought Blethen Jones is the girlfriend of the notorious Alexander McGovan. That hardly makes her innocent. Maybe she's meddled in club business, or they have targeted her due to whom she's connected to."

Frankie bared his teeth. Clenching his fists and dragging in a deep breath to stop himself from killing his junior agent. "Come here, boy!"

The pale-faced agent hesitated at first. Stepping forward, Frankie grabbed him by the scruff of his shirt before he planted his leading foot.

The agent froze. The terror in his eyes, showing the fear that Frankie imagined consumed every fiber in his body.

Frankie's glare was beyond terrorizing as he ground out through gritted teeth, "You may have graduated top of your class, boy, but it's clear you haven't brought yourself up to speed on this case and I don't do sloppy. Blethen Jones is an innocent civilian. Who she acquaints herself with is no concern of yours, especially when the Bureau is also responsible for her being the target of a serial killer."

"Sorry, sir, I mean Agent Reed. I meant no disrespect."

"Your slapdash investigation skills and lack of knowledge on this case are very disappointing, agent. I suggest you study the case files in their entirety before casting aspersions and making assumptions. Maybe then you'll bring something useful to the table."

Frankie released the horrified agent. "Leave," he breathed.

The inexperienced agent rushed toward the door in haste.

"Agent?" Frankie called, providing an evil and serious stare. "Let's be clear. My superior officer brought you onto my team in my absence. Our superiors may have seen something in you, but I have yet to see a glimmer of talent since my return. The point being, I'll toss your ass back to street beating if you're unable to demonstrate the basic competencies of the job and I couldn't care less how special you're perceived to be. There's no room for showboating time wasters on my team. You earn your spot here. Understood?"

"Understood, Agent Reed."

"Good. Now don't come back until you've given this case the attention it deserves. And close my fucking door!"

The pouting agent left Frankie to ponder in his thoughts.

Frankie knew he had to find Jericho fast, and he had to warn Sunnyville of an impending attack on B's life. Jericho was going to find her and, when he did, B would meet her maker if Frankie and the Gray Wolves failed to protect her.

The morgue reeked of death as if the grim reaper himself was present, as Frankie walked the eerie, gray corridors to the coroner's office. There wasn't a single window in sight to release the pungent smell of decay wafting into his nasal cavity as he approached the cold steel door to the coroner. Frankie didn't hesitate in opening the door. Jericho had made him immune to corpses these past months. The only difference this time, the chilling words carved into his victim's torso were now addressed to B, confirming her as his next target.

The resemblance seemed less uncanny in the flesh with Frankie making a mental note of all the subtle differences between the victim and B. The aesthetics were identical for sure, only the victim was at least a foot shorter with a larger bone structure than B, and upon closer inspection, her nails had been bitten down to nothing, and her eyebrows met in a mono brow. Frankie found himself a little insulted on B's behalf. B was far more athletic and would never bite her nails.

A strange wave of relief washed over him after seeing the body. Despite knowing B was safe in Sunnyville, Frankie almost felt that he had to see for himself that she wasn't the one lying on the stiff body tray.

The coroner distracted his thoughts as he gazed upon the victim.

"It just makes you count your blessings, doesn't it? This woman had half her life left in her until that sinister monster stole it. I tell you, Frankie, this job just gets harder and harder."

Frankie sighed. "Yeah. It's a tragedy alright."

The coroner returned the victim to the refrigerator. "You caught the perp, then?"

Frankie sighed. "Unfortunately, not."

"I hope you catch the monster soon. I'll sleep better knowing there's one less serial killer roaming the streets," the coroner said, removing his medical gloves.

Frankie followed him to the sink, observing his disciplined hand-washing regimen. "Anything new with this victim, doc?"

The coroner shook his head. "Apart from the carvings on her torso. Were you hoping for something else?"

Frankie shrugged. "Nah., I got what I need. I'll see you round," he said, making way for the exit.

He couldn't wait to leave the building, to relieve himself of the rotten stench engulfing his pores. He wondered how the coroner and staff could stand breathing in the stale air for a minimum of forty hours a week.

*Probably used to it!*

Stepping out into the icy darkness of night, Frankie dragged in as much of the freezing air as he could muster. Attempting to flood his lungs with the fresh air, Frankie peered up at the night's sky, relieving himself of the carbon dioxide in his lungs before smiling up at the radiant-looking stars. He loved to star-gaze. It was one of his favorite pastimes. He would often stargaze with Madoc and Rhys, and the starlit sky gifted him with beautiful memories tonight.

*Oh B, we gotta end this! I can't lose you, too!*

# CHAPTER TWO

# Lovers on the Ridge

B and Zander sat on the ridge in Portland staring out into the distance, Zander behind B with his arms wrapped around her.

"It's so nice to get a quiet minute with you," he said, nuzzling into her neck. Her scent mesmerized him as he inhaled her essence.

"Play your cards right and I might even cook for you tomorrow night?"

"Steak and BJ night sounds good," he teased, "A home cooked meal followed by ravishing you by the fire. I've missed that!"

"That's not my fault, good boy. We'd do it more often if you weren't too busy with club business," B scolded, her eyes stern and fixated on the valley.

*Great. She's pissed already. Nice start Zander!*

"Come on now. I'm trying to maintain a balance between the club and the business. Even you dinnae expect the success it's had. You need to employ more staff, sweetheart. I wouldn't be so stretched then." Zander pleaded.

"My business isn't the problem, Sunshine. It's the club. You have plenty of new members and prospects there. Seriously. How much work is there to do? You're only running an MC and looking after my business when I'm coaching."

"And ensuring we support their families. That's a full-time job on its own darling and you wanted this, remember? You wanted me to lead, and that's what I'm doing. You forget, this was yours and Noah's vision. I'm merely trying to help it into fruition."

B turned to look at him. The hurt in her expression was clear and growing. "Scottie, I didn't expect the club to take up all your time. Mackie seems to thrive in Uskiville with the club and the business, so why can't you with your fantastic brain? How are we supposed to grow our family if you're never around? You have nagged for children of your own and there's no chance I'm doing that alone."

Zander snarled, almost baring teeth. "Dinnae compare me to him. I have more to be concerned with down here."

"Oh, sorry! I didn't realize I was a concern."

"Welsh Cake," he sighed.

"Don't Welsh Cake me. I'm sick of being cast aside and you have no idea how hard it is to raise children. Don't get me wrong, I wouldn't change my experience of motherhood for anything, but it's bloody exhausting and you dividing your time and putting me last doesn't work for me."

Zander stared at her, paying attention to her resurfacing rage.

B continued. "Family clearly doesn't mean much when it comes to me anymore, does it? And I refuse to bring up your children while you prioritize the family who are more important to you at present."

"Whoa. Jesus, Welsh Cake. I understand you're hurting, but that's just stone cold. Everything I do is for you. I fucking knew this would happen. It's why I dinnae want to lead."

B kneeled, attempting to stand, and Zander pulled her into his lap, attempting to hide the hurt he experienced. Inhaling a deep breath, he looked into her eyes. Fear replaced the fire as she turned away from him. He pressed his head to her temple and stroked her back. "I've no' deserted you, darling. I promise to make everything right again and this bullshit about raising our future bairns alone. That's no' gonnae happen. I'll sort it out, but you need to hire someone to run the gym.

It's over-extending me with you out coaching and teaching most days."

B didn't look at him, her tension crushing him as her rigid body sat in his lap, her attention lost in her thoughts.

"Hey, look at me."

B shook her head.

Zander closed his eyes. "Please, Welsh Cake. I hate seeing you upset. I understand you're wary of strangers after all that's happened, but you need to hire people and trust that I'll let nothing happen to you."

"And I do. I locked the fiery dragon away and threw away the key, didn't I?"

"Yeah, and I appreciate that. Now, if you won't hire externally, please at least consider Hyde's offer to take my place as the gym manager? He's smart and excels under pressure. I will have plenty of free time then, and you like him. You trust him."

B pursed her lips, her head snapping to face him, providing her usual indecisive stare.

"Just think about it, please?"

"Fine. I'll consider it! But my birth control stays until I see more of you. It's pointless being in a relationship with a guy who's never home."

Zander's face became stern. "That's no' fucking fair. You're being a bitch now, and I wanted to spend some quality time with you today."

"Only because you've remembered I exist. You must be getting your end away at the club because you've not been near me," she screamed.

Zander's face crumpled. His brow furrowed as he attempted to find his words.

"You really believe that shit you're spewing? How dare you? I've no' looked at anyone. I'm knackered because I'm doing everything you've asked and have done since the day we fucking met. Welsh Cake, I'm stupid soft with you and I'm trying here. I never wanted to fucking lead. Accepting the Prez seat was the only way to keep you, and you have the audacity to question my loyalty? For fuck's sake, woman!"

B stood up, attempting to leave once more, tying her hair up in a bobble. "Let's just go home."

Zander grimaced. "You've wanted to come here for weeks, and you want to leave after five minutes of giving me hell?"

"You're bloody right I do! I imagined our experience differing from bickering and causing pain to one another," she said, walking away.

Zander stood before chasing after her, stopping her by grabbing her around the waist. "How about you tell me what's really pissing you off instead of picking a fight with me? You're only a nasty bitch when you're hurting, and I know you know I have always been faithful to you. So fucking spill, otherwise you'll go over my knee."

B couldn't look at him. He could see she was trying her best to stifle a giggle at his remark.

"*You* are what's pissing me off," she said.

"Yes, but something else is bothering you. Something bigger. You're in your 'fuck everyone and everything and I dinnae care who I hurt' mode. You have been for weeks. Even the laddies are treading on eggshells. This isn't healthy for our family."

B escaped his grasp. Only Zander's determination to get answers encouraged him to continue. Grabbing her T-shirt, he pressed. "You've been closed off again. Like you were when we first met. I dinnae like it. We're a team now, remember? Cut you and I bleed, so please start talking to me, darling."

B sighed, releasing a sharp breath. Her shoulders were still tight around her ears as she raised her head to meet his gaze. "He's coming for me, Scottie. I know he is, and Frankie won't pick up the phone. It's been three months!"

"He's just overloaded with work, I expect."

B rolled her eyes. "I'm not bloody stupid. Something is wrong. Every time I get my life together, something happens. And I'm tired. I want to build a future without all these bloody roadblocks. Why does this shit keep happening to me?"

Zander sighed into a smile for her. Taking her hands, he brought them to his lips. Kissing her, he held her head to ensure she maintained eye contact. "It's no' happening to you. It's happening *for* you."

B narrowed her eyes. "Fuck my life! What? Some fucker trying to kill me is beneficial to my life? What silly pills are you taking, Boyoh?"

"Darling, the world is bigger than us, and for whatever reason, this situation with Jericho is happening. We can either bury our heads or confront it head on. Either way, I'll be ready!"

"So, you agree, this is obstructing our future?"

Zander shook his head. "No, this is a tiny fucking pothole in a huge highway. Nothing is impeding our future. We have everything we ever wanted, well almost," he said, gesturing to her stomach. "Nothing is going to happen to you because you are fortunate to have a Prez whose soul you fucking own and an enormous pack of wolves supporting you. We would all die for you. You know that."

B nodded. "It feels like I'm a prey waiting to be hunted. When I caged my inner Dragon, all this fear and anxiety rose from the pit of my stomach. I feel weak, vulnerable, insecure even. and I don't like it."

"That's because you're not used to trusting people. You're getting there, and I'm proud of you for it. You just need to let everything go and understand I got you. I promise I will have his head sooner rather than later. You'll see," he said, giving her a wink.

"No. You'll give him to Frankie and let the FBI deal with him."

Zander scoffed. "Aye."

B scowled. "I fucking mean it, good boy."

Zander raised his hands. "Okay, I heard you. Now can we please just enjoy each other's company?" he said, pulling her to sit down again. "Here, you're all tense. Allow my magic hands to ease that tension and, while you're at it, finish that story about how you came up with the club patch? Christ knows how many times you've tried to tell it."

"You promise you'll come home early tomorrow so we can have a proper date night? I can't cope with five minutes here and there anymore. It's killing me, Scottie."

"I'm sorry, darling. I'll do better, and I promise you'll have my undivided attention tomorrow evening."

"No wolves keeping us company? I mean, Tyr is a lovely boy, but I want my Prez."

Zander kissed her shoulder. "You and I. Steak, a bottle of wine and you in my favorite red dress. No interruptions. I'll make amends for making you lonely. Now, allow my hands to relieve your tension. I don't plan on leaving here until you're relaxed and happy."

"That may take a while, Sunshine."

"We'll see," he said, unbuttoning her jeans.

# CHAPTER THREE

# The Last of the Original Nine

Jericho waltzed into Blaze's old compound. It was difficult to see what remained of Blaze's former club in the dark night sky. The sound of scurrying feet was his only inclination toward their whereabouts.

"There's only four of you left, by my count. Now don't be shy. I demand your presence as your superior."

A man emerged from the shadows, donned in camouflage, wearing his Pitbull cut. His buzz-cut appeared as sharp as his knife as he stepped into the light reflecting from the building behind them.

"Who are you?"

"I'm the destroyer of dreams. The man who takes what can't be taken. I'm one of the original nine. And to whom am I speaking?"

"Sully. Blaze's former club chaplain. Now show me your patch."

Jericho grinned, waving his arms in a theatrical dance. "I'm wearing it. Can't you see the Pitbull among the expressive art?" he asked, pointing to the Red Pitbull on his decorated cut.

"What the fuck is all over it?"

"The tattoos of my enemies, of course. Everyone needs a trophy or two," he twirled around, showing off the skin-filled cut.

"That's disturbing," Sully said.

"No, that's a colorful expression. Come now, Sully. We have work to do, and as your ranking officer, I demand you swear allegiance to me as your Prez."

Sully stepped closer. "And how do we know you haven't picked up that cut anywhere?"

"Nobody could create art like me, pretty boy. Besides, impersonating a Pitbull? That's a death sentence and blasphemy frankly. Now watch your tongue."

Three other men stepped out from the shadows; their aggressive stares fixed on Jericho.

"Prove you're a Pitbull. Show your patch or my guys will fillet you," Sully shouted.

"Don't make idle threats, silly dick! Atticus contacted me. Informed me of Blaze's demise. Now my question is, how did you four escape the clutches of the FBI? And don't lie to me. Liars get punished," Jericho sneered.

"We're not telling you shit until you show us your tattoo, asshole." Sully snapped, pumping his chest as if he was gearing himself up for battle.

Jericho raised his hands. "Oh, alright. Honestly, so uptight. Pretty, but uptight," he teased, removing his cut.

Another man attempted to reach for it, and Jericho pulled out a switchblade from his pocket. "Look, don't touch," he snapped.

"It's one of hours. Sergeant at Arms," the man shouted to Sully.

Maintaining a watchful eye while removing his pink T-shirt, Jericho's temper soared. He disliked showing his body to strangers. Rocky was the only man who had ever seen the damage beneath his cut, and removing his clothes stung as much as the memories of Rocky did.

Sully gave Jericho an inquisitive stare as he revealed the Red Pitbull patch on his back.

The other three men gawked in horror at Jericho's burns, accounting for fifty percent of his torso. His patch was the only area of his skin unscathed.

"Jeez, dude! You look like a burned kid's figurine. Who melted you?" another man taunted.

Jericho paused for a second, his childhood trauma replaying in his head. "Come see it. You can check the authenticity of my patch," he said, ushering the man closer.

"Why is it on your back? Everyone else's is on their forearm. It's what separates us from other clubs. Pitbulls aren't afraid to show who they are," Sully said.

"My arms are covered in burns, in case you haven't noticed," Jericho hissed, directing his attention to his scarred limbs.

The man who had approached stopped and stood less than a foot away. "God, dang! You're one crispy son of a bitch!"

Jericho cracked his neck in readiness before moving swiftly to plunge his switchblade into the man's chest, guiding him to the ground.

Sully and the two remaining men rushed to their fallen brother. "You killed him," Sully said in astonishment.

Jericho shrugged. "He was disrespectful," he said, his expression unfazed as he removed the blade, wiping the blood onto a handkerchief he retrieved from his jeans pocket. "Now, gentlemen, allow me to introduce myself. My name is Jericho Walters."

The men gasped, stepping back with wide-eyed expressions.

"Judging by the fear in your eyes, I'm guessing you've heard of me?"

"You're Jericho?" Sully asked.

"Let me guess, you were expecting a big tree trunk of a man. The type that makes men cower. Oh, gentlemen, gent-tle-men, have you not learnt from your brother's demise? Size doesn't matter, and neither does my feminine voice. It's what's in here that makes me more dangerous than any man alive," he said, tapping his temple.

"What is it you want?" Sully asked.

"The same thing as you, I expect. To wreak havoc on those who caused us pain. To seek revenge for our fallen comrades. The Mauler and Blaze were my brothers. Now, I'll ask you again, how did you evade the FBI?"

"We weren't in town when shit went south. Blaze worried the

bitch wouldn't show, so he sent us to collect her and ensure she made it to the farm. Only she must have taken another route," Sully explained. "By the time we arrived, the farm was swarming with Feds. We thought it best to head here and wait for Blaze to call."

"Only Blaze was already dead?" Jericho responded.

Sully stared at the ground. "Yeah! Artemis called. He escaped long enough to explain what had happened. We planned to regroup, only the FBI nabbed him."

Jericho got dressed. "Yes, yes, Arty, called me on Blaze's cell. I informed him I'd return after I dealt with some other business."

"Yeah, he said you'd help us. That was before he died in his cell months ago. What took so long?"

"Like I said. I had business to attend to. Besides, planning takes time," Jericho said, swaggering toward the club house.

"Where are you going?" Sully shouted, his impatience growing.

"To take my place in the Prez's office. We have a church meeting tomorrow, gentlemen. Right now, I need my beauty sleep."

"Wait! Becoming Prez requires all our votes," his brother in arms shouted again.

Jericho didn't bother to turn around. "I already have them unless you want to meet your pal in the happily never after. Bring the body, he has something I require for my cut."

# CHAPTER FOUR

# Deceit

The sun had long gone down when Zander sat in church staring at his cell phone. Frankie's name flashed along the screen, making him sigh as he answered. "More developments?" he asked.

"Another one. More likeness to B, and this time he's stated his intentions. I sent you an image," Frankie said.

Zander opened the message to reveal the disturbing image of Jericho's latest victim. The floor fell out of his stomach at the resemblance between Jane Doe and the woman he loved.

"Christ! Where is he?" Zander growled.

"This was Contra Costa, thirty-two hours ago. That's six now, and he's close. He's left body after body across the country. His intensions are clear. He's coming."

"And we'll be ready."

"Prez, he's evaded all security footage until he wanted us to see him. He wants us to know he's arrived. Now maybe it's time to free the Dragon from her cage?"

"No chance!" Zander snapped, tapping his fingers on the table.

"Then her death is on your hands."

"Christ, you're as dramatic as Welsh Cake!"

Silence loomed before Zander heard Frankie's wrath. "You know what? You're just as bad as Ari and Mackie. They caged the Dragon, and they got burnt. Your words brother! They lied to her, tried to change her, and now you're doing the very thing you freed her from. Shame on you. I thought you were a better man."

"Watch your tone, cop!" Zander threatened, leaning into his cell phone as if he was ready to fight.

"Fuck you! I don't answer to you. I'm not your pack, and B is my family. Now she needs to be informed, so she can prepare herself for the darkness ahead. He will find her, and he will kill her if she's as weak as you've made her."

"Frankie, we got this. Now I asked you out of respect for Welsh Cake to keep this quiet, and I won't tell you again. She remains in the dark on this."

Frankie released a heavy sigh, showing his distaste. "Look, I get it! You're the Prez and she agreed to support that, but don't change the woman you fell in love with. What scares you so much about her Dragon side, anyway?"

Zander's temper flared. He rose from his chair to pour himself a drink to calm his unease. "I'm no' changing her Frankie. I'm teaching her to trust. To have faith in the ones she loves. It's no' healthy living in attack mode. I should know, I lived there long enough."

Frankie's maniacal laugh forced Zander to pause, his words ringing true with the troubled Scot so much it made his heart ache as Frankie continued.

"That's what you don't get about her. Her strength makes her, her. That chaos you see is passion. The fire in her eyes is desire, and you're dimming her light, diminishing her soul. You've lied to her about this since Christmas, and she's going to find out."

"No. We'll put this to bed without her knowledge."

"And then what? Keep her as a good little old lady until she snaps? Because she *will* fucking snap. Haven't you learned that already?"

"My old lady is my business." Zander huffed into his whiskey.

"See, that's where you're fucking wrong! Your old lady is a fucking sister to me. I know and understand her a damn sight better than you, and I won't let your pride get her killed. You have nothing to prove, Prez. She loves you for you. You don't have to prove how strong you are to her. You've already won!"

"Winning has fuck all to do with it."

"So, inform her of Jericho's intensions or I will. I miss her, and I've done nothing but avoid her because I won't lie to her, and Zander, I want to be honest with her; I want to see my sister. She's the only family I have."

Zander puffed out his chest, narrowing his eyes as if Frankie were in his presence. "Stand down, Frankie. I'm warning you. I will sort this out for her. We're planning a family, and I want her to know she's safe and can rely on me. Dinnae hurt her by telling her things she cannae handle."

"The only reason she can't handle it is because you've killed her passion. She'll not live to grow our family if you stop her from being who she is. Now Jericho's coming for her any day now. So, get your fucking affairs in order and tell B. I arrive in Sunnyville tomorrow morning." Frankie shouted before ending the call.

Zander tossed the phone onto the oak table, shaking his head.

*Why dinnae anyone understand I want the best for her? All I want is for her to relax and trust her loved ones, and when I capture Jericho, she'll see she can rely on me; see that I'll never let her down.*

Jimmy interrupted his thoughts as he entered the room. "You alright, man? You've been in here a while."

Zander tossed his glass onto the cabinet. Reaching his arms above his head, he stretched into another sigh. "He's near Contra Costa, and he's coming for her."

"Shit." Jimmy slumped into his VP spot to listen to Zander. "How do you know he's coming for her? All the messages have been for Frankie."

Zander retrieved his cell phone displaying the image Frankie had sent him. He handed it to Jimmy, witnessing his face turn red with anger.

"Sick bastard," Jimmy said, shaking his head. "What's the play here? You gonna tell her now?"

"No. I want to do this for her. God knows I want to tell her everything, but she'll lose her shit and I dinnae think I can handle a batshit crazy Dragon on top of hunting Jericho. She knows he's coming, and she's barely holding on. I just want to destroy the fucker so we can get on with our lives."

Jimmy ran his hands through his scraggly hair. "She's getting pissed off with all these extra hours she thinks you're doing, though. Why not just explain you've been searching for him?"

"Yeah, I had both barrels yesterday. I dinnae want to worry her. She's anxious enough already. I need to nail him, and fast."

"You gonna kill him?"

Zander tilted his head toward him and pursed his lips. "He's a threat to our family, Jimmy. He's gotta go. When we flush him out, I'll end him, and we'll leave him somewhere for Frankie to find."

"You understand Frankie will lose it and Welsh Cake will chop your nuts off for this. You could lose her, man. Don't be stupid about this."

Zander gripped onto Jimmies shoulders, squeezing his authority into his VP, his tone deadly. "I'm no' letting him live. He's too dangerous, and she'll no' be safe until he's in the ground."

"Fair enough. What's the plan?"

"Hyde and the prospects will stay on the laddies. Tyr, Eddie, and Sandy can stay on Welsh Cake with me. You and the rest of the patches go hunting tonight and guard the club."

"And what about when she's at work tomorrow and Thursday?"

"I'll chaperone her to and from work. Tyr, Eddie, and Sandy will clock anyone entering or leaving the building. Dinnae worry pal. I got this! I just need to convince Frankie no' to tell her about Jericho tomorrow. We're this close to having the life we've always wanted," he said, releasing him and showing to the inch between his thumb and forefinger, "and I'm no' letting anything impede that."

Jimmy raised his hands in defeat. "You're the Prez. You lead, I follow, brother."

"Thanks, man. I'm gonnae brief everyone and get home to her. She's busting my balls about being here all the time, and if we dinnae catch him soon, I'm gonnae lose her. So, we must put this whole Jericho bullshit to bed."

"Got you, brother. I'll call everyone in."

# CHAPTER FIVE

# Date Night!

B scurried around the grocery store with her own personal security guard, Tyr, gathering all she required for the perfect dinner date with Zander. The excitement almost overwhelmed her. It seemed like forever since they'd last had a date night. She planned to prepare one of Zander's favorite meals as she raked through the steaks on the shelf for the best cuts of meat.

Hurrying around the supermarket like she was a contestant on a game show, B picked out potatoes, two bottles of Merlot, some strawberry tarts, and the finest vanilla ice-cream for dessert. Madoc and Rhys were spending some quality time with their father, leaving B and Zander to enjoy a romantic evening.

After paying for her groceries, B packed everything into her truck and headed home. She wanted to spend the afternoon pampering herself, ensuring everything was perfect for their evening together.

B unpacked the groceries and pre-set the table before venturing out again to her local salon with Tyr in tow. She had an appointment to get her nails and eyebrows done before coming home to run herself a hot bath. Immersing herself in the tub, allowing the bubble bath to soothe her skin, B unwound. Her mind fixated on date night with the man she loved.

B had missed him these past few months and was relieved he'd agreed to the date night. Their sex life had dwindled in recent months due to Zander's absence. Sex had become a weekend luxury if B was lucky. Zander always arrived home long after B had gone to bed and B had early starts on weekdays. On the weekends, B nagged for him to stay home, only Zander insisted he was required at the club. He would then go on scheduled ride outs or get so inebriated; he'd pass out before B seduced him. Sunday mornings were a dead cert. Only B wanted more from the man she had fallen in love with.

B figured tonight would be different, especially after their raunchy romp at the top of the valley the day before. Zander had convinced B that times had changed, and they would resume their relationship of old. His chivalrous demeanor after their falling out had B eating out of the palm of his hand. She was aware of how intoxicated and compliant she was when he turned on his charm. His seduction skills always melted away any frustrations she had in the blink of an eye.

After a long soak, B washed her body with her favorite body scrub and shaved her legs and underarms. Pampering herself felt good for a change.

Wrapped in a towel, she moisturized, applied her make-up and Zander's favorite perfume and curled her hair into loose curls. Zander loved her hair like that.

Rummaging through her drawer, she located her sexiest lace underwear along with stockings and suspenders.

B's arousal and excitement fizzed inside her as she dressed in her sexy treasures. Then she stood in front of the mirror, capturing her best pose, and sent the image to Zander.

*I hope you're ready for me, Scottie?*

Her dress was all that remained before heading downstairs to prepare their meal.

Walking into the kitchen carrying her stilettos, she received wolf whistles from Tyr and Eddie who had stopped by to see Tyr.

"Phwoar! Dragon, Prez's onto a promise tonight," Eddie teased.

Tyr slapped him across the head. "Don't be so disrespectful. That's Prez's old lady. He'll cut out your tongue if he hears you talking like that."

"What? I'm paying her a compliment."

"Think about what you just said. You're paying our extremely jealous Prez's old lady a compliment." Tyr said, tilting his head in question.

"Oh, right! Gotcha. Apologies, Dragon."

B laughed, placing her stilettos by the door and donning an apron from the kitchen cupboard.

"You do look beautiful, Mrs. Prez." Tyr smiled.

B blushed. "Thank you, Tyr! That's very sweet of you. I made fresh cookies this morning. They're in the biscuit tin."

"Chocolate chip?" he asked.

"Triple chocolate. You're favorite, if I'm, correct?" B confirmed.

Tyr's face lit up and he raced to the biscuit tin.

"Help yourself to coffee and whatever else you fancy until Scottie arrives."

"Thank you, Mrs. Prez," Tyr said, scarfing a cookie.

A stunned Eddie looked at B in astonishment.

"Problem, Eddie?" she asked.

"Yeah! He scalds me for paying you a compliment, yet he does it and gets cookies?"

"My favorite cookies." Tyr added, popping a whole one into his mouth.

B laughed, retrieving the steak and potatoes from the refrigerator. "He's more subtle with his compliments, good boy. Besides, Tyr has become part of the furniture these past few months. I've gotten to know him and his favorite snacks. If you stick around long enough, I'll make yours too. There's no favoritism among wolves unless you're the Prez. He gets all of me," she said, giving him a wink.

Tyr had become protective of B these past months, asking Zander's permission to watch over her, and B enjoyed his doe-like presence. She saw him as someone who just needed a mother figure. Despite Tyr's handsome and menacing demeanor, she recognized the insecurities behind his eyes. He would become bashful whenever she thanked him or displayed a compassionate gesture like giving him a cwtch when she thought he needed one.

Tyr mentioned little about himself, only that his brothers were bullies and his parents allowed it, but B had been around enough lonely bikers to know when they had hidden traumas. He always appeared envious of her relationship with Madoc and Rhys, and whenever B asked about his family, he would clam up. So, B did what she knew best by always baking him his favorite cookies and wrapping a comforting arm around him to make him feel better when he appeared down in the dumps.

Tyr was a big softie at heart and the perfect gentleman, making B feel relaxed in her own home. At twenty-four, he was the youngest fully fledged member of the gray wolves. B never worried about inappropriate comments or unnecessary unease from Tyr, like she did with some of the new members of the club. Tyr had become part of her close circle, and B had become protective of him, adopting him as one of her own. She would always have his back.

B cracked on with the cooking, leaving Tyr and Eddie to entertain themselves and before she realized, it was a quarter to seven.

She rushed to her bedroom to put on her lipstick, adding an extra spray of perfume for good measure then returned to the kitchen. Slipping into her stilettos, she oozed confidence: an experience she'd been lacking in recent months. Pouring two glasses of red wine, B then served up two steak meals, figuring she would play the good housewife by having Zander's meal on the table for his arrival.

Sipping her wine, B checked her watch again.

*Seven-forty-five.*

She checked her messages to discover Zander hadn't even opened her last message. The image of her in her sexy underwear remained unopened.

Anxiety ripped through her like a wolf tearing its prey apart.

*Where is he? He promised.*

B stared at the stone-cold meals sitting on the well-laid table.

*Nine-thirty-seven. He's stood me up for the last time!*

B poured the last glass of red into her glass, finishing the bottle of wine, while battling back tears of disappointment.

Tyr knocked on the open door. His arctic eyes provided a surprising sympathy that almost broke B's heart. "You alright, Mrs. Prez?"

B swallowed the hurt in her throat. She finished the large glass of wine and set the glass down on its placemat, removed her napkin, tossing it onto her plate. "Fine, thanks, good boy. I'm going to bed. Please inform Prez he'll be sleeping on the couch for the foreseeable future."

Standing, she straightened her dress, attempting to leave the dining room.

Tyr stood in front of her, smiling and giving her biceps an encouraging squeeze at her misfortune.

"Prez loves you. He's been held up with club—"

"Business, I know," B snapped. "Sorry, Tyr. I know you mean well. Your loyalty is admirable, but the fact remains that Prez's priorities lie elsewhere."

"It doesn't mean his feelings for you have changed. He's stretched and stressed right now."

B stepped around the Viking-like wolf. "Aren't we all, good boy? See you tomorrow. Usual time."

# CHAPTER SIX

# My Club, My Rules!

Jericho spent the night in Blaze's office, ignoring his subordinates for most of the day until calling his first church meeting.

Standing at the Prez's seat, he used a dirty rag to wipe the dust-off Blaze's old throne.

*Now Blaze, don't be mad. I'm sitting here instead of you. It takes both brains and sadism to make a great Prez.*

Taking a seat, he picked up the gavel, twirling it in his hands like a baton.

Sully and his men stopped short of the church door. "Make yourself comfortable," Sully grunted.

"Oh, I have!" Jericho said, placing his feet on the table. "Take a seat, VP," he said, gesturing to the seat next to him.

Sully's sour face lightened into a smile. "You're serious about revenge?" he said, sitting in the creaking, wooden, dining chair.

"I never joke about revenge, and I have plenty to administer," Jericho said. "You, I have promoted you!" he joked to the first soldier-looking man standing behind Sully. "Sergeant at Arms for you. You," he said to the second man. "You look thug-like. Road Captain for you! And you," he said, leaning toward the last man, "You're the secretary, of course."

The men took their seats. Their weary expressions were obvious as Jericho continued with the sound of his own voice soothing him. "The rest we'll figure out as we go."

"Not exactly enough of us to be a club, let alone revenge." Sully stated.

Jericho waved his hand, dismissing the comment. "Quality, not quantity, brothers. Besides, we're starting a recruitment drive."

The three men gave him suspicious glances.

"First things first. I require expendable cannon fodder. Desperate men, tempted by a quick buck and a desire for belonging and power. We'll give them a cut, call them our prospects."

"It'll be nice to order some grunts about," Sully said, taking out a cigarette.

"And order about you shall. However, these grunts as you call them can be used as bait. A means to an end. We'll recruit more promising prospects after we've ended the Gray Wolves."

Sully puffed away on his cigarette. "And how do you propose we do that, Prez? They have money and power. We'd need an army to take them down."

"Oh Sully, on the contrary, we're the only army we need. Well, us and our cannon fodder. See, I've planned this to precision. I've been tormenting both the FBI and the Gray wolves for months," he explained with pride. "And now it's time to bite off the hand that feeds them."

The three men appeared puzzled.

Jericho removed his feet from the table. Leaning forward, he clasped his hands together wearing a salacious grin. "You need me to spell it out? I'm going to kill their Dragon. My plan is in place, everything is set. All I require is your allegiance and several desperate delinquents I can dress up in Pitbull cuts."

"I hate to break it to you, Prez. Two big fuckers before you have tried and failed."

Jericho removed his blade from his cut pocket, stabbing it into the hard wooden table in frustration. "Yes, but they were stupid. God rest their souls. I am not. I'm calculated, conceited, and have a flare for the dramatics. My name will be in lights one day, gentlemen. That, I can assure you."

"Okay, then, what's the plan?" Sully asked.

"You wonderful Pitbulls are going to find me an army. Tempt them with this," he said, slamming twenty-five thousand dollars onto the table. "And give them each a cut. They have one job. Take out anyone wearing a Gray Wolves cut. Hunt to kill boys, hunt to kill."

"And us? Are we disposable cannon fodder?" Sully asked.

"No! No!" Jericho shook his head. His sadistic smile and tone encouraged. "You set them their task and lure the Gray Wolves somewhere quiet to wipe them out. Use your disposable assets. They do the dirty work. We'll have Sunnyville to run as our own once I'm done."

"What?" the three men shouted in unison.

"Oh, you two found your tongue, have you? I thought you'd gone mute and left VP here to do your bidding."

The two men cowered.

"Don't recoil into your shells now. I need men, not feeble mice." Jericho said.

Sully diverted the attention back to him. "And while we're doing that, what are you doing?"

"I'm hunting down Dragon and adding her to my cut. Leave the details to me. Here, put your cell number in here." He handed Sully his cell phone.

"And you think we can pull this off?" Sully asked, puffing away on his cigarette and punching his cell number into Jericho's phone.

"I don't think. I know. Gentlemen, have you been watching the news by any chance? There's a serial killer at large, you know, and all the victims share an uncanny resemblance to a certain Dragon."

"No!" Sully guffawed, bulging-eyed in disbelief as the others' chins dropped to the table.

"You're yanking my chain," his new Sergeant at Arms said, with escalating confidence in his voice.

Jericho sat back, relaxing in his chair, smiling. "I told you, gentlemen. I've got the brains to wipe the Gray Wolves off the face of the earth. Now, first order of business, slaying a Dragon."

# CHAPTER SEVEN

## Finito!

It was a little after ten when Zander returned home. Tyr and Eddie sat at the breakfast bar eating the remains of the biscuit tin when Zander entered, tossing his keys on the side table.

"Where is she?" he asked.

Tyr finished the cookie in his mouth. "She got fed up and went to bed about twenty minutes ago. She told me to inform you, you're sleeping on the couch tonight, and for the foreseeable future. I tried to talk to her, Prez."

Zander ran his fingers through his thick mop of hair. "That bad, eh?"

"She just seemed disappointed." Eddie said with remorse. "She set the table real nice. Candles and everything. She was all dressed up and seemed to think you were coming home earlier."

"Shit! I promised her a date night! The Church meeting diverted my attention and then we went hunting down cold fucking leads." Zander said, heading to the dining room.

As he stood just inside the room, the disappointment in himself tore through him. The exquisitely decorated table, set. B's favorite red candles had melted down to almost nothing and an empty wine glass sat opposite Zander's full glass of untouched wine. The beautifully cooked, untouched meals sat on placements at their seats, reflecting the effort made by his old lady.

Zander's imagination saw B sat at the table in her favorite red dress, her disappointed face staring at him as she sat alone waiting for him.

Banging his head against the door frame, a savage pang of anger burned in the pit of his stomach.

*How the fuck did I forget?*

The last few months had consumed him. He wanted nothing more than to keep B safe, spending day after day, night after night following unsuccessful leads, attempting to hunt the hunter.

Zander was determined not to repeat his mistake after almost losing B to Blaze and Glen. He wanted to be her hero, wanted her to drop her guard and feel safe around him and she had begun to do so until his absence created distance between them.

Everything Zander did, he did for B. Only she had no knowledge of his attempts to keep her safe. Instead, he made her believe it was work, so she didn't worry or worse, release her inner Dragon. Zander didn't want to risk his beloved's safety, so he lied to her knowing she would want to help.

After collecting himself, Zander chugged his wine and returned to the kitchen.

"You two can return to the club. Jimmy will bring you up to speed."

Tyr and Eddie climbed off their stools and headed to the front door.

"Good luck, Prez," Tyr said, patting him on the back.

"You're gonna need it," Eddie said.

"Get the fuck out!" Zander snapped, slamming the door behind him.

B was sound asleep when he entered the bedroom, her long, blond curls spiraling down her back as she hugged a pillow. His pillow, reminding him of his continued absence.

Her red dress and provocative underwear were strewn across the floor, suggesting her anger when she relieved herself of them.

Zander sat on the edge of the bed, pursing his lips together. He removed a stray hair from her face, causing her to stir, watching as she nestled herself further into the pillow.

*Look at her!*

*Fucking perfection, right there!*

*What the fuck are you playing at, Zander?*

*You're gonnae lose her, man.*

*Fix this!*

Swallowing hard at the thought of losing her again, he removed his shirt and slipped out of his jeans and boxer briefs. Zander was determined to apologize and make things right with B, ignoring her suggestion to sleep on the couch. He wanted to show her how loved she was.

Upon climbing into bed, the cool sheet tickled his skin. He removed the pillow from B's grasp, gently jostling her awake.

B's eyes opened, unamused. "Sco—"

Zander covered her lips with his and slipped his tongue into her mouth. B attempted to push him away at first, striking his chest with the palms of her hands, until he kissed her harder, cupping the back of her head to bring her closer. Taking a breath, he whispered: "I'm sorry darling. I really am. I'm making the changes as we speak."

B pushed him away, rolling away from him, fluffing her pillow to make herself comfortable. "I've heard it all before. Broken promises and bullshit. Now get out of my bedroom. You're not welcome, and thanks for waking me, asshole."

Zander spooned into her naked body, holding her tight. "I'm sorry!"

B removed his hand. "Not interested. Find some fucking bunny at your precious club to tend to your needs."

"No! You're the one I want! I came home to you."

"Fuck you, Sunshine!" she said, storming off into the bathroom.

Zander sat up. "How many times do you want me to apologize? I get it, I fucked up. Now, please, let's talk about it."

A minute later, he heard the toilet flush and the water running. B stepped out of the bathroom, her face like thunder.

"Welsh Cake."

B opened the closet, removing her suitcase.

"What the fuck are you doing now?" he asked, climbing out of bed.

"Packing your bloody shit! I'm done with you and being yours."

Zander snatched the case. "No fucking way!"

B became frantic. "Yes, fucking way! I'm not putting up with this shit anymore. You had your chance, Sunshine, and you blew it, good and proper. I'm nobody's afterthought. It's over. Finito! Now, piss off out of my house."

Zander stood, shattered by her words. "Welsh Cake."

B walked to the balcony doors, opening them. "Don't make this harder than it already is. You stood me up like a bloody bunny tonight and for what? To ride bikes with your brothers. Well, bash on, because that's a game I refuse to play anymore."

Zander watched her step down onto the balcony, resting her hands on the reinforced railings. He couldn't breathe. The air too thick, the prodigious shock dismantling him, his body weakening at the thought of losing her. He couldn't think of anything else since learning of Jericho's pursuit. He knew he'd risk losing her. It was hope that kept him going all this time. Hope that he'd kill Jericho without jeopardizing his relationship with B.

Lowering himself to the floor, he sat against the closet, observing the naked, wounded warrior of a woman standing on the balcony. No words could fix the predicament he found himself in. His brothers had warned him multiple times about the ramifications of his actions. Only Zander believed their love for one another would conquer all ailments.

He was unclear how long he had sat dumbfounded with his head in his hands when the balcony doors closed. His head jerked to see her standing with a distraught expression on her face.

"You haven't left?" she asked.

He shook his head.

B placed her hands on her hips, her impatient stare bored into him as she hissed. "What do you want from me, Scottie? I can't be a bunny that you pick up and put down when it suits you, and I refuse point-blank to be bruised by your actions anymore!"

"That was never my intention," he whispered.

"Then why keep doing it? Are you punishing me for something? Because I don't have a clue how I've wronged you, if that's the case."

"No, Welsh Cake."

"Then why treat me like dirt? Like I don't matter."

Zander's eyes threatened him with tears. His frown turned to remorse and sadness. "Because I'm a foolish jackass who thinks I can handle everything; never wanting to admit I feel like I'm carrying the entire world on my shoulders. You're the last person I'd ever want to lose, and now I've fucked the very thing I was trying to protect."

B sat beside him, planting her head against the closet, her eyes closed in despair.

Zander could see the last few months had taken their toll on her, as she banged her weary head against the hardwood. B's face appeared drained of the fiery embers that had lit it up the day they met. Just like his sleek, black mop of hair had become seasoned with a sprinkling of salt and pepper due to the events that had transpired these past months. They were exhausted.

He reached for her hand, squeezing her icy fingers, praying she wouldn't pull away.

B held them back, instilling a glimmer of hope into his broken heart.

Zander pulled her hand to his lips.

"Can you forgive me one more time? Welsh Cake, I'll never fucking let you down again. No more broken promises. You have my word."

"Scottie, this is the last chance you'll ever receive, and you far from deserve it!"

"Understood, darling. I understand I've pushed you beyond the point of no return," he said, staring into her eyes with all the love he could muster. "No more neglecting you. You will always be my priority, woman. I'll do whatever it takes to make this right."

"Last chance, good boy," she reiterated, "Hyde can manage the gym and you can hire externally if you promise to background check and triple-check their papers."

A wave of relief washed through his veins, diminishing the adrenaline that fueled them. "Thank you, beautiful. That means everything to me."

"No bloody security team, though. Tyr is doing a fantastic job of looking after me. He doesn't impose on my life. Frankie will manage the security of all the businesses once he returns home."

Zander gave her his best sympathetic smile. "Welsh Cake."

"Don't!" she snapped. "I know what you're thinking and one, you're wrong. He will come home. He's never broken a promise."

*Ouch! I suppose I deserved that.*

B continued, with venom in her voice. "And two, I want to be clear that I don't give a toss about club rules. My business, my money. My fucking rules trump the MC's rules. He's coming home to his family!"

Zander pursed his lips. Certain club members would show contempt given Frankie's dramatic confession and club exit. Several members remained loyal to Mack. Zander gathered Frankie's absence had contributed to B's insecurities, resulting in inconsolable guilt on his part.

*I better inform her I'm responsible for his absence. She'll probably kill me. Never mind, end our relationship. I need to be honest. How do I fucking tell her?*

"Okay, darling. Leave it with me, and I'll call a church meeting," he said, stroking her cheek.

B cracked half a smile, clambering to her feet, dragging Zander with her. "Bed. I've got work tomorrow."

Zander allowed her to escort him into their king-size bed, heaving the covers over them. Spooning and hugging her as if his life depended on it, he lifted his head to whisper into her ear. "Punch me if this is inappropriate, but I feel terrible for standing you up tonight. I only request that you let me make it up to you."

B smiled, turning into his heavy chest. "You're a dickhead, but you're *my* dickhead and yes, you can make it up to me now and every bloody night until you stop breathing, Boyoh."

Zander managed a smile, still damaged by the events of the night, albeit relieved of being granted one last chance. "Darling, I'm happy to oblige," he said, ascending down her chest in a trail of tender kisses, eliciting her soft moans.

Her hands rifled through his hair, tugging on it, forcing a raspy growl from his lusty lips. Her body responded to his touch, her arching back inviting him in as he continued to travel south.

Desperate to please her, he reciprocated her moans with more forceful kisses, his arousal consuming him as he tasted her skin. Spreading her legs, he allowed his lips to linger in the creases of her pelvis, breathing warm air and delivering delicate kisses to her pubic region.

"Mm…" B moaned. Her breaths were quick and shallow.

Zander grinned, relief washing over him as she raised her hips to meet his watering mouth. He loved to please her, make her writhe with pleasure. Her impatient whimpers were like sweet symphonies as she waited for him to connect with her.

"Beautiful," he whispered, nipping her inner thigh between his teeth. Grabbing her ass in the palms of his hands, he pressed her to his lips. Covering her clitoris, he stroked her with his tongue with long and bold strokes. His arousal grew more urgent as he tasted hers.

B's pleasurable moans heightened his sexual tension and enticed him further with her hips. Zander continued to tantalize her with his tongue, B's elegant writhes welcoming his yearning erection.

Zander's unswerving desire to make amends to the woman he worshipped captured every twitch, every moan as B gave herself to him, reminding him of her love for him. After one last taste of her, Zander reached her gaze. The innocence and desperation in her eyes reignited a fire in him. B was like an angel displaying her vulnerability.

So pure as Zander became lost in her, his eyes riveted, entering her with gradual intent. Indulging in everything she offered.

His eyes remained fixed on her, witnessing every emotion as he gave himself to her. Tucking his arms underneath her shoulders, he reached for her hands, grasping them above her head, displaying his devotion to their unity.

B's eyes complemented his. His slow and steady thrusts, enthralling her sex as she battled her composure, driving her hips to replicate his rhythm.

"Feel my remorse, darling. I only ever want you," he gasped, his arousal reaching its peak.

"I want you, Scottie. Lose yourself in me," she whimpered.

"Oh, darling. I want to be lost in you forever," he said as he thrusted harder, delving deep inside her.

"Yes! Don't stop!"

"Fuck!" he gasped; his tone higher pitched. The struggle to hold on was crystal clear across his anguished face. He drove again, teasing her G-spot.

Zander reveled in B's intimate cries with every thrust, his eyes still soul searching as she moaned with pleasure.

"You still want me, darling?"

B responded in a loud and desperate plea, arching her back in desperation. "Yes!"

Zander's heart skipped a beat, his erection throbbing in excitement and despair. "I'm sorry for hurting you, Welsh Cake. Watch me make it up to you," he managed in a high-pitched war cry.

Under pressure to cope with his arousal, he released her hands and pulled back onto his knees, slipping out of her temporarily. Taking hold of her ankles, he lifted her gently to re-enter her, opening her legs as he did so.

He broke into a rapid pace, his volatile thrusts devouring her with his dominance and size. He watched her grip onto the sheets tightly, holding on as if her life depended on it.

"That's it darling, come for me, show me how much you still want me, beautiful."

"Scottie!" she begged, barely managing to keep up with his tempo.

"I'm giving you all I have. Take it," he commanded in desperation, anticipating her orgasm. Her silky-smooth essence soaked his hard shaft, forcing him to resist his uncontrollable release.

The pressure on the base of his spine surged through him uncontrollably as he fought to please her. His energetic thrusts caressing her G-spot until her screams harmonized with her vibrant orgasm, suffocating his hard cock as she released.

Securing herself around him, B demanded his climax as he gave himself to her.

"I'm there," he rejoiced, driving into her without remorse as his body took over. The mounting pressure compelling him to erupt in an electrifying climax of his own. Every emotion raced through him as he became intoxicated by erotic pleasure. Surge after surge of penetrating and blinding explosiveness engulfed him as he released in guttural relief.

"Oh, Oh. Fuck! Christ darling, I cannae stop," he cried as he slammed through his climax, losing himself in her satisfied eyes.

Stilling into one last thrust, Zander released her legs, collapsing onto her, weakened by the remnants of his pleasurable release.

"My God."

"Thank you, handsome," she said, kissing his neck.

Zander panted through his words, looking down upon her sweat-glistened face. "Every day until I stop breathing, is going to be special, Welsh Cake. Things are gonnae change. I promise. All I want is you and our family."

B smiled at him.

"Are you sure we're alright? I need us to be okay, darling," he said, showing concern.

B nodded as if she could not speak.

"Say something, please?"

Zander watched her bite her lip as if she was choosing her words.

Fear flourished through his shattered body as he waited for her to speak.

"I want you to comprehend that you broke my heart tonight. The Blaze incident left me shattered, and I promised myself to never feel let down by you again."

"Darling. It'll never happen again."

"Scottie, you will never make me feel like I've been placed on the shelf until you decide to dust me off and play with me again. I am in love with you, but just to reiterate, I'm not your bunny or submissive."

Zander tried to talk, his dry throat almost forbidding words from exiting as he processed what B had said. Clearing his throat, he acknowledged her uncertain expression. A far cry from the passion that had engulfed them just moments before.

"Shit. Welsh Cake I'm sorry. I'm disgusted with myself for making you feel like that. I hear the contention in your voice, and you've made yourself crystal clear. All I ask is that you allow me time to make the arrangements to rebuild your faith in me."

"Just don't let me down again," she said in a faint voice, running her fingers through his sweat-soaked hair.

Zander climbed off her and sat up in bed. Taking her hand, he dropped his head in shame. "Right, I'll start now. We need to talk. Open and honest from here on out."

"Bloody hell. You've met someone else. Haven't you?" B said, sitting up and tugging the covers to her chest.

Zander's heart jumped into his throat. "What! No! Jesus. I want you, you daft cow, only you. Christ, what am I doing to you?"

"What the bloody hell am I supposed to think of that comment?"

"Not fucking that. Jeez, woman!"

"Then talk to me."

Zander saw how fragile B had become. He'd made her feel vulnerable, made her lose faith and trust in him instead of instilling her with confidence, empowering her and placing her trust in him.

Caressing her cheek, he calmed. "I've spent the last few months trying to track down Jericho. I hate that he's out there intending to harm you. It's why I've been away so much. We need to end this and move forward with our future together."

B's jaw-dropping expression was unmatched by any that had crossed her lips tonight. "Why didn't you tell me?"

"Because I dinnae want you looking over your shoulder every day. I wanted you to feel safe."

"And what did you discover?"

"Nothing but an old photograph," he sighed.

"We said no more lies, Scottie. You promised," she whispered.

"I know," he said, wrapping his arm around her. "I want to gain your trust by being the hero you deserve. Jeez! You had to rescue all of us from Blaze, and I almost lost you."

"I had no choice, good boy. I wasn't about to lose my family to a fucking bampot! Bloody hell, Scottie, when will you realize you have always been my hero? You've been my protector since the day we met. You don't have to keep trying so hard."

He caressed her clammy cheek with his free hand. "Darling, I want to be the best version of myself for you."

"And you are, so quit acting crazy. Now what's happening with Jericho?"

Zander fell silent again, fear rising deep within once more. He didn't want to stress her out.

"Please tell me," she whispered.

"He's killed six women with a striking resemblance to you and left them for Frankie to find. Frankie wanted to tell you. He refused to lie to you, but I ordered him not to. It's why he hasn't been around. I'm sorry, Welsh Cake. I've fucked up again. Jericho's coming but understand we're ready for him. You're heavily guarded, and when this prick shows his ugly face, we'll nail him."

"And I don't doubt that handsome," she said, forcing a smile. "I just don't understand why you felt you couldn't tell me. Keeping me in the dark again isn't appreciated; look where that's got us before."

"Aye, I know, and I apologize. I feared you going down the 'fuck it! My inner Dragon will slay everyone, and I'll shut everyone out,' road."

"It's what I know. Especially when I'm lied to," B snapped.

"And that's what I'm trying to change. My fear overcomes my honesty when it comes to you. This primal instinct to protect you kicks in. I'm no' trying to change you darling. I just want you safe. When I catch Jericho, you won't have to worry or be defensive again, and we can grow old together in fucking harmony."

B choked back a sarcastic laugh. "Nice sentiment, Scottie. Only, I put Dragon back in her cage to show you how much I trust you, but you lying to me, deciding for me and trying to protect me, does not differ from Mack and Ari. It stops now!" She kicked off the covers. "Stop bloody wrapping me in cotton wool. You're making me anxious, paranoid, and scared. It ends now or we do! Does anyone possess a picture of this asshole? Knowing who's hunting me would help."

Zander took her hand, placing it in his lap. "Understood. It won't happen again, and as for the picture; I only have an old mug shot. Frankie is coming over tomorrow with some surveillance footage. He says he changed his identity to escape incarceration. The picture I have is useless. No wonder we have gotten nowhere. We're going to distribute an updated image around the club so everyone remains vigilant and can recognize him."

B released a loud sigh. "Good! Changing the subject. It'll be great to see Frankie. I've missed him."

"I know. Frankie only kept away because he refused to lie to you. That was my bad. You're probably fed up with hearing my apologies, but I am sorry for everything."

"There just words unless you mean it, good boy. Has the man I fell in love with returned and back to coming home at a reasonable time?"

"All of me, anytime, anywhere. I'm back and yours only."

B nodded in silence as Zander breathed a sigh of release onto her cheek, kissing it. The weight of the world released from his shoulders. He had detested keeping everything from her these past months. Pulling her into his chest, he stroked her back.

"I love you, Welsh Cake, and I will nail this bastard for you!"

"I know you will! Why do you think my inner Dragon has remained in her cage? It's because I have you to look after me."

"You're damn right. Thank you for understanding."

B played with his chest hair, her voice innocent: "No more chances. Property of the Prez or not. You keep anything from me again, my inner Dragon will rip off your head and breathe fire down your neck. I'll chop your bits off, and we're done for good."

Zander gulped into a nervous chuckle. "Fuck. I'm glad she's fucking caged but, you're sexy as fuck when you're angry."

# CHAPTER EIGHT

# Mack's Back

B was in the kitchen clearing the breakfast plates when she heard Mack's unwavering mouth as he entered.

"Where's my bestie?" he bellowed with a huge smile on his face. Scooping her up in his arms, he kissed her cheek.

"Mackie, what a lovely surprise!" B said, beaming with glee.

"A month is too long, Dragon!" he said, setting her down to study her. "Glad to see you're still wearing the necklace."

"I never take it off. Where's yours?" she asked.

Mack retrieved his shamrock and dragon pendant from beneath his T-shirt. "Here, of course!"

"I've missed you Mackie!" B said, imposing on his space and placing her head to his.

Mack cupped the back of her head, holding her there. He always made her feel safe in their clinch.

B closed her eyes, not wanting to move as exhaustion battered her bone-tired body.

"Hey, you alright?" he asked.

B opened her eyes and nodded.

"Christ! Do you have to be so fucking up close and personal with my old lady? God, that best friend shit does my nut in!" Zander said, entering with his coffee cup and newspaper, plonking himself at the breakfast bar.

"Sorry, Prez, but best friends never quit. Even if they do become property of the Prez," Mack teased, giving B a cheeky wink.

Zander growled his usual growl. B knew he didn't like how close Mack got, especially when he knew Mack still loved her.

"Nice to see you looking healthy again, good boy," B said, lightening the mood.

"Thanks. I've been bulking. It's nice to feel myself again."

"It looks good on you," B said as Zander grimaced from behind his paper.

"I'm glad you think so. Ari doesn't like it. She thinks I make a better skinny guy."

"Tell her to wash her mouth out. You looked fucking ill and gaunt at Christmas. Besides, real women like something to hold on to," she teased, giving Zander a wink.

"Not anymore. Ari thinks I should take up running and become lean. She's even trying to feed me wheatgrass, for fuck's sake."

Zander raised an eyebrow, smirking. "The baby-making project? For the record, I'll no' be partaking in shit like that when we try to conceive," he said, turning to B.

B laughed as she readied herself for work, and Mack continued.

"Nah. She's on a health kick. Besides, I've put the brakes on that shit. The woman's obsessed. I told her, I'm more than my fecking sperm. Honestly, I'm beginning to think that's all she wants me for."

"That's not true Mackie, she loves you," B said.

"I dunno. Something's off with her. I needed a break, so I figured I crash here tonight, if that's cool with you both?"

Concern washed over B. "Of course. Are you sure you're alright?"

"Aww, I'm fine Dragon. Just catching my breath. I can't seem to do anything right. No matter what I do, it's wrong. She's even got us attending marriage counselling sessions. I just need a day to detox."

"Shit. Take all the time you need. We could do with you here with everything that's evolving, anyway," Zander said, flicking through his newspaper.

"Why? What's happened?" Mack asked with concern in his voice.

B turned away, fear and anxiety flurrying through her, as her shaking hand poured her glass of water.

"I'll fill you in at the club, brother. Welsh Cake is leaving for work in a minute."

"Fair enough, but can I pinch a moment with her a second? I need help with some personal Ari shite. You know, woman stuff!"

"Oh, fuck that! I'll leave you women to it and get the truck ready," Zander said, leaving the room.

Watching him leave, B waited for Mack to turn to her. He still knew her better than anyone else, and she knew Mack would never ask her anything regarding 'woman stuff.'

Mack's face hardened with urgency. "What's happened? You're not yourself."

"I'm fine!" she pressed, drinking her icy water.

"Don't bullshite me, Dragon. You're nervous and you look like shite."

B choked on her water with nervous laughter. "Don't sugar coat it, Mackie. Say it like it is!"

"Dragon, you know me and I sure as hell know you. You're different and you've lost your confidence, and you look scared. Now explain."

B pursed her lips. Her tell when attempting to hide her emotions. Experiencing fear felt alien to her. Unnerving, even. B was always strong, but switching off her Dragon tendencies transformed her from formidable to fragile.

Mack placed his hand on her cheek. "Dragon, please? You can tell me anything."

B closed her eyes. "Jericho is coming to kill me. He's killed six women likened to me and I'm next. Frankie and Zander have been trying to catch him for months, but now it appears he's coming for me."

Mack's face grew into a ballistic ball of fire. The rage spewed from his seething lips. "And nobody thought to tell me this?"

"I found out the extent of the situation myself, last night. Frankie and Zander kept me in the dark, too."

"Let him come. Dragon, you've dealt with bigger psychopaths than him. We both have. So why do you look so scared?"

B gulped. "Because I caged the Dragon months ago, and now, I feel weak. I hate it, Mackie. Dragon is part of me, but I promised Scottie I'd keep her caged. He's desperate to be the hero here. He needs this."

Mack scratched his head and furrowed his brow. "I'm not following you."

"Mackie. I think he feels a little inadequate after the Blaze situation. I need to allow him to be the one to deliver Jericho to Frankie."

"What. Fecking what?" Mack said with an increasing temper. "Dragon, you can't suppress who the fuck you are to make Prez feel better. What the feck? No. You are amazing, just as you are. Shame on him for putting this on you! I'll make this right."

B grabbed his arm to stop him leaving to confront Zander, watching Mack track her movements. "Please Mackie. I can do without it. I need my best friend."

Mack turned to her, taking hold of her arms. "Dragon, no one is worth your love if they're trying to change you. You taught me that years ago. Your fiery tendencies make you who you are. Don't dim your light for his insecurities. He needs to step up and match your energy, not lower your vibration, gorgeous. I love every piece of you, mind, body and fecking soul. I always will. Besides, change right now is dangerous. I'm sure Frankie has explained, you'll need to be yourself if you come up against Jericho."

B's voice trembled. "What happens if I can't get her back? What if I'm stuck as Vulnerable Vera forever? I can't live like this. I'm scared Mackie, and I hate it!"

Mack pulled her into his embrace. "Aww, my sweet, sweet fecking Dragon; always looking after everyone else's feelings other than your own. It's time to take control of your life again, and if Prez can't see you as the shining star that you are, he doesn't deserve you."

A single tear escaped B's right eye. Battering it away in frustration, she held Mack a little longer, burying her head in his shoulder to hide her tear-stained cheek.

"Uh hum," Zander said from the doorway. "Ready to go, sweetheart?" he asked.

B pulled away, giving Mack her warmest smile as he nudged her chin with his fist.

"Have a good day at work." Mack said as he turned to Zander. "All good, brother, promise."

B arrived at school, parking her truck in her spot with Zander, Mack, Tyr, Eddie, and Sandy in tow. Tyr, Eddie, and Sandy would ensure no uninvited visitors entered the school, remaining inconspicuous as they guarded the school's perimeter.

Zander and Mack would return to the MC, where Zander planned to brief Mack on the Jericho situation.

B clambered from her truck as Zander approached her. His warm hands around her waist made her smile.

He whispered into her ear. "I love you."

B turned to him, wrapping her arms around him. "I love you too, Scottie."

"You sure you're alright?"

B whipped her head back, rolling her eyes. "Fine. Scottie, I keep telling you. I'm no damsel, so no more treating me like one. Now, I've got track to teach." She shrugged out of his grasp to grab her gym bag.

"I'll be here when you finish. Have a good day," he said, kissing her cheek.

B locked her truck and made her way onto the sidewalk near the school's entrance, giving Tyr a confident pat on the back as she passed.

Glancing over her shoulder at the entourage of bikers in the parking lot, B witnessed Zander watching her with stern eyes.

*He's afraid.*

Jerking her head away, she glimpsed at Mack, who gave her a smile and saluted to her, easing her tension. Waving to him, she headed inside to take on the day.

*You got this B! Just another day at work.*

The morning flew by in the blink of an eye, with B sinking into her office chair to eat her lunch. She had just polished off her egg sandwich when the janitor knocked on her door with his huge trash bin.

"Uh, sorry Mam! Can I collect your trash, please?" A tall, well-spoken man asked. He appeared menacing with his bright green eyes and scarred cheek, his ginger hair, and well-spoken tone, his only apparent warming features.

A puzzled expression covered B's face. "Where's Gonzalez today? He normally collects my trash."

"A family emergency, apparently. Head office assigned me to cover."

"Shame. Hope he's alright," she said, turning for the trash can.

"No, no. Allow me please?" the well-spoken man said. "You continue with your lunch, and I'll be out of your hair in a second.

B turned to sit back in her chair as the man stepped behind her seat to retrieve her trash can when she felt a sharp pain in her neck. Reaching up, she took hold of what appeared to be a syringe, staring at it as her senses dulled and her vision evaded her.

"Dragon, oh Dragon," the well-spoken man sang with delight, until everything went dark.

# CHAPTER NINE

# Friend or Foe

"Morning, Men!" Zander grunted as he waltzed into church armed with a coffee and a cigarette pressed between his lips, with Mack trailing behind him.

All members were present, minus Eddie, Tyr, and Sandy, who remained on task at the high school.

"Still in the shit with Welsh Cake, judging by your tone. And you were hoping to get lucky last night?" Jimmy teased.

"Oh, I got lucky alright. That was the easy bit," Zander said, taking a seat in his Prez chair and plonking his cigarette in the nearby ashtray. "Telling her about Jericho after, not so much. I hate I lied to her about it."

"We tried and tell you, man. How is she?" Jimmy asked.

"Hard to say. She's still pissed with me, though."

"Hard to say," Mack scoffed. "You've broken her!"

"Excuse me?" Zander snapped.

"No offense, Prez, but I think I know Dragon better than anyone, and this caging the Dragon shite. Fecking stupid if you ask me. At least I just wanted to keep her in Uskiville. You are trying to change the very essence of her being!"

Zander slammed his mug onto the table, splashing hot coffee

everywhere. "Christ! You're as bad as Frankie. I'm no' trying to change her. I'm trying to make her see she can trust me. She doesnae need to fight anymore. She has me!"

"Haven't you learnt anything from our past mistakes? You're caging her, just like I did, only I made her strong. What the feck have you done, other than make her weak? I've never seen her looking so vulnerable."

Zander took a long drag on his cigarette. "Who fucking asked for your opinion?? You're a guest here, and if you want to continue wearing that patch, you'll watch your fucking tone."

"I'm still the fecking Founder, but fair enough. I'm just trying to explain what she tried to convey to me this morning. More fool you if you don't want to hear it. You'll lose her before long." Mack said, getting up to leave.

Zander watched him open the door until curiosity got the better of him. "She say something to you, Irish?"

"Yeah, I know a lot, but we shouldn't discuss it here in church," Mack said while eyeballing the ceiling.

Zander studied Mack's stern face. His unwavering loyalty to B and the club was commendable. Pressing his cigarette into the ashtray, Zander rose from his seat. "Give me a minute," he said to his pack, ushering Mack out of church and into the quiet bar.

Pouring himself a whiskey, he offered Mack a shot.

"It's a bit early for me, thanks," Mack snapped.

"Suit yourself!" Zander said, downing his shot and helping himself to another.

"So, Welsh Cake confided in you?"

"She's my best friend Zand. What do you expect?"

"I expect her to confide in me if she has a problem. We had a heart-to-heart last night and now I discover she's running to Mr. Perfect for comfort. I mean, after all the shit you and Ari put her through, she still trusts you. I've tried everything, but she never fully opens up."

Mack pulled out a bar stool for Zander to sit on. "She doesn't want to upset you. She's trying to please you because she fecking loves you."

Zander sat on the bar stool, shaking his head. "What do you mean, please me?"

"Dragon believes you need the win with this whole Jericho shite. She thinks you're feeling less than after we all had our asses handed to us by Uncle Mauler and believes that's why you want to cage her dragon."

Zander's face flushed with embarrassment. "What. That's bullshit! I told her, I just want her to be happy, relaxed and understand she doesnae have to fight for herself anymore."

Mack stifled a chuckle. "Brother, she understands that, but trying to tell a dragon not to be a dragon is futile. Those fiery fecking eyes you fell in love with. That's in her DNA. It's who she is. It's fecking special. Why would you want to change that?"

Zander bowed his head. "because she's strong and strong people don't need an anchor. That part of her is incredibly fucking powerful. When in attack mode, that lassie dinnae need anyone and can lose her sincerity. If she continues living like that, she will lose her beautiful vulnerability forever. I dinnae want to harden her, brother, because I'll lose her. I'll become a sultry boy who she tosses away when she gets bored."

"Feck, Zand. You couldn't be more wrong. Dragon, in all her glory, loves you. Whether it's in 'attack mode' like you call it, or in the broken and vulnerable state she's in now. You are everything to her, but your paranoia will destroy what you have. Don't make the same mistakes I did. Trust me, it'll haunt you forever."

Zander pushed his glass away. "I've failed her time and time again. If I can just show her, just once that I can look after her. I wouldn't feel like I'm less than a man around her."

Mack placed a reassuring hand around the back of Zander's neck. "Listen, brother. She's never once seen you as a failure. She's changing everything about herself just to please you and it's hurting her. Dragon has never compromised her identity for anyone." Mack stressed.

"Maybe."

"Feck maybe! Today was the first time I ever saw Dragon scared, and it breaks my heart that the man she loves wants her to live like that. She's making herself unhappy to please you Zand, and before long, she's going to realize that feeling small and frightened doesn't align with her. When that day comes, she'll resent you and feck you off, if you don't fix things now."

"And what if she becomes a fiery mess again? How do I match that energy? Keep her from doing something stupid?"

"Prez, Dragon is a lot of things, but she's not stupid. She's as clinical as you are. She always has a reason for her actions and, as for the fiery mess part, just embrace it man. Match her fecking energy brother and I promise you, once you do, you'll never want to see her as anything other than the take-no-shit dragon she is."

Zander pressed his palms into the bar. "Fuck! Why is everything so hard?"

"Because the easy shit isn't worth doing. Zand, I get it, you've had a rough start, but once Jericho is gone, you're home free. Now sort your shite!" Mack said, slapping his back.

Zander conceded. "I'll call her at lunch. Dragon will be back in full force by the day's end. Thanks, pal!"

Mack embraced him before turning back to church.

"Hey, Irish."

"Yeah." Mack paused and glanced over his shoulder.

"You really think Welsh Cake and I are endgame?"

"Yeah, I do! If you ever hurt her, though, I'll hunt you down and torture you worse than you torture your prey."

Zander chuckled. "I'd expect nothing less."

Mack gave him a curt nod and headed back to church, leaving Zander to ponder.

Zander didn't sit long before Frankie arrived, suited, and booted with a stern look on his face. His sideburns had grayed somewhat, no doubt, under the stress of his manhunt.

"Prez," he said, removing his sunglasses to reveal a stare that matched his tone.

Zander stood and puffed out his chest. "Looking like a true cop with your standard issue gun holster and badge," Zander snapped before bursting into a fit of laughter and embracing him.

"Nice to see you, Frankie. I apologize for the heated conversation yesterday. You were right. I told Welsh Cake everything last night. She seems a little uneasy, but she knows."

"Thanks, brother. Is she embracing her inner dragon again yet?"

Zander scratched his forehead. "That one's taken Mack to talk some sense into me this morning. I'll make that right when I call her at lunch today. That reminds me. You're early. More developments?"

Frankie placed his hands on his low back, creating a subtle crack. "Negative. The threat is imminent, and I want to make sure we're all singing from the same hymn sheet."

"You think Mack will let sleeping dogs lie?"

Frankie shrugged. "Depends on whether he's still hissing like a little bitch about me being FBI."

"Oh, he's still bitching alright."

"Should be fun in church today, then."

Zander laughed. "Just do me a favor. When he throws the first punch, drag his ass outside to have your throw down. Welsh Cake will kill me if I wreck Noah's bar."

"I'll lure him like the grizzly bear he is."

Frankie followed Zander into church to be met with a menacing stare from Mack.

"What the feck is the traitor doing here?" Mack snarled.

"He's here for B's safety. Without Frankie's insight, we would be screwed. Now let's get started." Zander said, showing Frankie to a seat opposite Mack.

As they took their seats, Zander grasped the gavel to start the meeting and as the gavel struck the table, Mack landed a punch to Frankie's nose, busting it wide open.

"Filthy traitor!" he spat, returning to his seat.

Frankie retrieved his handkerchief from his suit pocket to wipe the excess blood from his nose. Everyone stuck, stunned, to their seats, watching his movements, waiting for retaliation.

"Feel better, Mackie Boy?" Frankie said, baring a bloody smile.

"Not even close, asshole. You betrayed me and the club."

Frankie rose to his feet without saying a word. He slipped out of his suit jacket, removed his holster, and unbuttoned his shirt, folding his clothing over his chair, before making way for the exit. Turning back to Mack, he grinned. "Come on then, Mackie Boy. Show us what you're made of."

The pack went wild, hammering their hands onto the table as Zander raised an eyebrow at Mack, who appeared a little dumfounded.

"A dispute between brothers has to be settled," Zander teased.

"He's not my brother," Mack snapped.

"Maybe not, but the air needs to be cleared if you're both planning to stay at my house tonight. Or I can give Welsh Cake a call. That'll unleash the Dragon."

Mack curled his lips. "Then you better make sure I don't kill him. God knows what I'll do to him when I face him out there."

Zander laughed, raising his hand to the pack, encouraging them to watch the wolf fight. "Have at it, fellas."

A cheer erupted as everyone dived from their chairs, rushing outside.

Mack squared up to a shirtless Frankie who towered over him in the busy parking lot. "I'm gonna enjoy beating the crap out of you."

Frankie laughed, before cutting Mack with a deadpan expression and jabbing him in the throat, knocking the wind from his sails as customers leaving the parking lot stared in horror.

Walking away, he laughed as if he was enjoying himself, waiting for Mack to compose himself. "Come now, Mackie Boy. Don't keep a Fed waiting. I wouldn't be the first to beat you in this parking lot, right?"

Mixed emotions rallied around the parking lot as Jimmy turned to Zander. "You gonna stop this shit? It's bad for business."

Zander smirked, taking a seat on a nearby picnic bench. "And ruin the entertainment? Not a chance, brother. Besides, I can't have half-cocked and unfocused wolves right now. I need them on point for Welsh Cake. I'll let them work off the excess testosterone and once Frankie puts Mack in his place, I'll tell them to put their dicks away."

"Mack isn't in the wrong here, Prez. Frankie betrayed him. Betrayed the club."

"Yeah, but he's also throwing his career on the line to help Welsh Cake. Besides, Mack's trying to cozy up to her again, and that trumps their shit."

"But he helped you this morning."

"Yeah, and I'm grateful for that, but it dinnae mean he doesnae need to be reminded of his place, and Welsh Cake would have my balls in a vise if I touched her precious Mackie."

"Oof! That's got to hurt!" Jimmy said, diverting their attention back to the fight where Mack had returned the favor by taking his fist to Frankie's stomach.

Frankie and Mack went punch for punch, delivering blow after blow to one another.

"Is that all you got, Mackie Boy?" Frankie said, spitting the excess blood out of his mouth, decorating the parking lot.

Blood poured from a cut above Mack's left eye. "I'm just warming up, traitor!"

Frankie ushered Mack forward with his fingers. "You talk a lot of shit, boy. Remember who trained you. I can see your chest rise and fall quicker than your wench dropping her panties for you. Fucking harlot!"

"I'll fecking kill you!" Mack roared, tackling Frankie to the ground.

Frankie laughed as he swept Mack onto his back with ease, punching him in the face. "That's for B, asshole. You had the whole fucking world at your fingertips, and what did you do? Destroy your best friend. Look at the danger she's in now, because of your vengeance trip. You ruined everything!" Frankie said, delivering another blow to Mack's face, the blood from his nose and mouth spraying over club members.

"Feck you! You brought her in on your trumped-up case, forcing her to square up to Blaze." Mack screamed as he dug his thumb into Frankie's eye, pushing him off him. Crawling to his feet, Mack booted Frankie in the ribs. "You were my best friend. You're the one who ruined everything and now you die!"

Mack attempted another kick to Frankie's ribs, only for Frankie to catch his leg and drag him to the ground.

The pair rolled over the concrete, tearing lumps out of each other, the rage between them fueled by their prior actions.

Zander intervened. "Right, enough! You've had your pound of flesh. We got work to do!"

Jimmy and Zander dragged them apart with Frankie still laughing his sadistic laugh.

"We good, Mackie Boy?" Frankie said, extending his hand,

Mack swiped his hand away. "Feck you!"

"Come on, let's work together for B."

"Why she still treats you like family. I'll never know," Mack said.

"She trusts me and understands I only want to help her. What have you done to help her, Mackie Boy?"

"Get fecked!"

"No, seriously. She allowed you into her life. Gave you everything and all you did is take. You kicked her when she was down, and you think that's okay because you're in love with her?"

Zander snarled. His hands were still holding Frankie back. Frankie's words infuriated him. B was his and he couldn't stand the thought of someone else wanting her.

"She's my best friend. I'm happy for Dragon and Prez. Loving her is not something I'll apologize for; she's my family. I never wanted to hurt her."

"Funny, that's all you've done!" Frankie smirked.

Mack stepped forward with the aggression of a wild animal until Zander stepped between them, palming their chests to separate them.

"Look! None of this blame game shit matters anymore. What's done is fucking done! Right now, you two need to put your differences behind you because there's a sick son of a bitch gunning for the woman we all fucking love, and if anything happens to her because you two are busy measuring your dicks to comfort your bruised fucking egos, I'll kill you both whilst you sleep, and no, Welsh Cake won't fucking stop me."

Frankie sighed. "Prez is right, Mackie Boy. I know I betrayed you when I infiltrated your club. I didn't expect to find a family. Best friends who I would die for. I understand you won't forgive me, but you betrayed me, too, brother."

"Betrayed you, how?" Mackie snapped.

"When you brought Ari to Uskiville, you let her consume you, and in return, that unleashed a disease upon our family. That disease has spread to Sunnyville, to B and she will die if we don't eradicate it. So, help me, please? If not for me and the club, for B. For our best friend." He extended his hand to Mack once more.

Mack walked away from Frankie, breathing in a clear breath for everyone to see. Shaking his head in despair, he turned and placed his hand in Frankie's. "Fine! But this doesn't mean we're brothers again. This is for Dragon."

"Understood." Frankie said, shaking his hand and giving him a nod.

"Right. Hyde, clean these silly pricks up, whilst the rest of us figure out a plan to catch us a killer. You two meet us in church afterwards. Oh, and you can both explain the state of yourselves to Welsh Cake tonight. I'm no' getting in the doghouse for you pricks fighting."

# CHAPTER TEN
## Awake!

B woke to the distinct smell of burnt bacon. Her head pounded as she opened her eyes to find herself gagged and bound to a steel cage by her ankles and wrists. Her eyes wandered as she captured her surroundings. She appeared to be in an old, derelict warehouse.

The sun beamed through the broken skylight and the clear patches in the dirty windows. Old invoices littered the floor, and in the building's far corner, a makeshift living space. An army green pop-up tent, a fold-up camping chair, and a singular camping stove with a used pan on the burner. The smell of cheap cologne wafted toward her as her capturer approached.

*The janitor*!

Only there was no janitor. It dawned on B to whom the heavy footsteps and ginger hair belonged. The different colored embalmed tattooed skin decorating an old Pitbull cut and his inauspicious grin, as he played with a jagged switchblade upon his approach, unnerved B. Jericho had abducted her from the one place, she thought she was safe and under the nose of all she loved.

*The school security guards wouldn't have batted an eye at Jericho passing himself off as a janitor. Gonzalez had plenty of interchangeable staff.*

*Maybe he used a name badge or the delivery entrance to charm his way into the school?*

B's confused mind spiraled in disbelief as Jericho walked across the cold warehouse floor. The man who left a trail of death on his way to capture stood only twenty meters away from B.

*Scottie will come for me!*

His footsteps were now loud and proud as he danced toward the music of his own melody. Camp-like, as he began singing theater style.

*Oh, I've caught myself a dragon.*

*And now I'm gonna play.*

*I've caught myself a dragon.*

*This bitch is gonna pay.*

Fear vanquished B's pores as her attempts to break free failed her. The plastic cable ties cutting into her ankles and wrists as she rattled the cage in desperation.

B was defenseless with Jericho, free to do what he wanted to her.

"Well, hello my dear. I don't believe we've been introduced. Jericho Walters," he said, removing the filthy gag from her mouth.

B glared, repulsed, terrified, and mute.

"Excuse the makeshift facilities. I had to pitch-up somewhere until I convinced the other Pitbulls to make me their new Prez."

The mention of the Pitbulls made her skin crawl. They had inflicted immense torment on B, and now she remained in peril from their worst sociopath.

"I have to say I'm confused and a little disappointed, Dragon. Someone bold enough to murder my friend, and you have no words. Blaze was one of my very few friends and you took him from me after extracting evidence for your Fed friend. Tell me, is Agent Reed enjoying the gifts I left him? Yours is going to be my best gift yet," Jericho said, removing his cut.

"Fuck you!" B said, trembling and tracking his movements as he neatly folded his switch blade, placing it along the edge of the table. Emptying his pockets, he placed a plastic food bag, tweezers, and a bottle of embalming solution in a neat line on the table like an obsessive, compulsive psychopath.

"Come now dear, manners cost nothing. Now fair's fair. You outed me to the Feds and killed my friend, and now I'm going to torture you and gift you to Agent Reed."

"You can try, asshole."

Jericho stepped within breathing distance. "I believe I have the upper hand here. You're trapped, Dragon, and you'll be dead and delivered to your loved ones before they realize you're missing. You might as well accept your fate. Nobody is coming to rescue you and I can assure you; you'll not break free. Now sit back and enjoy the music. It's beautiful, isn't it?"

"There's no music playing, you fucking whack job!" B growled, baring teeth.

"Hehe! There's always music, Dragon. It's a continuous melody for me. A sweet, sweet lullaby playing over and over. It used to torment me, but now it's part of me. You can't hear it?"

"No, because I'm not fucking nuts!"

Jericho snatched his switch blade and turned on his heels, gripping her throat with one hand, placing the blade a millimeter from her eye. "Don't fucking call me that!" he breathed before releasing her. For twenty-two years, Mom called me that daily. I soon showed her. "Shut up, shut up!" he said, fisting the side of his temple.

The hairs on B's neck stood on end.

*Holy shit. This psycho is going to fucking murder me.*

Her attention returned to Jericho, who took his blade to her gym T-shirt, cutting it down the middle from collar to hem before yanking it, tearing it from her body. The burning sensation she experienced as the cotton dragged against her skin was nothing compared to what she was about to endure.

"Wonderful," he admired. "I bet you spend a fortune on skincare."

"Touch me and you die," she snapped.

"Hehe, oh I love the sass. Woo! Come now Dragon. Stop with the scared girl's pretense. I want to see you shine like the star you are," he said, twirling around with his arms out-reached, theatrically. "I wanna see the carnage, the fire, even if I have to coax it out of you," he said, returning to her and taking down her gym shorts.

"You sick bastard. Is this the only way you can get a woman, you ugly prick?"

"Ew, Dragon. Gross! You may have the Gray Wolves falling over you, but not me, sister. You don't have— How can I explain? You don't have the right tools. All of this..." he said, gesturing to her body, "The whole boobs and pussy thing, disgusting. Now, your Prez, mmm now I'd love to play with him. I see the attraction there. The things I'd do to *him*."

The disgust on B's face radiated as he licked his lips.

"Oh, you're disappointed that I'm repulsed by you," he pouted. "No, dear. I came to terms with my sexuality right after I plunged a knife through Rocky's heart. See betrayal is cold. I developed feelings for him; thought we understood each other's wants, needs, and desires. I gave myself to him. He was the first person I ever trusted, and it was all lies. He took my body for his own gains. Seeking gratification from me when he intended locking me away like a caged animal."

"You were in love with him?"

"Oh, I fell hard, Dragon," he said, pressing his hands to his heart. "My heart belonged to him until I discovered he was blue. A vile Fed. He had files upon files of damming evidence on club activity, including drug runs and my victims. My cut had fewer tattoos back then, but I have flourished since."

He directed B to his grotesque tattoo covered cut. There must have been over one hundred tattoos embalmed and stitched onto the black leather, preserved by a varnish-like shine.

*Those poor people, murdered by this monster.*

"Killing the man, I love freed me, Dragon. I no longer feel pain anymore. Now, I'm just tying up loose ends," Jericho continued.

"Then why strip me? If it's an attempt to scare me, it's not bloody working!"

"This is just art, princess. I need a blank canvass and you're it, and I know all about the property of the Prez tattoo on your backside. I'll be taking that, too."

B rattled the cage, trying to break free. "You're a sick man."

"I call it creative expression. Now these will make a fine addition to my cut," he said, gesturing to her tattoos on her near-naked body.

B spat in his face.

Jericho glared at her in disgust. "Now, that's not nice. I'll take your Dragon's head for that."

B screamed in pain as he took his blade to her ribs. The jagged blade took her breath away as Jericho dug into her flesh without a moment's notice to remove the head from her dragon tattoo, waving the blood-soaked skin in her face.

"Precious!" he said, kissing it and turning his back on her to tend to the fleshy dragon head he'd stolen from her.

B wailed in frustration, rattling the cage detaining her. Blood wept from her wrists as her fruitless attempts to break free broke nothing but her skin. Sweat poured from her head as warm blood from her beheaded Dragon tattoo seeped down her torso, decorating her peach lace thong in a sea of red. Nausea provided her dehydrated lips with a watery mouth as she swallowed down the bile in her stomach. B lost her identity the moment he took it from her. The very essence of her being. Jericho had taken the head of her dragon, and it destroyed her.

# She's Gone!

Zander demanded order in church as his phone rang. Madoc was calling him.

"Shut the fuck up!" he screamed, banging his gavel onto the table.

Answering the call, he heard panic in Madoc's voice.

"Zander, something's happened. My mum is missing!"

Zander's heart sank. His face was white as a sheet as he placed the call on the loudspeaker for his brothers to hear. Church went dead silent from his reaction; a pin drop could be heard.

"What do you mean, she's missing?"

"She didn't turn up for class after lunch." Madoc's strained voice could barely convey his words. "Her office: there was a needle, and a note left for Uncle Frankie. The police are on their way. Zander, I don't know what to do. Rhys is crying his eyes out, and my dad isn't answering his phone. Please, come and help us."

Zander dropped his head in anguish. His face turning shades of purple as pain and anger ripped through him.

"Dinnae worry, laddie, me, and the whole club, along with your Uncle's Frankie and Mack, are on their way. Sit tight. We'll get her back soon."

Zander hung up the phone, speechless.

Jimmy attempted to interrupt until Zander lost his mind, picking up the oak table to throw it. "I'll fucking kill that son of a bitch!"

Mack and Jimmy grabbed hold of him. "Clear fecking head, now, Prez. Let's get her back!" Mack snapped.

"Get onto Tyr. Find out what the fuck's going on?" Jimmy snapped at Hyde.

Frankie sat tapping furiously on his phone, while the other members straightened the table.

They all stopped to watch him.

"Come on, you bastard, where are you?" he shouted into his phone.

"What the feck are you doing?" Mack asked.

"She's wearing the necklace you gave her, right?"

"Yeah," he shrugged, looking bewildered. "She was wearing it this morning. Why?"

"I placed a tracker in it before you gifted it to her. I'll have her location in a second if this piece of shit loads."

A glimmer of hope reached Zander's consciousness as his heart rate continued to race in rapid succession.

Mack grimaced. "You fecking what? That was a gift!"

"Yeah, and I always warned you, you'd be the death of her. That tracker could save her fucking life right now."

Zander couldn't breathe. Four seconds for the tracker to appear felt like an eternity.

"Fuck! We're gonna need back up. She's at the docks. Somewhere between the shipping yard and the desolate warehouses. My money is on the warehouses," Frankie said standing and ripping his suit jacket from the back of his chair.

"Christ! They stretch for miles, Frankie." Zander said, clawing his hands down his face.

"Then we better fucking move. I'll call it in. Let's go!"

Zander turned to Jimmy. "Jimmy, I need you at the school, please, brother? I need you to take care of the laddies, and I demand to know what those three numpties were doing when my old lady was taken."

"You got it, man. I'll handle it. Go bring her home."

# CHAPTER TWELVE
## Tortured

Jericho continued to work on B, removing her identity in sequential succession while she screamed in pain. After he removed the head of her Dragon, he turned his attention to her 'property of the Prez' tattoo.

Zander had insisted B and all members of the Gray Wolves Motorcycle Club have a tattoo before leaving Uskiville to mark his promotion as Prez.

B was first in line. Zander convinced her to have the tattoo on his favorite part of her anatomy: her backside. Instructing Mack to tattoo the Gray Wolves patch with "property of the Prez" inscribed around it, and as the club's tattooist, Mack was happy to oblige.

Zander had B's Dragon tattooed onto his chest with "Property of Dragon," inscribed around it. He then instructed all patched members to have B's dragon on their chests with the Gray Wolves signage around it: the club's tribute and appreciation to B for all that she had done for the club.

B's left glute muscle spasmed as Jericho dug into her flesh. The tattoo removal lacked precision, but the tattoo was treated with embalming solution and stored carefully, suggesting its importance to Jericho's twisted trophy collection.

B's cold and clammy body weakened: exhaustion taking hold. The fight had never really entered B's soul today. Zander had tamed her inner Dragon, leaving B in a heightened state of anxiety in the weeks leading up to today, and now she was in a state of resolution, resigning herself to her impending death.

She'd lost all hope of being rescued. Jericho's MO had been made known to her. He tore the flesh from his victims to wear as a trophy and, after toying with their emotions, he plunged a knife into their heart. That was the destiny she resigned herself to now.

The dragon was dead, and she would follow.

A lump formed in her throat as her thoughts drifted to her boys, her world.

*How will they take it? How will they recover?*

Fear, anger, and desperation rose through her as Jericho toyed with her once more.

"Pretty necklace. You won't be needing that anymore," he said, distracting her from her thoughts, snapping it off her neck and tossing it across the warehouse.

*If I'm going to die, I'm not giving that sicko the satisfaction of hearing me cry.*

"Fuck you! You nut job! You fucking psychopath. Got your heart broken so you take it out on the world. Newsflash asshole, nobody cares! The world doesn't care. People go through worse shit, and do they take it out on innocents? No, you're a special kind of whacko. What's the matter, Mommy didn't love you enough?"

Jericho slapped her across the face. "Shut up, bitch. Shut your God damn mouth."

B spat her blood at him. "Oh, touchy. Let me guess. She despised who you became. Saw your sick little tendencies growing up and all she felt was shame. Am I right?"

Jericho fisted his head again. "Argh, I said shut up. Shut up! All you women are the same. You're evil, and you don't know what love is. Women like you just take, twist and cause pain. My momma was the same. She loved my sister. Worshipped her. And what did I get? Nothing but abuse."

"Oh, boo bloody hoo. Grow the fuck up, good boy. Everyone has inner child wounds. The difference being normal people work through them. We don't carve people up because we can't face our own demons. You pathetic prick!"

"Ahh, but my momma was different," Jericho said, turning away. His voice was quiet. "Momma only wanted pretty girls. And me? I tried to be pretty for her, but it disgusted her. So, she made me uglier than ever by setting my shirt on fire. It stuck to me as it seared my skin. Well, who's laughing now? I showed her, and now I'll show you, Dragon."

# CHAPTER THIRTEEN

# Ticking Clock

Frankie led the team of Gray Wolves along the highway and down onto the docks, scanning potential places Jericho might've taken B. He was like a bat out of hell, swerving in and out of traffic with his foot on the gas.

"How much farther?" Zander spoke into his microphone.

"A couple of miles. Must be near the old paper factory."

Racing along, Frankie attempted to drown out his fear, keeping his eyes fixed on B's tracker. His thoughts returning to the last time he had seen her. Their last embrace on Christmas day.

*Hold on B, we're coming!*

Guilt absorbed him as he cast his mind back to all the calls he refused to answer, refusing to lie to her. Only now, he'd do anything to hear her voice.

B had become Frankie's family. He couldn't lose her to Jericho, too. He'd already taken enough from him. The frightful evening of Rocky's death taking its turn in his frantic mind now. Cradling his best friend in the pouring rain as he lay dead in his arms. Jericho's artistry displayed in all its glory as Frankie shed tears over his corpse.

*No! I'm not losing anyone else.*

He made a sharp right turn, almost hitting Zander off his bike.

"Christ, pal! Are you trying to fucking kill me?"

"Sorry Prez. The tracker moved. Hang right along the water." He turned right onto another road.

Frankie moved closer to the tracker, watching as he closed in on the red flashing beacon of hope for B's survival. Frankie knew the clock was ticking and her time was running out. After she'd been held captive for hours, Frankie prayed for her survival. Who knew how long Jericho kept his prey before they met their maker?

# CHAPTER FOURTEEN

# Plunge

B knew she was taking a risk, toying with Jericho's emotions. Taunting Jericho whilst she was bound to a steel cage wasn't her brightest idea; it was her only idea and the only weapon she had to disarm him.

*If I can get into his head, I can buy me some time. He may kill me quicker. A risk I have to take.*

"Hey, can I ask you something?" B said to Jericho, who was busy with his tweezers and embalming solution.

"What?" he snapped.

"What about your father? You've not mentioned him."

Jericho shrugged. "Died when I was four. What of it?"

"What was he like?"

Jericho turned to approach her, smiling a sinister smile. "He was kind. He wasn't like me," he said, digging the tweezers into her arm. "You think you can appear to my softer side, Dragon? You're out of luck. I don't fucking have one! Before I kill you, I'll capture the blue butterfly on your thigh. My patience is wearing thin with you, and Agent Reed needs his gift on time."

"Why taunt him? You took his best friend already."

"And now I'll take another one. A brother and a sister. A matching pair and twice the torment," he teased.

"Why?" she asked. "Rocky was the one who hurt you, not him."

Jericho tilted his head in amusement. "Oh, he played his part."

"How? By avenging his best friend, his brother?"

"That and because of what Rocky said with his dying breath," he said with a casual shrug as he cut into B's thigh.

B bit into her lip, once again refusing to provide him the satisfaction of enjoying her apparent pain as Jericho continued.

"Oh, alright. I'll spill," he said in a humorous tone. "You know, I've never had a girlfriend before. This is fun," he teased, removing her baby blue butterfly with his tweezers, and placing it on the table. He turned to face her, sitting back onto the table, swinging his legs in sadistic glee.

"Okay, so before Rocky and I had our heart to heart, shall we say? Hehe. He decided he would cut me deeper than death itself. See, that little scamp had me all kinds of crazy for him. I was head over heels in love. Torturing him brought on a whole new meaning of love for me. So, I was busy taking my mementos," he said, gesturing to B's tattoos on the table, "and that's when he told me. Now buckle up, sister. This is the juicy bit."

B listened, desperate to understand.

Jericho's hands gestures provided the dramatics as he continued. "I was grateful Noah wasn't up to killing my dreamboat, my secret love. He was a young pup. He wasn't ready for that, but me I was an angry, broken man. Rocky destroyed me. Yes, the man I'd fallen for told me his heart never belonged to me as he was in love with his marine fancy, his best friend. He told me no one could ever love a monster like me. He just enjoyed taking me so he could torment me once he arrested me. I mean, the audacity, right?"

*Oh, my days! Rocky was in love with Frankie!*

"Did he ever tell Frankie?"

"Oh, who cares? I plunged my knife into his heart faster than a toupee in a hurricane. You know, nothing like a gay man scorned and all that," he said, jumping up onto his feet. "That concludes today's lesson. Agent Reed is getting his just desserts because the man I loved chose him. I kill you and he has nobody left to love. It's bittersweet, don't you think?"

"And me? I deserve this because I got a confession out of Blaze?" B asked, keeping him talking.

"Oh. honey, no. It's not like that," he said, stroking her sweat-glistened forehead. "Blaze was a brother to me, yes, but only by biker code. I'm killing you only to hurt Agent Reed. To be honest, I'm a little sad I'm ending your life. We've spent the day bonding. Unfortunately for you, the heart wants what it wants, girlfriend."

Retrieving his blade from the table, he stepped toward B.

"Can I have one last request? Like the movies, right? I mean, you said yourself we've bonded today?"

"I won't deny a last request. You have been fun. Name it," he said, placing his blade in his back pocket and retrieving a pen from a different pocket to take notes.

B's smile confused him. "Remember my face when Agent Reed slices your throat? You will die by his hands, and I'll be fucking dancing on your grave, asshole." B burst into a fit of hysterical laughter, infuriating Jericho, who once again retrieved his switch blade to charge toward her.

"Say hi to Rocky for me, Dragon, and don't worry, I'll wear your badges with honor," he said placing the blade at her sternum.

B stared him down as the knife pierced her skin. "Come on you psycho, what are you waiting for? Bloody do it!" she screamed.

A gunshot interrupted them as a bullet tore through Jericho's hand.

B whipped her head around to see Frankie's face wreathed in fury, pointing his gun at Jericho.

*Oh, thank fuck!*

Jericho seethed, picking up his blade with his good hand, attempting to attack B again. Frankie intervened with haste, shooting him in his bicep, stopping him in his tracks.

Racing over to the scene of the crime, Frankie disarmed Jericho as a multitude of FBI agents and angry bikers swarmed the building.

"Got you, you sick son of a bitch." Frankie snapped, kicking Jericho in the ribs as he read him his rights.

Once Jericho was cuffed, Frankie's colleagues dragged him to his feet, allowing Frankie to deliver a fist to his stomach, knocking the wind out of him.

Relief washed through B like an ocean wave, the ordeal too much for her. Her consciousness failing her fragile body, and the sound of Zander's voice distorted as she lost her battle with the waking world.

B woke in hospital with a fright as Zander, Mack, and Frankie stood at her bedside. The doctors had taken care of her wounds and taken some blood, requesting a full blood work up following the injection she received to subdue her.

"Hey, darling. Welcome back." Zander said, kissing her cheek.

B dismissed him, looking straight at Frankie.

"Where is he?" she asked, climbing out of bed, ignoring her pain receptors crying out, making her aware of her injuries.

"Whoa! Steady there, B. He's locked away. We got him. Now get back in bed."

"No chance. Get me access to that sicko!"

Frankie took a step toward her. "B, I know you're upset..."

"Upset?" B laughed. "No! Angry, pissed. Fucking evil, maybe. That guy needs to die."

"Welsh Cake, listen to yourself. You're no' thinking straight," Zander said, placing his arm around her, ushering her back to the bed.

B shrugged him off in an instant. "Don't touch me, asshole. I'm not your property anymore in case you haven't bloody noticed. That sadistic fucker took your mark from me after you promised to keep me safe. Place my trust in you. Pfft. Jericho had a knife at my heart today and all because I allowed you to tame my inner dragon. You made me weak, good boy. That's never happening again."

Zander palmed the wall, a gaunt appearance on his face as he whispered to her. "Welsh Cake, please? I'm sor—"

"Save it. I'm done listening. I keep getting screwed over repeatedly. No more," B said, with fire in her eyes.

Turning to Mack, she placed her head on his. "Mackie, I need your help. He took the head of my dragon. If Frankie won't give me access to that sicko, I need to go back to Uskiville with the boys today."

"Over my dead fucking body!" Zander snapped.

B ignored him. Her eyes fixated on her best friend, pleading with him.

Mack smiled at her, gripping the back of her neck. "You know what, Dragon? When someone is stupid enough to cut off the head of a dragon, two new heads grow back fiercer than ever before. Uskiville will always be your home. Whatever you need is yours."

"Stand down, Irish, or I'll have your throat." Zander bellowed.

"Easy, Prez. Maybe a few days away will do her some good?" Mack said.

"Have you got rocks in your head? No fucking chance!"

B faced off with Zander, "and you're going to bloody stop me? All I've ever done is love you and it's made me weak. I need a break from you. From Sunnyville, from fucking everything. I'm going to my cabin, and you're staying here. I need to think seriously about my future, and I can't do it around you."

Zander loosened his collar and rolled up his sleeves. "Fuck!" he wailed, punching a hole in the wall.

B ignored his tantrum, too consumed by her wounded pride; it angered her as she bayed for Jericho's blood. "When can I get out of here?"

"As soon as the docs dismiss you. I want a statement before you leave." Frankie said.

"You want my statement? Jericho Walters will die by my hands."

"B stop this!" Frankie said, taking her arm. "I know you're hurting bu—"

"You have no fucking idea what I am, Frankie. What that monster did. What he told me about Rocky, about you. Don't bloody tell me what I'm feeling because you have no fucking clue."

Frankie removed his hand, raising his arms in defense.

"Good. Now, if everyone has finished telling me what I'm doing and how I'm feeling, I'm going home to see my boys. Mackie, can you come back to the house and help me pack, please?"

"As soon as you get the all-clear, Dragon, and not before."

# CHAPTER FIFTEEN

# Congratulations Agent!

Frankie entered the hospital ward where Jericho was spending the night. He'd received treatment from the doctors who displayed contempt toward him for being a sinister serial killer. Their lack of compassion showed throughout as the felon remained cuffed to his bed.

Armed officers guarded his private room and down the ward corridor. They deemed Jericho high-risk, a danger to all.

Acknowledging his subordinates, Frankie entered the room to find Jericho sleeping. Anger seared through him as acid wreaked havoc on his stomach. Rocky's killer was now in his clutches and Frankie would bring him to justice after years of waiting.

Digging his thumb into Jericho's wounded bicep empowered him as he watched him wake, wincing in pain like a weasel.

Frankie released him, placing his cell on the table to record the conversation.

"You have my attention, asshole. Aside from killing my best friend, what desperation brought you to come after me? Wrong move, silly dick, and B's safe, by the way. You lose!"

Jericho cocked his head, providing a mischievous smile. "Did I, though? Rocky is dead. Oh, watching his life leave him was beyond remarkable. You should have seen it."

Frankie punched him in the face. "Keep going dirtbag, I got time."

Jericho licked the fresh blood from his lips. "I wouldn't be so sure, Agent. Dragon will fall sooner rather than later, despite my incarceration. I have spies everywhere. Once a Pitbull, always a Pitbull. I have marked her card, and you will witness another best friend's death. Anyone you have ever loved, or love will die. I'm will haunt your dreams until my last breath."

"Empty threats don't scare me. Look at you. A psychopath looking for attention."

"Don't call me that," he sneered.

Frankie roared with laughter, clutching his abdominal muscles. "A psychopath? That's what you are. Tell me, why kill all those women?"

"It was fun, and I had to leave a trail of breadcrumbs. Although the grand finale went awry, I have contingencies in place. I like Dragon. She's a firecracker! We bonded over you. I think she likes me. I'll see her again."

Frankie gripped hold of Jericho's hospital gown with vexation in his voice. "You're a deluded asshole. Killing innocents for fun and, as for B, she doesn't bond with people like you."

"On the contrary. We're BFFs now. Well, until she breathes her last breath. She can say hi to Rocky for you. Compare deaths."

"Fuck you! It's over! You're not going anywhere. Now tell me why you killed him."

Jericho smiled, closing his eyes, he laid his head back onto his pillow. "You'll have to ask Dragon. She knows all the deets. Now if you'll excuse me, I have to get my beauty sleep. A Pitbulls job is never done! I'll see you real soon, Agent. We have a long relationship ahead."

"We're seeking the death penalty, Dickwad, and I'll watch as you burn in hell."

"I don't think so. I'll be on a comfy psych ward. Untouchable and you'll visit often."

Frankie strolled to the door, frustrated by the lack of clarity over Rocky's murder. "See you never Jericho. Rocky will be laughing, knowing you're in custody."

"Oh, that smile. Shame how it vanished as I plunged my blade into his chest. Dragon will fill in the gaps and I'll be seeing you soon. Real soon."

Frankie snatched his cell from the table after almost forgetting it, taking one last glance at the crazed lunatic, sitting in hysterical laughter. Slamming the door in anger, rage fueled him. He thought he'd feel better or relieved after bringing Jericho to justice, only he felt more angered that Jericho was still breathing. B had almost died, and his oldest and best friend deserved more than his murderer lapping up a life in the psych ward. Psychopath or not, Jericho was still making threats. Threats requiring attention. Jericho was correct. Although he was in custody, he remained a threat and could not be trusted.

Frankie entered the department to be congratulated by his team and superior officer.

"Well done, son. Years of hard graft finally paying off. With Jericho behind bars, we can talk about that promotion you have always wanted. You've shown resolve, professionalism, and much resilience and I'm proud of you."

"Thank you, Sir. I will have the paperwork on your desk by tonight," he said, shaking his hand and walking the short distance to his office.

Closing the door behind him, he shrugged out of his blazer, tossing it onto his chair.

*This asshole is gonna keep coming until he gets the needle.*

Reaching for the bottom drawer in his desk, he retrieved a bottle of B's Welsh Whiskey. Holding the glass bottle, the red dragon decorating it reminded him of his best friend.

*She's not safe until he dies. Fuck! I gotta get out of here.*

Placing the bottle back in the drawer, he slammed it shut and headed to Uskiville.

# CHAPTER SIXTEEN

# Going Home

B informed the boys they were going to surprise Ari, baby Alex, and the boys. After packing their suitcases, B set her house alarm, and they headed for her truck out front. They were loading the last of the luggage when B noticed Tyr arriving, parking adjacent to her truck.

"Give me a minute, Mackie Boy, please?"

Mack took the case, handing it to Tiny, and ushered Madoc and Rhys into the truck as B approached Tyr, who had cut his engine, removed his helmet, and was storming toward her.

B could see how flustered he was. His face was bright red and the same remorseful stare in his eyes she had seen a thousand times before when Zander had stood her up, stared back at her.

"Hey, Tyr…"

He hugged her tightly, oblivious to her injuries. "Are you alright Mrs. Prez? I'm sorry, I had to see for myself and apologize for allowing this to happen on my watch. I didn't see him enter. This is my—"

B released herself from his grip, interrupting him. His beautiful features pained with regret. "No, my lovely. This wasn't your fault and I'm fine. I just require a few days away to recover."

"Are you disappointed in me? I failed to protect you."

B couldn't help but laugh. "Look around, good boy. You're not the first and you won't be the last. Besides, you haven't failed me. We had no idea who we were dealing with. He just outwitted us, that's all. Please don't beat yourself up about it."

Tyr's face hardened as he stared at the ground.

B caressed his cheek, making him look at her, giving him her best smile. "You're a good boy, Tyr. You're young, bright, and talented and wasted in the bar. When I get back, I'm going to bring you into my security team. If you want that?"

Tyr closed his eyes; she could see he was struggling. "I don't deserve that. I need to face Prez's wrath for letting you down."

"You tell Prez I'll break his handsome face if he lays a finger on you, good boy."

Tyr smiled, removing her hand and straightening himself up like a soldier standing at attention. "No, I disappointed myself and my Prez today and I'll face the music like a man. I would offer to come with you, but I doubt Prez will ever trust me again."

"Oh Tyr, you're such a sweet boy. Don't worry, I'm fine. I'll be back before you know it and I'll talk to Prez about a security placement. I won't have you waste your life in a bar. You're so much more than that."

Tyr nodded, placing his hands in his pockets. "Thank you. You sure you'll be, okay?"

"Absolutely. Now, promise me you won't allow this to get you down."

"Promise."

B gave him a hug and kissed his cheek. "I'll come by the club when I return to check on you."

"Thank you, Mrs. Prez. I'd like that."

He turned to leave, and B called out to him as she climbed into her truck.

"Hey, Tyr."

"Yes, Mam?"

"Never change. You have a perfect soul and I'd hate to see you harden like most of the MC. Take care, my lovely."

Mack, B, and the boys hit the highway shortly after her release from the hospital, leaving a furious Zander heading for the MC.

B couldn't wait to escape Sunnyville. The past months had proved heavy on her heart and soul. She needed time to figure out her next steps. Consumed by anger and revenge, B's mind fixated on delivering justice to Jericho as Mack drove her truck back to Uskiville, towing his bike whilst Tiny followed behind.

Mack was the first to break the silence.

"Talk to me, Dragon," he said, eyes fixated on the highway.

B stared out of the passenger's side window. "About?"

"How you're feeling? Your plan of attack? Anything. You're never short of something to say, so don't start now."

B winced in pain, glancing back to ensure Madoc and Rhys had their air pods in. Convinced they were not listening, she began.

"Mackie, I'm ashamed of myself. I need to reignite my inner dragon. This submissive version of myself isn't who I am. I've become soft and all because I didn't want to offend the man I love. The stupidity came back to haunt me! Jericho's incident wouldn't have occurred if I had stayed true to myself. I thought Scottie loved me for me but he's just like—"

"Like me?"

"Mackie, I—"

"No. Say it, Dragon. Prez is just like me."

B placed her hand on his forearm. "Mackie, I never meant it like that. And for the record, you tried to cage me, not change who I was. You always celebrated my fiery side. You just suffocated me. Totally different."

Mack laughed. "Because that's so much better?"

B couldn't help but laugh.

"You're wrong though." Mack said to her straight. "Prez worships you. We all do. How he kept his shit together after taking that call from

Madoc, I'll never know. I was dying inside. That guy just wants to be your hero, Dragon. The problem is, in your story, only you can be the hero!"

B narrowed her eyes. "That's not true!"

"Bullshite, Dragon! You always have to save yourself and others. You always need to feel in control. Today, you lost that, and that's why you want Jericho's head. He took control away from you, worse than anyone else has ever done. Today you were weak, somebody else's prey, and now you're wounded by it. Prez didn't change you or tame your inner dragon. You did! You did that and now you're projecting the blame. Now suck that shite up. Own it, heal from it!"

B sulked, resting her head against the window. "Remind me never to come to you for sympathy."

"You want sympathy? Look in a fecking dictionary. You chose your path. If you don't like it, change it. Dragon, you taught me that, remember?"

"I taught you too well, and why do you think I'm here, asshole?"

Mack chuckled. "Yeah, I got that at the hospital. So, what's the plan? Have an 80s style training montage while doing yoga up the valley?"

"Piss off!"

"I'll put you through your paces."

B glanced over her shoulder and made sure her boys remained engrossed in their phones. Turning back to Mack, she tilted her chin. "You're going to teach me how to shoot!"

Mack whipped his head to make eye contact, distracting him from the road. "What?"

"You heard me. I'm in Uskiville for some R&R as far as Sunnyville and Frankie are concerned, but you and I have work to do, Mackie Boy."

"No!"

B kicked the footwell in frustration. "What do you mean, no?"

Mack lowered his voice to an angry whisper. "I'm not letting you throw your life away because your ego got bruised. Besides, you fecking hate guns and there's only one reason you would want to learn how to fire one. You can't get to Jericho in prison. So what? You think you can walk into the courthouse and bang? That's it?"

"That's my intention!"

"Are you crazy?" Mack's ballistic rage disturbed the boys in the back of the truck. "Sorry boys. Plug back into your music. My road rage has gotten no better."

Rhys had Madoc gave him an amusing glance before adjusting their earbuds. Mack waited until he was sure they were submerged in their own worlds before nudging her thigh.

"Ow! For fuck's sake. I'm trying to heal there!"

"What the feck, Dragon. Are you fecking nuts? Law enforcement will arrest you before you get to him. Is this prick worth more to you than your family? Your livelihood? I don't fecking think so. Christ on a bike!"

"He has to go, Mackie. What he's done. He killed innocent women because they resembled me. He has taunted Frankie, and Frankie has no clue about half of what's gone on. If he knew, he would kill Jericho himself. That man does not deserve to breathe for what he's done."

"Then let Frankie do it! You don't get to play God, Dragon, and what happened to black and white?"

"Haven't you been taking notice? I've not been white in a minute."

Mack shook his head, tapping the indicator to turn left. "You'll always be white to me, Dragon."

"To hell with white. That sicko will continue his reign of terror from his cell. You know it. I know it! So, help me, please?"

Mack released a loud sigh. "No! I'm not letting my best friend throw her life away like this. You want your tattoos fixed, I'm your guy: want to grapple? Great! But a suicide mission, not fecking happening. I'll imprison you if I have to."

"And how well did that work out for you last time?" B teased, her grin wide and bright.

"Dragon don't be an asshole. You've come to me because you know

Prez wouldn't help, and I agree with him. Let this shite go. He's going down. He'll never get out."

"And I'm always going to be in danger whilst he's breathing."

"We'll keep you safe."

B cackled. "Because you've all done a stellar job so far. I'm finished with the cascade of lies, Mackie. It's time to put it to bed."

"Dragon, I'm telling you to leave this alone."

"Mackie, I'm doing this, and if you won't help me, I'll find someone who will."

# CHAPTER SEVENTEEN

# Incarcerated

The hospital discharged Jericho into police custody following medical treatment. The custody officer processed him and directed him to a holding cell, where he waited for his defense attorney to arrive. He made no bones about demanding his phone call.

Using his uninjured hand, he established contact with Sully.

"I see things didn't go according to plan, judging by the hordes of Feds and wolves at the warehouse," Sully teased.

"On the contrary, all best laid plans require adaptations and ulterior exit strategies. Even my plans have plans. Now I'll admit my incarceration came a little premature. However, I have a team of seasoned Pitbulls aiding me on the inside. I assume you called my attorney?"

"I did. He should be there already. So, what's next?" Sully asked.

"Is the cannon fodder ready to execute our plan?"

"Ready when you are."

"Start with the strays. I'll have a cell phone as soon as I've transferred, so wreak havoc on your end until I provide my next instruction."

"You got it, boss!"

"And Sully, let me remind you, I'm just as dangerous in here as I am out there. Remain vigilant and I'll see you soon."

Following his phone call, officers dragged him into an interrogation room where his defense attorney waited.

The suited attorney informed him of his options.

"There's no way out of this, Mr. Walters. The charges are quite substantial. I can attempt to get a plea bargain, but this is a slam dunk for the DA."

"What do you mean? I'm certifiably insane. Diminished actuality will suffice."

"I'm not sure that's the best option. You're a serial killer. Not to mention a cop killer."

Jericho bared teeth. "You're not listening. That is my only option here. You want me to prance about demonstrating a lack of awareness of my surroundings? Headbutt a wall, bite your fucking nose. Just say the word."

The attorney continued. "They'll interrogate you, and I can suggest a psych evaluation. Without knowing the details, I am limited in what I can do."

Jericho broke into a theatrical song. "Okay, but just remember, I know where your precious family lives. So, your ass is on the line too."

# CHAPTER EIGHTEEN

# Played Like a Fiddle!

Frankie stared through the reciprocal mirror at a mute Jericho, witnessing the district attorney's interrogation.

"This asshole is playing the DA like a fiddle. That bullshit vacant expression isn't fooling anyone," he said, gesturing to a dribbling Jericho.

"Easy Frankie, they're just getting started."

"Come on Ray. He's like a wet fucking newspaper in there. Let me go ruffle his feathers. I'll get him to talk."

Ray reached up, placing an arm around his shoulder. "Give the DA a chance. They know what they're doing."

Frankie propped up the mirror's frame, eagle-eyeing the serial killer as the DA posed another question to be met by silence. He could feel the inferno rise within him as the nervous DA attempted another question.

"As you can see, my client is incapable of comprehension, therefore he cannot answer your question," the nervous defense attorney said.

"Fuck this!" Frankie snapped, rushing out of the room, brushing off his superior officer en route to the interrogation room.

Anger burned through his soul. His all-consuming rage was now the driving force of his expression. He flung the door open wide, frightening the suited men whilst Jericho's expression remained unaltered as Frankie gripped him by his prison issue jumpsuit.

"Talk, you sick son of a bitch, or I'll *make* you," Frankie said, spitting at him.

Ray attempted to pull Frankie away as the DA stood with the defense attorney to protest.

"Unhand my client, Agent, or I'll ensure you lose your badge. My client is incapable of basic communication and this abuse of power is shameful," the defense attorney shouted.

Frankie released Jericho, dropping him into the metal framed chair, approaching the defense attorney, who gulped in fear. "Are you fucking kidding me, asshole? He's taunted us for months! He was more than capable of killing six women and attempting to kill another." Frankie slammed his hands onto the metal framed table, causing its legs to buckle. "He was perfectly fucking capable of avoiding security footage and leaving sick messages on the victims' bodies addressed to myself and another victim."

Frankie turned and gripped onto Jericho shoulders, applying pressure to the top of his wounded arm, attempting, and failing to prompt a reaction. "This sick fuck has been clinical since he killed an officer of the law, and he made a phone call. I even have a recorded confession on my phone from the hospital. So, tell me, how the fuck does he not comprehend the questions?"

The attorney's sheepish expression provided Frankie with all he needed to know.

"Oh, I see. He's got his claws in you," Frankie nodded. "Threaten your family, by any chance?"

The attorney's eyes widened as he mopped beads of sweat from his forehead. "I don't know what you're accusing my client of Agent, but—"

Frankie cut him off. "Save it asshole. You're already dead in his eyes," he said, shaking his head at him.

Turning to the DA, he grimaced. "This asshole doesn't get diminished actuality! Take it off the table, you simple-minded fucking job's worth. He's fucking playing you! You have a duty of care to the citizens of this state by seeking the truth beyond all reasonable doubt. You swore an oath to uphold the law. He murdered innocent people, and he's a fucking COP KILLER! Now do your fucking job, you sack of shit, or you're just as bad as he is."

Frankie left the room, barging past Ray as Jericho remained unfazed and continued his act of insanity, adding rocking and holding himself in his chair to lay further foundations for his case.

Frankie made haste for his office, whacking files from other agents' hands and barging past anyone in his path. Entering his office, he double palmed the items on his desk, sending everything flying like a paper airplane before it crash-landed onto the floor.

A guttural rasp ripped through his body as he white-knuckle rode the wooden desk, rattling it as if he was undertaking an isometric exercise.

Ray rushed in behind him, closing the door.

Frankie green-eyed him. "That bastard isn't getting off lightly. For all we know, he has everyone in his fucking pocket. I promised Rocky's mother justice: promised *myself* justice. He doesn't get to waltz around in a padded-fucking cell after we've all endured so much pain!"

"Frankie. Allow the DA to do their job. Justice will be served! Your barging in there could have compromised the case."

Frankie released the desk, dragging a palm through his hair. "I'm sorry, Ray. It's just, it's been a hell of a few years and now we have him, I can't allow him to be awarded leniency."

Ray stared at his feet. His hands twitched in his pockets as he stepped toward Frankie. Retrieving his hip flask from his inside pocket and unscrewing the cap, he took a small sip and handed it to Frankie.

Frankie pursed his lips, snatching the flask and guzzling its contents. He stared out of his window to be met with a sea of office buildings in front of him.

"Do I need to enforce annual leave here, Frankie? If you're unravelling, son, I need you to step away."

Frankie placed Ray's hip flask back in his pocket. Nodding in acknowledgement, he straightened his tie, composing himself by taking a deep breath. "No sir. Listen. I lost my head for a second. It won't happen again!"

"Can you promise me that? Because it's my ass on the line here, too."

Frankie turned to face him. He couldn't afford to be pulled from the case now. He was determined to see justice prevail till the end. "Ray. It will not happen again! Come on. How long have you known me? How many times have I lost my temper?"

"This being a first worries me."

Frankie's voice became low. His crazed stare and heavy breaths resolved into a composition of business and composure. "Ray, I'll follow your lead on this if I have to. I have to see this through. I'll never forgive myself if I screw this up."

Ray palmed his face with both hands. "We'll get you through this, Frankie. Just keep your cool and we'll nail this bastard. He'll fry for sure!"

Frankie closed his eyes, attempting to hide his contempt for Ray's naivety. Jericho was spinning a web of deceit, and Frankie knew from the DA's gaunt expression, he was ready to hand Jericho a deal of some sort. In Frankie's opinion, the below par DA had no fight in him. He didn't command the room and demand Frankie leave after his outburst: Frankie could smell the fear on him and that just wouldn't do. No, Frankie himself would have to ensure justice prevailed to ensure B's safety if the judicial system failed him.

# CHAPTER NINETEEN

# Long Live the Pitbulls

Jericho refused to answer questions throughout his entire interrogation. Instead, he continued to display his vacant expression and, after two hours of non-conversing and a lengthy spell in a holding cell, his case was presented to a judge. The judge denied Jericho bail and ordered him to be remanded into custody to await trial, allowing both the DA and defense to build their cases.

Jericho blew Frankie a kiss as officers escorted him into a prison transfer vehicle with four armed officers and transferred him to Wellridge Maximum Security Prison, where his belongings were taken, and he was issued with inmate clothing.

The over-run prison provided Jericho with his own cell in protective custody. He was just settling in when another inmate drew near, mopping the floor, and handed him a book.

"Long live the Red Pitbulls," he said, showing his tattooed patch on his right forearm. "Thank you for taking care of us on the outside. We appreciate you feeding our families after Blaze's murder. You have brothers here supporting your cause, Prez. Anything you need is yours."

Jericho opened the book to find a burner cell phone. "Why thank you kindly, Isaac. Tell me, how far are we with our Pitbulls in wolves' clothing?"

"Marcus and Topher contacted Sunnyville two months ago, requesting aid from the Pitbulls, just as you requested. Jimmy the VP responded, took care of their business on the inside in return for an owed favor."

"Interesting, and the wolves are none the wiser?"

"No. The wolves are too arrogant to see beyond their egos. Marcus and Topher's loyalties have and will always lie with the original nine Pitbulls. They expect the club will establish contact now you've arrived."

Jericho tapped the book in his hands, laughing. "Oh, this is good! Thank you, brother."

"I'm here every day around this time. What you need is yours!"

"I require Marcus and Topher's cooperation. Can you convince them it is in their best interest to comply with my demands? I have another assignment for them."

"That, I can arrange."

"Splendid. I'll be in touch tomorrow with further instruction."

# CHAPTER TWENTY

# Zander's Wrath

Tyr, Eddie, and Sandy sat at the bar, waiting for Zander to enter the club. Sandy's knee twitched, and Eddie had bitten down all his fingernails as nerves set in. Tyr sat with a clear look of disappointment etched across his face, like he was ready to accept his fate.

Zander hurled the bar door open, stopping everyone in their tracks as the big heavy bar door smashed into the drywall. His menacing demeanor commanded the room.

Sandy gulped as the heavy-footed Scot stomped toward them, clenching his fists on approach.

Tyr was the first to step up, standing at attention. "I'm sorry Prez, I—"

Zander punched him hard and fast, gripping his blond hair and bringing his knee to strike his face. Dropping the Viking-like figure to the floor.

"You were meant to keep her safe! Call yourselves wolves!" he bellowed, grabbing Eddie's cut to scream in his face.

"I-I..."

Zander head-butted him in the nose. The blood decorated his white shirt and cut.

Dropping Eddie, he turned to a terrified Sandy. "Welsh Cake's done plenty for your family. She almost died keeping them safe, and this is how you return the favor?"

A quivering Sandy had no words, trembling on his bar stool.

Zander's disappointed glare bored into him, right before he back-handed him across the face. A clear sign of Sandy's incapacity to receive such a blow from the Prez. Zander may have been seething, but he had no intention of killing his brother in arms. He was projecting his disappointment onto the ones who let him down, let his old lady down.

Standing in anger, displaying his dominance, he cast his eyes around the room to a terrified club house. Families stood in fear as sweat poured from his crazed face. Mopping the sweat with his T-shirt, he took a breath before acknowledging them.

"Welsh Cake's gonnae be fine. That bastard tortured her by cutting off her tattoos. She's headed back to Uskiville to rest a wee bit while we take care of things here. Jericho will die for what he did to her," he said, unable to contain his anger.

The bar echoed in agreement, and everyone watched as Hyde's five-year-old daughter Luna approached him. Tugging on his jeans. Zander knelt to face her.

"A bad man hurt aunt B?" she asked.

Zander's heart melted. He hadn't realized Hyde's daughter was present. "Yeah, sweetie, but aunt B is okay and will be back real soon," he said, giving her a wink.

Luna placed her hand on his cheek. "Are you okay, Uncle Zandie?"

Zander closed his eyes, scooping the little girl into his chest to kiss her cheek. "I'm alright sweetie. Uncle Zandie didn't mean to scare you with his big, old, grumpy roar. How about we put some music on so you can show me some of that dancing you love? Come on," he said, turning to the jukebox.

The rest of the bar scurried around with Hyde, cleaning up the trio of wolves who had suffered Zander's wrath. Jimmy encouraged normality to resume by ordering a free round of drinks as Luna chose songs on the Juke box.

Zander studied her as she placed coins into the machine and selected the music. His dream of having his own child with B by his side seemed to slip further away from him. He longed to have one of his own and was surprised B had agreed to bringing his child into the world, especially since their tumultuous relationship was still in its infancy. Only now the woman he loved couldn't stand being around him, let alone become a mother to his child.

Setting Luna down, he patted her head before she ran off to Hyde. Glancing around the vibrant bar, he couldn't help the hurt in his heart. Surrounded by an entire community of bikers under his command and protection, witnessing families sitting and laughing together, Zander never felt so alone.

*We never stood a chance. Constant battles for the club, but to what end? To lose the woman I love. I became Prez for her and where is she now? With her best friend, the man who caused this shit storm and I'm in the dark. Why can't I be happy with the woman I love? When will we get our shot at happiness? God, I miss her.*

Jimmy interrupted his thoughts by bringing him a beer.

"Thanks man."

"How are you holding up?"

Zander walked with him to the bar, consuming the contents of the beer bottle in one gulp. "I'm losing her Jimmy. I just want her back."

"How long is she there for?"

"Christ knows. I know Mack is getting more comfortable with her, mind, and she's getting further away from me."

"Then go get her. Take no shit, drag her dragon ass home," Jimmy said, waving at a prospect to hand them each another beer.

Zander took the beer, snapping the cap off. "That won't work Jimmy. I promised to keep her safe and let her down time and time again. Maybe I dinnae deserve her."

"That's baloney and you know it."

"I dinnae know anything anymore, pal," he said, taking a sip of his beer. He noticed Jimmie glancing at a red-headed woman in ripped jeans and a blue vest across the bar. "Friend of yours?" he asked.

"Sort of. T saw the waitress vacancy, and we hit it off."

"You vet her? You know what Welsh Cake's like with strangers."

Jimmy sheepishly wiped the sweat from the back of his neck. "Uh, not exactly. We, um, got to know each other pretty quick. I invited her here. She's hopefully brought her documents tonight, and I was hoping to get to know her a bit more."

"Congrats, brother. I'm happy for you."

"I can send her packing. Bros before hoes always."

"No, you deserve this. Go on, get lost," he said, shoeing him away. "I'll be fine. I'll have a few and stay here tonight."

"Good idea man. I'm here if you need. Just holler."

Zander watched Jimmy take hold of T by the waist and lead her outside. Perched on the bar, he retrieved his cell from his back pocket.

*No new messages.*

He dialed Mack's number, only to be met by voicemail again.

*That Irish prick is ignoring me.*

Tossing his cell on the bar, he finished off his beer and reached over the bar, snatching another bottle, before wallowing in self-pity.

# CHAPTER TWENTY-ONE

# B's Home

Mack pulled onto B's drive at the cabin after an hour of silent treatment from B.

She grabbed her things and huffed up the cabin steps, entering and slamming the door behind her.

The house boasted its familiar scent of fine timber, varnish and spring as B opened the windows to allow the fresh air to circulate.

The boys headed straight to the pool, where Junior met them with a spectacular splash by dive-bombing into it. Remy followed suit as B watched them thrash about the pool as if they'd never been separated from their best friends.

B grabbed a bottle of good stuff, settling into her favorite spot on the porch. She began to unwind when Ari appeared.

"Hey, I heard what happened. Are you okay?"

"Fine, Ari. Just enjoying a quiet drink."

"You look like shit."

"Bloody charming. Any other delightful observations up your sleeve, or can I chill the fuck out on my porch?"

"Mack said you were a pleasure today. B, having been attacked numerous times myself—"

B raised her palm to Ari. "Let me stop you there, good girl.

I'm no fucking damsel. I don't need a BFF, counseling or any other shit to feel better. What worked for you was for you. Not bloody me. I'm not one for crying over spilled milk, so save your pity or whatever fucking drab you were about to spill from your mouth."

"Well, it didn't take long for gentle B to wear off. How long did it last keeping that bitch locked up? I see Dragon is back with a vengeance."

"You're damn bloody right. No more having the piss taken out of me."

"Oh, so this is a pity-party?"

B snarled. "Nope. Just making things clear. Let's not forget, I'm constantly on the receiving end of the shit you caused. A fire you started."

Ari stared at the porch. "B, when are you going to let things go? Please?"

"How about when people stop trying to kill me?" B snapped, pulling herself to her feet. Taking the whiskey from the table, she descended the porch steps toward the valley.

"See you around, Ari. I'm glad the white picket fence fantasy is working out for you while the rest of us collect your karma."

B sat in her familiar spot, angry at the world, guzzling whiskey.

She'd been there long enough to consume two-thirds of a bottle when Tiny approached, startling her as he snapped a twig under his feet.

"Easy Dragon. Let me peel you off the sky. You jumped a mile high then," he said, raising his hands in defense.

B smiled, shaking her head as she pulled herself onto her feet, stumbling as she did so. "You took me by surprise, you big, scary bastard."

"Had a few there, Dragon?" he teased, taking her by the elbow to steady her.

"Just clearing my head."

"Haha, clearing it? I doubt that. Come on, let's get you home."

Staring at his gun secured to his waistband, she smiled. "Tiny, you can teach me how to fire a gun, right?"

"No chance! Mack has already briefed me on the drivel you're chatting. It's a shit plan, Dragon. I have connections who can handle this quietly. Consider it as a thank you for helping me and my mom here. I owe you, after all."

"Nah, he's mines. I'll not get you in troubles with your Prez," she slurred.

"That Prez has asked me to come drag your ass home. Zander has been on the phone four times already and it's driving Mack mental."

"Urgh! I can't deal with that right now. I got shooting to plan."

"Not right now, you don't. You couldn't shoot shit at the moment."

B released herself from his grasp, taking his gun from the holster. "Yeah, I could, watch me," she said, removing the safety.

"Fucking hell, Dragon. Quit playing around. It's dangerous."

"You said I can't shoot. I say I can. So, I'll show you."

"You're pissed and this ain't funny. Now give me the fucking gun."

B turned to point the gun toward a tree at the edge of the ridge and fired, missing the tree by miles.

"You're a fucking lunatic!" Tiny said, snatching the gun from her hand. After putting the safety on, he slammed it back into his holster.

"Hey."

"Don't fucking 'hey' me. Now you're going home," he said, tossing her over his shoulder and stomping off into the clearing.

# CHAPTER TWENTY-TWO

# Frankie

Frankie arrived in Uskiville with nostalgia crashing down on him. Uskiville had been his home for years, albeit undercover. It was home. Precious bonds and memories were made here, his family lived here, a family he still loved very much.

Parking next to B's truck, Frankie headed up the steps and into her cabin to be met by four strapping teenagers raiding the fridge that Ari had stocked prior to their arrival.

"Glad to see nothing's changed," he said, startling the boys.

Madoc was the first to greet him, rushing over to embrace him. "Uncle Frankie, we've missed you so much."

"Missed you too, kid."

Junior, Remy, and Rhys followed suit, embracing their uncle with a transference of love and warmth.

It dawned on Frankie that he hadn't thought about how his absence had affected the boys he'd watched grow up. Blue or black, he was their uncle. It didn't matter to them if he was FBI or a Gray Wolf. He was family.

"So, what's it like being an FBI agent, Uncle Frankie?" Remy asked, before Mack entered from the back porch door interrupting him.

"Frankie. I'm out back," Mack said in a serious tone.

Frankie nodded. "I'll catch you boys soon, alright? Be good," he said before making his way outside.

Mack handed him a beer as he stepped outside, and Frankie narrowed his eyes. "What's this?"

"What's it fecking look like? A beer."

"We're having beers again now. Careful Mackie Boy. You'll have me thinking we're brothers again."

"Feck you! Look, I need your help with Dragon."

Frankie raised an eyebrow, dropping himself on the outdoor seating. "I thought you had this covered. That's what you told Zander before you left Sunnyville."

"Yeah, I didn't have all the details then."

"What details?"

Mack took a large gulp of his beer. Taking a seat next to him, he looked Frankie dead in the eyes. "She wants me to teach her how to shoot."

Frankie choked, spluttering cold beer everywhere. "Come again? I don't think I heard you right."

"You heard right. She wants me to teach her how to shoot so she can walk into the courthouse and take out Jericho," he said, pinching the bridge of his nose with his thumb and forefinger.

Frankie stood to lean against the thick porch pillar. "Can't say I blame her. He did a number on her. She'll calm down in a few days."

"She won't!"

Frankie coughed up the remains of the inhaled beer. "Nah. The day Dragon fires a gun is the day hell freezes over."

"She's serious. I've told her no, but she says she'll find someone who will if I don't."

"I'll talk to her. Where is she?"

"Where do you think? I've sent Tiny to fetch her. She tore strips off Ari earlier, and I'm not ready to face her drunken wrath yet."

"We—"

A gunshot interrupted them.

Frankie and Mack's wide eyes met. Stunned, they launched their beer bottles and ran toward the valley.

"If that lug head is teaching her to shoot, I'll kill him," Mack spat, gasping for breath on a sturdy incline.

They had just turned a corner to be confronted with Tiny carrying a red-faced B, seething at him.

Tiny set B on her feet. "She's your problem now. Psycho bitch!" he said, stomping off down the valley.

"Prick!" B shouted after him.

"What the feck happened up there, Dragon?" Mack demanded.

"I stole his gun to practice shooting. He got pissed and here we are," she said, gesturing to her surroundings. "Wait, where's my good stuff? That bastard stoles it."

Frankie burst into a fit of laughter. "Oh, someone's had a skinful. Come on, I'll make some tea and we're going to talk."

B's eyes became heavy as Mack stroked her head resting in his lap and Frankie made some tea. She had almost dropped off to sleep when Frankie returned with a tray of tea and biscuits in hand, teasing her with his impression of a Welsh accent.

"Right, good girl, sit your ass up. We need to talk," he said, placing the tray on the coffee table before jostling her awake to hand her a cup of tea.

B's eyes sprung open. "You know I don't talk like that, right?"

"I think I do a cracking impression of you," he teased again.

Mack took the tea from Frankie and handed B her favorite red mug once she sat up. "Here, sober up!"

B sat back, cross-legged on the sofa, caressing her mug, "can we get this lecture over with? I got shit to do."

"No lecture, B. We want to help," Frankie said.

Mack gave Frankie a death stare, who reciprocated with a tilt of his head. A telltale sign he had a plan.

B gave him an inquisitive stare. "You're going to teach me how to shoot so I can end, Jericho?"

"Uh huh!" Frankie said, sipping his tea.

"What happened to bringing him to justice the white way? What happened to talking sense into me? Good cop, bad cop, remember? Mack's always a bad cop with his quick-temper and you're literally good cop, attempting to talk sense into me."

"Do you want us to talk you out of it?" Mack asked.

"No, I bloody don't! So, what are you two up to?" B said, setting her mug on the table's coaster and crossing her arms across her chest.

Frankie sighed. "He's taken too much from me, B, and I don't believe this will stop until he's dead."

"What changed your mind? You said he'd get the needle."

"I'm not so sure anymore. His arraignment is being processed, but there's a slight chance his psych evaluation will provide mitigating circumstances which may see him dodge the needle. It's a longshot, but after seeing him in action, I'm convinced he'll push the defense to play the psych card. The DA will counteroffer if that happens."

B fell silent. Retrieving her tea from the table, struggling to compose herself, her hands trembled, spilling the tea, frustrating her as she fought back the tears.

Mack and Frankie stared at one another, unnerved that their best friend appeared broken. Frankie stood from his chair, taking her tea away to sit next to her. Wrapping his arm around her, he kissed her cheek to provide comfort, while Mack sat in apparent shock.

B remained mute, wiping the droplets of spilled tea from her jeans, as Mack's agitation and anger over B's suffering, became apparent.

Frankie attempted to get her to open up. "Talk to me, B. It's my understanding he's told you something to break you. The torture you endured is on me, and I need to rectify that. So, I need you to talk, okay? Mackie and I are right here."

B nodded, attempting to peel herself away from them.

Mack placed his hand on her thigh. "We're right here, Dragon. You can tell us anything. You know that."

Taking a deep breath, B gave Frankie a sympathetic glance. She hated that she had to divulge the details of Rocky's death to him. She wasn't sure it would be the closure he was seeking.

Fumbling her fingers in her lap, she attempted to muster the courage to open the conversation.

"Um—" she said, shaking the images of her torture from her head.

Frankie knelt before her. "Hey, hey! He's got you all kinds of fucked up. This isn't you B. You're strong. I get he hurt you. He rattled you, but he's in jail now, and I'm here for you. B, you're the only family I have left. You'll always be my sister, and I'll help you through this."

B nodded, sucking up the stray tears and nasal discharge. "Shit. Frankie. He's a special kind of evil. The things he did…"

Mack and Frankie's faces crumpled into crazed anger.

"No! Not that! He didn't touch me like that. He stole my identity with his sadistic brutality."

Relief washed over them, with Mack closing his eyes in solace. "Thank God for that! Take it step by step," Mack advised, while rubbing her back.

B nodded once more. "The tattoos were his act of violence toward me. Cutting them out of my flesh as if I was a piece of meat. And what he did to Rocky…" She closed her eyes in contempt for Jericho. "I need to ask you something, Frankie. It might sound, well, strange, but I—"

Frankie narrowed his gaze. "Ask away."

"Rocky. Was he gay?"

Frankie laughed. "What? No B. Rocky loved boobs and ass. He got his pick of women."

B shook her head. "You sure about that?"

"Uh, yeah. I would have known if he was gay, B. We were blood brothers."

B fell silent, unsure how to unfold the events of her warehouse torture.

*This is too hard. I can't do this!*

Frankie pushed the tea and biscuits aside, sitting on the coffee table to meet her line of sight. "B, what happened in that warehouse? To Rocky? He's tortured the two people who mean the world to me and I'm lucky you're still standing. You hold the answers I need."

B sighed. Her voice remained low and apologetic. "They were sleeping together. Rocky was in a relationship with Jericho while undercover."

Frankie stood with a firm hand covering his mouth. The disbelief in his tone showing contempt for her comment. "Nah, nah. You're wrong B. I'm sorry. He's messed with your head."

"He may be sadistic, but I saw it in his eyes. Jericho wasn't lying. He had no intention of keeping me alive. I was his next package to hurt you. I was being bloody tortured and gift-wrapped to get back at you."

"He was torturing you to get back at me? You outed him!" Frankie roared with flailing arms. "You got Blaze's confession B. That's why he came after you."

B shook her head, standing as she took his arm. "Frankie. Rocky told Jericho he never loved him; He was sleeping with him so he could taunt him after he took down the Pitbulls."

"Stop it B. Rocky wasn't gay. He would have told me!"

"He couldn't tell you, good boy," B whispered.

"What do you mean? We told each other everything."

B pulled him onto the couch. Taking both of his hands in hers, she watched how he studied her movements. "Frankie, Jericho tortured Rocky when he found out he was FBI. Rocky had incriminating evidence to put him away. Jericho had fallen for Rocky, only Rocky told him he was only sleeping with him to taunt him and—"

"And what?"

B closed her eyes, squeezing his hands.

"B, please?"

She stared into his eyes with all the sympathy she could muster. "Rocky was in love with you, Frankie. He told Jericho he could never love a monster like him because his heart always belonged to you, and that's when Jericho lost it and plunged a knife into Rocky's heart. He quoted, 'Nothing like a gay man scorned.'"

Frankie's mouth fell open. "Tell me you're lying." The truth inserted a quiver in his voice.

B shook her head. "Jericho admitted to coming after me to take the only other person you loved. He wants you to hurt like he hurts. He thought Rocky was the only person who ever loved him for who he was. Only Rocky's heart belonged to you. Even in his dying breath. I'm so sorry Frankie."

Frankie leapt to his feet, raking in jagged breaths. "This ain't happening!"

Mack stood to comfort him, placing a hand on his back. "VP, I know this is hard…"

"I'm not your fucking VP. I'm a federal fucking agent. All this to find my best friend's killer and it turns out he lied to me the whole time?"

B piped up. "Frankie, he was probably scared he was going to lose you. He must've known his feelings wouldn't be reciprocated."

"No, but I would have understood."

"But your bond wouldn't have been the same, brother. You know it and I know it. Of course, you would have accepted him for who he was but rejection? That hurts. You don't recover from that. It doesn't change your love for him, the memories you shared. You will always be brothers."

Frankie took hold of the mantlepiece to vocalize his anger. "Brothers. He couldn't even be honest with me. I tortured myself for years, blamed myself for his death when he was sleeping with the enemy. Jericho may have tortured Rocky for being FBI, but he died because he was banging a sicko. And I get persecuted for it."

"Frankie, he loved you."

"B, you almost died because he was too coward to convey his feelings. Telling a psychopath instead, providing him with the ammunition to come after me and the people I love, God damn it!"

Frankie's outrage sobered B up instantaneously. Witnessing the turmoil in Frankie's face and watching him pace the sitting room to digest the information divulged to him, hurt her heavy heart. She turned to Mack. "Grab the good stuff, please?"

Mack nodded and wandered off to the kitchen, and B placed her hands on Frankie's chest to stop him in his tracks.

"I'm so, so sorry. It broke me having to tell you that. I can't imagine how you must be feeling, but please take comfort knowing that you were in your best friends' thoughts in his last moments on this earth. He loved you, and that psychopath didn't allow him the chance to convey that to you."

Frankie choked, pulling her into his enormous chest. Tears ran from his cheeks, falling like raindrops onto her head. "I'm hurting, B. I have so many questions, and he can't answer them."

"I know. It sucks, good boy, but that's not on him. That's on Jericho."

Frankie whispered into her ear. his voice shaking, "and you? He broke you. I'm sorry, B. You didn't deserve this."

B stifled back her own tears, determined to remain strong for Frankie. "What doesn't kill you makes you stronger? You know this! Now, let's have a drink."

Frankie squeezed her into a bear hug. "He dies, B. You wanna learn how to shoot. We'll teach you. Let's head up the creek tomorrow. Spend a couple of days there. Just you, me, and Mackie Boy."

"I'd like that," B said.

"What do you say, Mackie Boy? For old times' sake?" Frankie said, calling to Mack, who remained busy in the kitchen preparing three whiskey tumblers.

"If that's what you both want? I'm here for whatever you need."

"Do you think Ari could watch the boys?"

"Yeah, I'll sort it, Dragon. Now get these down you," he said, approaching and handing them each a glass of their favorite amber liquid.

# CHAPTER TWENTY-THREE

# I Want My Old Lady Back

Zander barked at the prospects for the tenth time that morning. B had only left yesterday, and he was already struggling. All he desired was to hold the woman he loved, make her feel safe, and help her through her latest torment. Only B pushed him away in true B style.

Struggling with his emotions, he thrashed about the bar like an angry lion, snapping at friends, left, right, and center until Jimmy appeared to grow tired of his Prez.

Approaching him, he sat opposite Zander in a quiet booth in the bistro with a glass of water.

Zander's stern eyes were enough to make him cower.

"What is it, Jimmy? You've been hovering around here all morning. Speak your mind or let me be!"

Jimmy shrugged his shoulders. "Alright! You're being a jackass!"

"Really?" Zander said, raising an eyebrow.

"Yeah! You are! What happened to Dragon isn't anyone's fault. Not yours and not the prospects. You're being way too hard on them. Everyone's scared to breathe around you, Zand."

"Good! Stupid mistakes cost me, my woman. The trusty trio assigned to look after her should have kept her safe, God damn it! So, my pack will take what I dish out!"

"Make you feel better, does it? They fucked up, I get it, but you let her walk away. You lied to her, tamed her and pissed her off, not us. Ease up on everyone, including yourself. This is getting out of hand. What's she doing up there, anyhow?"

"Getting away from me and cozying up to Mack!" Zander sulked, stirring his coffee.

"And you're going to allow that? You're the Prez, for fuck's sake."

"She doesnae want me near her, Jimmy. She made that quite clear."

Jimmy threw his glass of water at Zander's face.

"What the fuck. Jimmy!"

"Wake up Prez. Stop fucking sulking! That shit about her not wanting you is God damn baloney, and you know it. She doesn't know what the fuck she wants, especially when she's like this. You want your woman back. Go fight for her. If you don't, Mack will have her moved back to Uskiville and you'll lose her forever."

Zander flicked the excess water from his drenched hair and hands. "I've already pushed her too far, Jimmy. I dinnae want to push her over the edge and lose her."

"You're gonna lose her anyway if she's up there with Mack. You said yourself, his relationship is on the rocks. Why don't you ride up with Hyde and Tyr? I'll hold the fort and handle things here."

"I'll think about it."

"Don't take too long. We know Mack. If he sees this as an opportunity to win Dragon back, he'll take it."

Zander rubbed his chin. "I said I'll see."

Jimmy handed him a stack of paper napkins from the windowsill. "Well, do us all a favor and quit snapping at us. It's getting old brother and I say that with all the love in the world."

"Aye."

Zander watched Jimmy return to the kitchen before punching the password into his phone. Dialing B's number, her voicemail again met him. B and Mack had returned none of his calls or messages and he couldn't bear the thought of them being alone together in Uskiville. It made his mind go to unnerving places. Flicking through his cell phone, he pulled up Tiny's number and hit the call button.

"Tiny here."

"Hey, pal. I'm trying to track down Welsh Cake. You know where she is?"

"Oh, hey Prez. I didn't recognize your number. They've headed up to the creek for a couple of nights. Left at sunrise. The reception is garbage there. Do you need me to pass on a message for when they return?"

Zander's blood boiled. The vein in his temple bulged as he screwed his face up in anger. "Na, I'm good pal. Say hi to your mother for me," he said before hanging up.

"More problems?" Jimmy asked, entering the room as Zander slammed his fists onto the table.

Zander slid out from the booth. "Yeah, that prick has taken her to the creek for a cozy fucking rendezvous. Keep an eye on shit. I'm heading to Uskiville."

# CHAPTER TWENTY-FOUR

# Marcus and Topher

Isaac entered the prison yard, walking around the basketball court to the benches along the furthest fence from the guards, taking watch where Marcus and Topher waited.

"What took you so long? It must be a hundred degrees out here. I'm sweating my nuts off!" Marcus said.

"I was in deep conversation with the Prez. Communicate with Jimmy, gather information and lure them here on Prez's order." He handed Topher a scrap of paper with an address scribbled on it. "The timing and execution of this is crucial to the Pitbulls future. So, don't fuck this up."

"How will Prez protect us? Sunnyville has plenty of loyalists here. Talking to you could put us in danger of being shivved."

Isaac peered around the yard. "We'll make it look good. Prez will bring you to our side of the yard if that occurs."

"Then what?" Topher asked.

"You'll both receive Pitbull cuts upon your release, and he's offering twenty grand to each of your families to cover expenses for the rest of your sentences." Isaac stared them down. "Payment on delivery of the wolves."

Marcus and Topher acknowledged each other with a subtle nod of their heads.

"We'll make contact today. We'll explain Prez is here. Say we're spooked about his presence and pull around here. Jimmy's a talker, he'll spill his guts thinking we're loyal to the wolves," Marcus claimed.

"Good. I'll meet you in the shower block tomorrow afternoon. Wait until everyone has gone to the mess hall to eat. It will reduce your chances of getting made."

"And you'll keep the rest of the Pitbulls in the loop. I don't fancy being shanked in here after this."

Isaac narrowed his gaze. "After what?"

Marcus punched him in the face, sending him to the ground, while Topher kicked him between the legs. Marcus dived on Isaac, attempting to choke him. "Trying to make it believable," he whispered.

Isaac fought back until gunshots fired overhead. A clear deterrent from the guards suggesting they disband as other officers made their way to them.

Marcus and Isaac disbanded, attempting to blend into the crowd of inmates near the basketball courts, only to be restrained by prison guards who dished out their own punishment, landing blows to each with their batons. The distraction provided Topher enough time to slip inside, rushing to his cell in haste.

# CHAPTER TWENTY-FIVE
## The Creek

B opened the cabin door, digesting a dust cloud so thick it threatened to constrict her airways.

"Bloody hell, Mackie," she coughed, fighting her way to open a window. "You said the cabin was clean."

Mack and Frankie strolled in behind her, dumping their bags onto the dusty floor.

"It's a bit of dust, Dragon. We'll sort it," Mack said, collecting the cleaning equipment from under the sink in the kitchen.

B headed into her bedroom. Dumping her bag on the floor and opening the curtains. Daylight reflected off the creek, shimmering in the morning sun as the ducks created elegant ripples across the creek's surface. B loved the view here. The peaceful glow when the sun set provided the perfect backdrop to the place she loved to escape to. She would often sit for hours in the window's apron, reading until she fell asleep. B also loved the cabin when the rain came and how it pitter-pattered on the window as she sat in front of the warm fire.

Preoccupied by her thoughts, she cast her mind back to her home in Sunnyville and how Zander would make love to her in front of their own fireplace. A distant memory compared to where her mind rested now.

Frankie tapped on the door, distracting her.

"The cabin is almost at your level of cleanliness. Are you ready for your first lesson?" he asked.

"Ready as I'll ever be," she said, pressing her palms into her thighs before standing to face him.

"You alright, B? You've not said much since last night."

"I'm fine. You? Last night was a lot."

Frankie kicked the door frame, his eyes fixed on the wooden floorboards. "Yeah. It's one more obstacle to overcome. One foot in front of the other, that's all," he shrugged.

B stepped forward, placing her hand on his arm. "But you don't have to get through it alone, big guy. I'm right here."

Frankie smiled, wrapping his arm around her and kissing her temple. "And I appreciate that. Now haul ass. God knows what Mackie's been setting up for you."

# CHAPTER TWENTY-SIX

Jimmy had just finished the morning rush in the bistro when T entered with a stack of dirty plates.

"You can breathe a little easier now. It's quiet for a second," she said, dropping the plates into the sink.

"Calm before the storm, babe," he said as he continued to prep for the afternoon rush.

T snaked his arms around his waist. "Can't we take a brief break?"

Jimmy closed his eyes. Her touch was almost too much to resist.

"Remember what I said this morning? I run this place. I need to stay on the ball."

"Aww, please. Just a minute, for me," she said, unzipping his pants.

Jimmy allowed a soft moan to escape his lips. T had shown interest in him since they'd met, and after a long time of playing with the bunnies. Jimmy wanted nothing more than to indulge, only he had to attend to the club and the rest of the business after finishing with the bistro.

"T, I crave you, but Prez is not here and I'm busy. There will be a truckload of hungry school kids arriving when school breaks out. I need to be prepared."

T provided her biggest pout. "I thought you had status here."

"I do. That's why I'm busting my ass."

"Funny, a real man would delegate. Are you a real man, Jimmy?" she asked as she took hold of his manhood.

Jimmy pressed his lips together in desperation. "Damn, T. You know I want you."

"Then delegate. Call one of your prospects to prep. Show me why I should stay at this job."

Jimmy didn't want to offend her as her hands massaged his erection. He grabbed his cell from the counter.

"Sandy, I need you to fetch the prospects to prep the food for the afternoon rush. I don't care what you're doing. It can wait. I'll be thirty minutes. Now get yours and the prospect's sorry asses over here."

Hanging up the phone, a satisfied gaze from T greeted him. "You're so hot when you're in charge."

Grabbing the back of her head, he pulled her in to kiss her before turning her away from him and slapping her backside. "Upstairs apartment. Go, quick," he said, chasing after her.

Jimmy and T lay sprawled out on the bed after their brief encounter.

T straddled him while Jimmy fondled her breasts with his free hand.

"You're some woman, T," Jimmy said, taking another drag on his cigarette.

"You're some guy, Jimmy. I'm enjoying working with you. Maybe I'll stay in town a little longer."

"You've decided to stay then?"

"Kind of. I like what I see here."

"That makes too of us," he said, dropping his cigarette into a glass of water on the bedside table before rolling on top of her.

"We have to go back to work."

"Do we, though?"

Jimmy laughed. "Yes! You've worked four hours before I wound up here. You're a bad influence. A beautiful, busty, bad influence."

T pouted again. "You didn't like it?"

Jimmy laughed. "I loved it, but I have to work. We have to work," he said, taking her hand and pulling her to her feet.

T stopped. "You'll make this up later? Ditching me for work, I mean?"

Jimmy laughed. "I'm not ditching you. You're coming too. Now move your ass."

"Yes, but I want to stay in bed, so you'll make it up to me later."

Jimmy huffed a playful huff. "I'll do whatever you want after the bistro is closed. You've not even done a decent day's work, and you're trying to wrap me around your little finger."

"Is it working?" she teased.

Jimmy raised an eyebrow, flashing her a smile. "A little. I like you, T."

"I like you, too. It's nice to have a big important vice president want me. It makes me feel looked after."

Jimmy kissed her soft lips. "Stick with me, babe. I'll make you feel special."

"Promise?" she whispered.

"Promise."

# CHAPTER TWENTY-SEVEN

# Shit Shot

"Feck my life, Dragon. It's one can. You've fired a multitude of rounds, and you still haven't hit the damn thing."

"Piss off, Mackie. It's your shit instructing. Aim and fire at the can? That's how you teach? Bloody hell. I got no chance of learning with you."

Frankie intervened as tensions reached the melting point. "How about we take a break? B can't help it if she's shit at shooting," he teased, giving her a wink.

B tipped her head to the sky and closed her eyes like a stropping teenager. "Why can't I bloody get this? Hours of practicing and nothing. What the hell?"

"You can't be good at everything, Dragon. I'm finding this entire experience rejuvenating. Especially now I know you're human," Mack joked.

"Fuck you, good boy. It's pissing me off. You said you'd help, and you've both sat there getting pissed. Wankers!" she snapped, dropping her gun on the ground, and stomping off inside.

"Oh, Dragon, come on. I'm sure you'll hit something eventually. Don't go!" Mack laughed, watching B flip him the bird before stomping up the four steps to the cabin.

He turned to Frankie. "Thank feck she's shite. So, what's the proper plan? I know you have one, otherwise you would have given her the lessons I got in Frankie's School of shooting. Which I didn't need, I might add."

"You fucking did! Don't get me wrong, you were good. I just made you awesome."

"Get stuffed!"

Frankie took another sip of his beer before changing the subject. "B's not throwing her life away for that piece of shit."

"Okay, So I'll ask again. What's the fecking plan?"

"You won't like it."

"Why not?"

"Because it involves you making a-fucking-mends for all the shit you've brought on her."

Mack cocked his rifle, taking a shot at the can laid out for B's target practice, putting a hole in its center. "What the feck does that mean?"

"It means we're taking that fucker out! We let B think she's training for it, and we take him out before the court hearing."

"How?"

"With your talent for sniping, of course."

"Go on," Mack smiled, putting the safety on his rifle and propping it against a large campfire log, swapping it for a beer."

"He'll get an hour a day of isolated, outdoor exercise."

"Yeah, in a high max prison."

"At the bottom of a hidden valley." Frankie winked.

"You're not serious!"

Frankie's glare became stern, his jaw prominent as he seethed. "You owe her, Mackie Boy, and I want him dead. I'm too closely connected to do it myself. My superiors would smell it a mile off. Now, I have a plan, but I need your full support to return to the Sunnyville chapter when this is over. I want my cut back to guide and support B. She's family and I'm determined to protect her. She's going to need it."

Mack sighed long and hard. "You're right. I can't sleep at night, worrying about her."

"You're always gonna love her, aren't you?"

"Always have. Always will," Mack said, chugging his beer like an anti-depressant and glancing at the cabin.

"You really think I can make amends?"

"I don't think, Mackie Boy, I know. You're fucking doing it! We'll discuss the details later. For now, we need to make her think she's getting somewhere. Now, do the best friend, head-but thing and bring her out for a drink. It'll be fucking dark soon."

Mack tossed his beer can into the pile of other empty beer cans a few feet away. "Frankie."

"Yeah."

"Do you think she'll ever love me?"

"She does love you. She always has."

"No. I mean, for real."

Frankie clambered to his feet and perched himself on the log next to him. "Look, she loves the Prez, and I thought he was good for her until his fucking head went and he tried to tame her. You," he said poking his chest. "You're the dickhead who didn't appreciate a good thing until it was gone. Mackie, you took the wrong road with B. Put yourself in the friend zone. Now I know she loves you, brother, even if she doesn't yet. But every time she puts her faith in you, you fuck shit up. You want her to love you and I mean really fucking love you, man? Show her the man she knows you can be."

"How?"

"By helping me take out Jericho."

"You think that'll work?"

"It'll be a start. You'll have a fight on your hands with Prez, though. Are you prepared for that?"

"I am. I'll do anything for her."

Frankie sighed, almost feeling sorry for him. "I know, Mackie Boy, and soon it'll be time to put your money where your mouth is. Risk your life, your freedom for hers."

"Whatever it takes, brother."

"So, you're in?"

"I'm in, and you have my support with Sunnyville. I'll sleep easier knowing you're keeping her safe," he said, getting up and strolling toward the cabin.

"Zander's a good man, Mackie. She's safe with him, too."

Mack turned on his heels. "She's safer with me. One day she'll come home to me, Frankie, and when that day comes, I'll welcome her with open arms."

"What about the harlot?"

Mack belly laughed. "Feck! You really fucking hate Ari, don't you?"

Frankie grunted. "She broke our family. Brought hell to our door. I should thank her, though; I would never have discovered who killed Rocky if she hadn't."

"Nah, I think I did a good job of breaking us, too. And what about you? You turned out to be a federal fucking agent?"

Frankie dragged himself up off the log he'd perched himself on. "It was always my intention to leave the FBI and remain in Uskiville. I went undercover and found my people. Where I truly belonged. I was hoping I could leave after I solved Rocky's murder and tell you about it in time."

"And I still would've wanted to murder you."

"True." Silence loomed for a few seconds until Frankie spoke again. "You didn't answer my question about the harlot."

Mack bowed his head. "You were right. I got caught up in finding my son and Ari was there. I care for her, but time has shown me I could never love anyone other than my dragon. Besides, I'm pretty sure she only wants my sperm. She wants a playmate for Alex. The trouble is, she doesn't even get me hard anymore."

"Shit."

"Yeah. Well, enough of this sissy crap, as Dragon would say. I'm going to fetch her so we can turn this pity fest into a proper family reunion."

Mack sat around the fire with B and Frankie. They hadn't spent time together since before Ari arrived.

"God, I've missed this," he said as he ate his campfire stew.

"Yeah, it's been good, man," Frankie added.

"And what about you, Dragon? Have you missed this?" Mack asked.

B shrugged her shoulders.

"Come on, Dragon. You're not still pissed about missing the can? You'll get it tomorrow for sure," he said, nudging her arm.

"Whatever?" she said, making another smore. She hadn't been able to stomach the stew she had made for dinner.

"Hey, don't be like that. It's been a minute since we've all got together. Let's enjoy this. We may not have another chance for a while."

B produced her finest half-smile. "You're right. Sorry. It's just the last time I came up here. Everything changed."

"Junior?" Mack asked.

"Yeah. Look, no offense. I'm glad you have him back and I love the kid to death, but everything that's happened since has been an utter shit-show. It would be nice to wake up and not have someone try to kill me," B said, staring into the blazing fire.

Mack smiled at Frankie, who returned with an encouraging nod of his head.

Mack sidled up next to B, hooking his arm around her. "Dragon, I'm sorry. I never meant to bring any of this to your door. All that's happened, all that you've been through, that's on me. You didn't deserve that, and I'm gonna make it right."

"Forget it, Mackie. We play with the cards we're dealt by the world."

Frankie moved to sit on the opposite side of Mack. "B, we're with you always. We'll make everything right and we'll get on with our lives, but for now, eat your big ass smore and drink your beer."

B couldn't help the growing smile curling her lips as Frankie continued. "Let's reminisce about the good old days when our biggest issue was Mackie's constant bitching about you kicking his ass at grappling."

B chuckled, almost dribbling the melted chocolate all over her vest.

"There's that laugh we love. And for the record, I didn't bitch. I took my ass whooping gracefully," Mack said.

B and Frankie burst into a fit of laughter, making B spit her bite of smores everywhere.

"What? I did."

"You moaned every bloody day, good boy. In fact, you sulked until lunch time."

"And, at the dinner table, in the bar, and if I beat you at darts. Fuck, you would whine like a pig," Frankie said, laughing.

"Alright, alright. What's this? Pick on Mackie night? Feck off!"

B and Frankie continued to tease Mack, reminiscing about the days of old for hours and drinking the evening away, until B stood up.

"That's me. I'm done for the night."

"Oh, don't go yet, Dragon. It's early and we're having a laugh. We've missed you!" Mack said.

"Likewise, Mackie Boy, but I need to sleep now, or I'll be too tired in the morning."

"So have a long lie."

B gave a stern gaze. "I've not got long to brush up on my shot, Mackie. If the DA brings the trial forward, I'm screwed, and I'll be looking over my shoulder forever."

Mack stood to face her, pulling her head to his. "Dragon, let me sort this. I created this mess. Allow me to fix it, please?"

"No, Mackie. I won't involve you. That piece of shit cut me open. He was ready to plunge a knife through my heart. He won't stop until he has his way, and he's killed me to get back at Frankie."

"Dragon, I am involved. I started this. Let me take him out, make amends."

"No. If I choose to shoot him, that's on me. You're not going to prison for me. Junior, Remy and Alex need you."

"And Rhys and Madoc need you. I fecking need you. Please don't do this!"

"I'm sorry, Mackie. Nobody else will suffer the fate of the cascade of lies. I'm doing this. Now I'll see you first thing," B said, pulling away and kissing his cheek before heading inside.

Mack turned to face Frankie, sitting with a sympathetic sigh. "Why does she fecking call it the cascade of lies?"

"Because her life cascaded into chaos when you began lying to her," Frankie confirmed. "Look, each lie triggered an unfortunate butterfly effect, attributing to every mishap and unfortunate series of events until the present day. B's a deep thinker. To her, everything that has gone wrong correlates to Ari showing up and you betraying her. As a result, she's accepted a new normal."

Mack listened as Frankie continued.

"B has always had fight or flight as her first regulatory process. Prez removing that fucked her up, and B has always been a predator, not a prey. Blaze and Glen may have tried to kill her, Jericho made her vulnerable, but it started with your lies. Now, B's assignment is to neutralize the threat."

"And she believes killing Jericho in cold blood is the answer."

"Mackie. It doesn't matter what she believes she's doing. I have a plan. Now take a load off and let's discuss."

# CHAPTER TWENTY-EIGHT
## Rideout to Uskiville

Zander drove through the country lanes leading to the cabin with Hyde and Tyr when Jimmy called.

"Yeah," he said, communicating via his helmets in call, Bluetooth.

"You almost there?"

"Two minutes out. Why?"

"Just checking. Listen, I received a call from Topher. He and Marcus have their panties in a twist about Jericho's incarceration. There's a lot of commotion building with the Pitbulls on the inside. Apparently, Marcus is in the hole along with one of theirs after a fight broke out."

"Auch, tell them to keep their heads down and ears open. They'll be released soon, but they're a liability. I dinnae know if they'll fit into the new environment we've cultivated."

"Already done. Any suggestions on keeping them out of harm's way? They're still loyal to the wolves."

"We haven't got any pull left on the inside to keep them safe, VP. They've been inside for years. They went in as Pitbulls, remember. Tell them we'll put some feelers out for reinforcements. It's all we can do. Remind them it's high time we collected on our favor, and we want to know everything that's going on, on the inside."

"Right man, good luck with Welsh Cake."

"Aye. Cheers, pal," Zander said, riding up to the cabin porch.

He clambered off his motorcycle, his hips stiff following the ride up to Uskiville. Stretching upwards, he headed to the cabin with both Hyde and Tyr by his side.

Frankie, sitting drinking whiskey on the porch alone, stood to greet them.

"I wondered how long it would be before you appeared," he said.

"Where is she, Frankie?"

"Sleeping. She's had a long day."

"She alright?"

Frankie nodded. "Of course."

"Wait! Where's Irish?"

"Inside sleeping."

"That son of a bitch!" Zander said, showing contempt, stamping up the porch steps,

"Whoa," Frankie said, manhandling him. "Not like that. Separate rooms man."

Zander caught his breath, shaking his head.

"Listen. B would never do that to you! Mackie, yeah, in a fucking heartbeat because he's always gonna love her. B adores you man, now take it slow. Down the hall, the second bedroom on the right. I'll forewarn you; she's bound to be fucking cranky with you."

Zander shook his hand. "Thanks, man. I'm no' here to cause an argument. I want her to understand how much I miss her."

"Fair enough. The wolves can have a beer here with me and sofa surf tonight," he said, handing them both a beer from the cooler box next to him.

"I appreciate it," Zander said before straightening his cut and heading inside.

Approaching the bedroom, he turned the doorknob and stepped inside.

B took his breath away as she slept curled up in the fetal position.

Zander eased the door closed before sitting on the bed next to her. He couldn't help but stroke her cheek and admire her beauty.

Startling her, B woke, her eyes wide like a deer in headlights as she bolted upright.

"Hey, hey. It's alright, it's me. Sorry I woke you."

"Bloody hell, Scottie, you scared me half to death. What are you doing here?"

Zander took her hand, kissing her gently. "I miss you. I couldn't bear being apart any longer. Please understand, I had to see you, darling."

B rested her head against the headboard, and her eyes hardened like black stones. "Scottie, we discussed this. I need time to process."

"Welsh Cake, please? I'll do whatever it takes to get you home."

"It's not as simple as that."

Zander inched forward, caressing her cheek. "I fucking love you, and I'm sorry for making you feel like you couldn't be yourself. Darling, I was wrong and just wanted you to feel safe."

"I know. This whole situation is messed up and I need to catch my breath, please? All I'm asking for is time."

Anxiety reared its ugly head as palpitations banged his chest like the beat of a hard drum. "Do you have any idea how hard that is, especially since I fucked up? I'm trying to make things right. Just give me that chance, please?"

"Bloody hell, that seems to be a common theme around here. How about everyone leaves me to sort my own problems? You tried helping. You all keep trying to help and I keep getting hurt. No more. I'm fixing things for myself from now on."

Zander dropped his head, the shame too much to bear.

"I've told you before. I'm no damsel. You want me back? Allow me to be myself. I need a few days," she said, shuffling under the covers.

Zander bit down on his bottom lip in frustration, while his heart sank into his chest. "If that's what it takes. I'll leave. I'll do anything to make you come home."

B pulled the blanket to her chest, holding it tight as she closed her eyes and Zander stood to reach for the door handle.

"Where are you going?" B asked. The impatience clear in her tone.

"Leaving, like you wanted."

"Bloody hell. I didn't mean now. It's past midnight. I don't like you riding in the dark. You know that!" B said, pulling back the cover beside her. "Sleep."

Zander half-smiled. A glimmer of hope filled his depressed mind as he walked around to his side of the bed. Removing his boots and clothes, he laid on his back next to her, staring at the ceiling, scared to hold her.

A moment of awkward silence passed until B whispered.

"Scottie."

"Yeah," he said, his voice low and croaky.

"Cwtch me, please?"

Zander sighed into a smile. He'd longed for her touch. He hated missing her. It always destroyed him when they were apart. B was his happy place.

Turning into her, he slipped his hand over her waistline, careful not to cause pain to her injured body. The silkiness of her skin felt at home to him. Pulling her into him, he nuzzled into her neck, breathing in her rich scent. Closing his eyes, she took hold of his hand, squeezing it to her chest.

"Don't let go," she whispered.

Zander's eyes pinged open. "Never, darling. I got you!"

*Fuck! She's scared.*

Wrapping her up tight in his arms, he whispered, "I know I let you down, darling. I promise, I'll not make that mistake again. Dinnae be frightened. Nobody will hurt you ever again."

B sighed. "Stop making promises you can't keep. The only person who can keep me safe is me, Scottie, and that's okay. Understand, I know how to handle myself. I just lost myself whilst I was falling for you, and I won't make that mistake again."

Zander's heart shattered. Her comment making him feel inadequate, like half a man even. "You dinnae trust me to keep you safe anymore?

Frustration rippled through her exhausted tone. "I didn't say that.

This past year has turned my life upside down. I've gone from being a reputable businesswoman to a hunted old lady. I refuse to be the hunted anymore. So, I'll become the huntress."

Zander turned her to face him. "I dinnae understand."

B wrapped her arms around his heavy frame, peering up at him, half asleep. "I'm going to put a bullet in Jericho. Take him out and any other fucker who makes an attempt on my life. I'm done with looking over my shoulder and I'm done with people trying to save me."

Zander attempted to comprehend what she was saying with his face showing his confusion. "Welsh Cake, you hate guns."

"You're right, but I hate Jericho more. He mutilated me, made me feel small. It scared me, and I'm never going to feel like that again."

"That's no' necessary, darling. I can have him taken care of on the inside. Call in some favors."

B played with his chest hair. "Favors that will probably come back to haunt us. No offense, Scottie, but everything Mackie did has been returning like a fucking boomerang. Like bad karma and I must have done some awful shit in a past life because it's coming for me. I'm ending this so nobody else has to suffer."

Zander kissed her forehead. "Listen to yourself. You're talking about taking a man's life here. Welsh Cake, I dinnae want that for you. We're meant to start a family, grow old together. I'm no' intending to visit you in prison."

"You're right, because if I end up inside, I don't want you wasting your life on me."

"What the fuck? Welsh Cake. No, this is no' happening. The psychopath isn't worth your life. Think about the laddies."

"At least I'll know they won't meet the same fate if that asshole is in the ground."

Zander sat up in frustration, throwing his arms in the air to show his objection clearly. "Darling, he's gonnae get the chair. You dinnae need to do this."

"He's going down the psych route. He can do too much damage to me if he lives."

"Then, I'll handle it."

"No, I need to do this!"

"You dinnae."

B fisted her hair in exasperation. "I knew you'd react like this. That's why Mackie is teaching me how to shoot. I love you, Scottie, and I don't expect you to understand my requirements, but I'm doing this."

Zander turned, towering over her as she lay beneath him. "That's why you came here, because you know he'll do anything to get right with you?"

"What does it matter, Scottie? You weren't going to help me. Now I'm tired." B said, hunkering him down so she could cwtch into his chest.

Zander held B tight in stunned silence. Confused by her frantic mind, he couldn't sleep.

*What am I gonnae do? I'm losing her!*

Wracking his brain for answers, he drifted off to sleep, only to wake the next morning to an empty bed.

Running his hand along the soft bed linen, he reminisced about the times they would wake up in each other's arms, content as their smiles illuminated the room. The familiar fleet of anxiety washed over him.

*I need to fix this.*

Dragging himself out of bed, he readied himself and wandered into the kitchen, where Frankie was making coffee.

"Morning," Zander said, leaning against the wall.

"Prez," Frankie said, handing him a mug. "Here, two sugars, right?"

"Aye. Cheers."

"You two alright now?"

Zander brought his coffee to his lips, inhaling the full-bodied aromas before pouring the hot, brown liquid down his throat in haste. "I dinnae think so, pal. I'm frantic here. She's shutting me out despite my desire to make things right. She's banging on about putting a bullet in Jericho."

Frankie wiped the kitchen counter-top with a cloth, tossing it into the sink. "You made her unguarded, scared even. B always retreats to what she knows when she's wounded. It's why she's here."

"Am I losing her?"

"That's up to you. You have a special bond with B, and I know you love her, but you made her feel weak. Mackie makes her feel safe and empowered. He always has and right now he's the one she needs. B needs to feel invincible again."

Zander lost his temper, kicking the dining chair into the table. "She's my fucking old lady. I'm what she needs."

"Yet, she's out there shooting cans with him."

"And you agree with this bullshit? What happened to law and order? Justice for Rocky?"

Frankie straightened the chair, pulling it from under the table to sit on. "That went out of the window once he took B. He won't give up until she's dead. I bear some responsibility for her involvement here. The shit she's endured, well that blood's on all our hands now."

Zander placed his mug into the sink, swilling it out under the tap before placing it on the draining board and joining Frankie at the table. "I dinnae understand, Frankie. She won't talk to me, let me in. All I got last night is she's learning to shoot to end that bastard and I'll no' allow her to throw her life away."

Frankie jabbed him in the shoulder. "We're in agreement. We're just letting her think we're teaching her. Mackie hasn't taught her anything and fortunately, B can't shoot for shit. We've got this, Prez."

"Aye? Then what's the plan?"

"Oh, no, you're staying clear of this one. You're too desperate to be the hero. Focus on fixing your relationship. Mackie will never give up on her. Can you say the same?"

Zander narrowed his eyes at Frankie. The anger in his voice demanding he listen. "Aye, of course. I would die for her, Frankie, and I want in on this. That prick needs to pay."

"And he will. B needs to feel like she's in control so we can eliminate the asshole before his court date."

"Well, if it's an inside job you're after, I got connections."

"Negative. He's already protected by old Pitbulls, and I can't have any loose ends once this is done."

Zander sat back in his chair. "Then how the hell you gonnae get to him?"

"All in divine timing, Prez. He's my prey, remember. You gave me your word. Now go to your old lady. Otherwise, you'll lose her."

"Aye, but you better keep me updated." Zander said, leaving the kitchen in a huff.

"And Prez?"

"Yeah?"

"Restore my hope in you. Embrace B and all her dragon tendencies. Be the man she fell for. She deserves that."

Zander gave a heavy nod. "Aye, she does. Thanks, pal."

Zander stepped outside to greet Hyde and Tyr. "We're heading off in ten, fellas. Go grab your stuff.

The two men headed inside, leaving Zander to observe B conversing with Mack. Zander despised seeing her laugh and joke with him while their relationship was crumbling. His resentment toward Mack was growing by the second and if he wasn't careful, he would push B into his open arms.

Walking the short distance to greet them, he witnessed B take a shot, missing her target by miles.

*Christ, she's gonnae shoot herself.*

"You wanna shoot, darling? I'll teach you. You'll no' learn much with him," he teased.

"Feck you!" Mack spat back as B lowered her gun to greet him.

"How many targets you hit, beautiful?" he inquired, taking hold of her free hand.

B kicked the ground, her apparent dissatisfaction overwhelming.

Zander raised an eyebrow, cocking the corner of his mouth into a wry smile. "That many, huh?"

Taking her around the waist, he whispered into her ear. "Take the time you need, and I'll be waiting to give you a proper lesson when you're home," he said, kissing her cheek and turning to leave.

He had taken about six steps when B shouted after him.

"You mean that?"

"Aye," Zander said, turning and giving her a seductive smile.

Zander's eyes tracked her movements, watching B lower her gun, placing it on the ground before approaching him.

"Tuesday 10am, Sunnyville shooting range?"

Zander nodded, smiling into his dimples. "It's a date."

B gripped his cut, pulling him into a passionate clinch.

Zander wrapped his arms around her, drawing her in to taste her.

*Christ, I've missed those lips!*

Releasing her, he gazed into her eyes. "You run to me, not your best friend. Whatever you need, I got you. Do what you must and come back home."

B nodded, backing away with half a smile on her face. "Tuesday."

"Looking forward to it, darling."

# CHAPTER TWENTY-NINE

# Mixed Emotions

B fought back the lump in her throat, watching Zander leave for Sunnyville. She wanted to tell him to stay, only she was so angry at herself for allowing him to diminish her power. Caging her inner dragon isolated a huge part of her life that kept her safe, and B believed in her heart Jericho would never have abducted her so easily if she'd had her wits about her. She also wanted Zander as far away from her mission to take out Jericho, acknowledging the ramifications of her intention to shoot him at the courthouse. The press alone would have a field day, not to mention she would be likely to get the chair or spend the rest of her life behind bars. To B, it was a small price to play for her family's safety and to end the ongoing torment thrust upon her by the cascade of lies. B didn't want Zander to receive the same fate, so pushing him away made sense.

"You're going to ditch your best friend and let Prez teach you how to shoot." Mack asked, distracting her from her thoughts.

"I'm still here, aren't I?" she said with a wink. "Mackie, I'm staying for a few days, and I told Zander I need to clear my head. And I meant it."

"So, you're going back to him?"

"Of course, I am," she laughed. "I know you think I'm stupid, but I love him. I know we can get through this if we can communicate better."

Mack nodded; his apparent wounded puppy expression created a whirlwind of guilt for B. She was painfully aware of his true feelings for her, and she had made it crystal clear that she saw them as friends. B requested Mack's help with her current situation as a friend and only that.

"Mackie. If this is too much for you, I can leave."

Mack puffed out his chest. "What? NO. Dragon, you've just got here. I can handle it. Look, I'll never hide my feelings from you again and yeah, it hurts like hell, but you're still my best friend and I want to be there for you."

B approached with caution to give him a hug.

"Uh, maybe put the gun down first."

"Oh, shit. Right!" she laughed, handing him the gun.

Mack placed the gun on the floor. Opening his arms, he welcomed her embrace.

"I miss you, Dragon."

"I miss you, too Sunshine."

Stepping away from her, he straightened himself out with a nervous cough. "Listen. I was hoping we could hit the beach this week. Take the kids!"

B's jawline jutted along with a harsh glare. "As long as you don't go diving off those bloody cliffs again?"

Mack laughed, "I haven't died diving yet?"

"Seriously, it's dangerous and I'm anxious enough at present."

Mack gave her a friendly shove. "Dragon, I know what I'm doing. It's a case of understanding one's surroundings: knowing where to dive. Besides, I used to go diving all the time before I enlisted."

B rolled her eyes at him. "I don't care. It frightens me. I'm not going if you plan to dive. Besides, you're teaching our kids bad habits."

"What if I dive from the little cliff? Would that make you feel better?"

B collected the empty beer cans, stacking them to create a bigger target. "Not really."

Mack threw a can at her, laughing as it ricocheted off her head. "Ow, Prick!"

"Sorry, I wasn't aiming for your head. Serious though, I could jump from the blue bridge and be fine. I'm not as stupid as you think I am."

B threw a can at his chest. "I never said you were stupid, Mackie."

He threw it back, just missing her. "Then trust me when I say diving from the little cliff poses no threat to my life."

"Whatever you say, Mr. Thrill seeker. You have to get your kicks somehow, good boy."

Mack grabbed her, playfully man-handling her.

"Watch my wounds, Good boy, or I'll have to choke you," B said, grappling with him like the old days.

They rolled about on the ground, trying to outdo one another before calling a truce, sitting on the hard mud to catch their breaths.

Mack puffed and panted through his beaming smile. "I've said it a hundred times already, but I've missed you, Dragon. I'm just so happy you're here."

B's face was a picture of amusement. "And I'll say it a hundred times back. I missed you too, Mackie."

"I didn't hurt you then, did I?"

"Fuck off. I'm invincible," she scoffed.

Mack smiled. "I know. Seriously, though. Your ordeal must have been terrifying."

B sucked in her bottom lip, allowing her eyes to cast over the creek. "To be honest, I've never felt so scared. He took the best pieces of me, Mackie."

Mack kneeled before her, gazing upon her. "You're wrong," he said, touching her temple. "Your best feature is in there and there," he continued, pointing to her heart.

B glanced up at him. The sunlight shone upon his face, reflecting from his crystal eyes. She had always thought he was handsome, only he appeared different today. More striking as he stood, embracing his feelings and conveying his thoughts to her.

The moment took B's breath away, creating a peculiar uneasiness within her as if she didn't trust herself around him.

"Sorry. I didn't mean to make you feel uncomfortable," he said.

"You haven't. It's just, something seems different about you, and I can't put my finger on what it is?"

Embarrassment made Mack's face turn beetroot. "Good different or bad different?"

B's lips curled into a radiant grin as she felt the warmth whistle through her body. "Good different. You've changed Mackie. Matured even and it looks good on you."

"I don't know whether that should offend me, given my age."

B bit her lip, stifling a giggle. "Sorry, I didn't mean to offend you."

Mack stood, extending his hand to pull her up onto her feet, almost pulling her into his solid chest. "It's just nice to see a smile on your face again. Someone as beautiful as you should never look sad."

B paused for a moment, collecting herself. She wasn't sure what the exchange was doing to her fragile mind, but she knew it wasn't right.

*I'm in love with Zander. No one will come close to him. This is just my mind messing with me.*

Regaining her senses, she discovered Mack was still holding her hand. Brushing it off, she gave him a friendly nudge. "Come on, Mackie Boy. You're supposed to be teaching me how to shoot."

Grabbing her rifle, she shrugged off her moment of sanity and resumed her shooting practice.

"When are you heading home?" he asked.

"Probably Monday night. I want to return to work, and I could do with all the help I can get with target practice. I'm bloody useless with this thing," she said, waving the gun around.

"Come on, you're not that bad. What does practice make?"

"Bloody frustration, Sunshine."

"Hey, how about we take a break and go for a walk?"

B huffed. "I'm running out of time, Mackie. Please, can we just keep practicing?"

Mack shrugged. "Sure, but you better fecking hit something soon. I mean, I've never seen you so shite at something."

"Not fucking helping, good boy," B said, taking aim.

"Say the word and I'll do this for you."

B took her shot, missing again. "Bloody hell! I need this Mackie to regain my strength. I feel like a superhero who's been stripped of her powers. Help me get my powers back, please?"

"You got it, but a little bird told me once that feeling powerless is all in your head."

B laughed. "It surprises me hearing that you listened to some of the advice I gave you."

"Maybe you should listen too? Your advice always put me back on track."

"I have to find my way on this, Mackie."

Mack stood in her personal space, staring into her eyes. "B, I'll follow you off a cliff, but I don't understand why someone as smart as you is thinking so irrational."

"Because being rational, having the sensible head has almost got me killed more times than I can count of late. Now, I fight fire with fire. I am a Dragon, after all."

Mack took the gun out of her hands, placing it against a nearby tree. "Just tell me, you're not doing this because you want an out from Sunnyville? Because if that's the case, I'll give you one."

B shook her head. "Mackie, I love Sunnyville. I love Zander, my life there. I'm doing this to feel safe again."

"In control, again, you mean?"

"What's the difference?"

Mack took her hand in his. "B, let me give that to you. Prison doesn't scare me. Allow me to rectify the damage I caused."

"And destroy me in the process, as I have to live with the ramifications of you going black again after I thought so hard for you to stay white?"

"But it's alright for you to go do it?"

B pulled her hand away. "No. I'll pay penance for my sins. Everyone will be safe, though. It's worth it!"

"Not to me."

"Then we can just agree to disagree, Sunshine," she said, picking up her gun. "Now shut the fuck up and let me shoot."

B, Mack, and Frankie cut their trip short after Frankie was called to the office.

"We can always stay here together?" Mack suggested. "Catch up on all we've missed these past months?"

Uneasiness swept through B. "Nah, let's go back and collect the boys. We can head to the beach this evening instead. I've not been to Barry beach to watch the sun set in forever."

"Sure, Dragon. Whatever you want."

B could sense the disappointment in him, only it made her more determined to fix things with Zander. She knew Mack loved her and she didn't want to hurt his feelings. However, Zander was her person, and he was hurting too and, in that moment, B knew she needed to return home to Sunnyville to where she belonged.

Sunset at the beach was a beautiful sight, bringing a brief minute of peace to B.

She watched as the children frolicked in the sea, splashing one another. It made her smile.

A hand pressed against the small of her back, making her jump.

"Sorry," Mack said. "I was shouting at you from the truck. I brought your tartan blanket. I know you get cold at the beach."

"Thank you," she looked him up and down. "Full wetsuit?"

"I'm going for a swim, Dragon, and it's a little nippy at this hour."

"Don't let me stop you."

"You'll be alright here, on your own?"

"Fine Mackie. Now go on."

B watched him run into the sea, playing with the children. He appeared to be the biggest kid there, laughing with them and dunking them under the water.

*You haven't changed that much then, Mackie Boy.*

B laid on the beach towel, wrapping herself in her blanket.

*Mackie's right, it's bloody chilly.*

Closing her eyes, she drifted off to sleep until Junior's shriek woke her with a fright.

"Aunt B, dad's being stupid again. He's going to jump off the enormous cliff again," Junior said, jostling her awake.

B sat herself up, frustration rippling through her as she scanned the cliffs to her left. Mack had just reached the top of the cliff when B stood up.

"Stay here, I'll get him."

B walked along the sandy beach thinking how pointless an exercise it was attempting to stop Mack from his stupidity. She knew he wouldn't listen, and she couldn't climb the rocks in her current condition. She was half-way to the cliffs When Mackie waved and dived into the sea.

*Bloody fool.*

B's heart always skipped a beat when he pulled stunts like this. She scanned the water's surface with her heart in her throat, waiting for Mack to emerge and once he had, her heartbeat resumed.

*Asshole.*

B Stamped her feet toward him as he swam back to the shoreline and emerged from the water, raking a hand through his hair as if he were in an action movie posing for a photo shoot.

"Oh, shite! You're pissed," he said, swaggering toward her. "I know I said the little one, but I love this, Dragon."

B slapped him across the face, stunning him into silence.

"Get off on scaring everyone, do you?" she screeched. "It ain't funny and it sure as hell ain't clever. You asshole." She slapped him again.

Mack raised his hands to defend himself. "Alright! Alright. I'm sorry."

B's blood boiled as she stared him down.

"Look, just because you think I'm not capable doesn't mean I can't do it."

B turned on her heels. "I didn't say I thought you weren't capable. I think it's reckless. You know it scares the kids."

"The kids or you, Dragon?"

B turned to face him; her face was full of rage. "Both, Mackie! You don't listen to or care about anyone's feelings. I believed you'd changed, but you're the same thrill-seeking, adrenaline junkie you've always been. You're like a big, bloody kid, and I can't handle your antics right now!"

Mack appeared disappointed by her comment. "Dragon."

"Forget it, Mackie. You do you. You want to go jump off the blue bridge. I won't stop you anymore! I've got enough shit on my plate to last me a lifetime."

Mack grabbed her wrist.

"Get off me," she said, snatching her wrist away. "While you're getting your kicks, some of us are trying to get off the adrenaline train, and witnessing shit like that doesn't help."

"Dragon, I'm sorry."

B walked ahead. She didn't want to fall out with him. "Forget it Mackie. It was a mistake to come back to Uskiville. You can't help me. I'll head home to Sunnyville first thing."

# CHAPTER THIRTY

# Tuesday

Zander sat against his sleek black motorcycle outside the shooting range, waiting for B to arrive. The blazing sun burned into his already tanned skin.

*Come on, darling. Dinnae keep me waiting, this is torture!*

Checking his watch for the third time in a minute, nerves kicked in, his cigarette the only thing keeping him calm while he expected her arrival.

*09:57. She's never late. Come on, Welsh Cake. You know I hate waiting.*

Zander had texted her the night before to ensure she was returning home, receiving a brief "yes," in response.

*09:59. Christ, she's no' coming.*

Dragging the nicotine into his lungs with a forced inhalation, the short-lived buzz did nothing for his anxiety. His attention turned to the familiar roar of B's truck engine making a right turn into the parking lot, with Tiny riding close behind as her escort.

*Thank fuck for that!*

Tossing his cigarette, he straightened his cut and tussled his hair, checking himself in his motorcycle wing mirror.

B parked next to Zander, allowing him to open her door and take her hand to escort her from the vehicle.

"I thought you kicked that disgusting habit?" she asked, staring down at the smoldering cigarette on the concrete.

"Aye, I've been a little stressed in your absence and they calm my nerves," he said, kissing her cheek. "I'm so glad you're back, darling."

"Me too."

Zander swiveled around to Tiny, who had parked up next to his bike. "Thanks for looking after her, pal."

Tiny nodded. "Always. Glad you have her back, though. She's been a right pain in my ass," he teased.

Zander chuckled. "I bet!"

"Prez, you have no idea."

"Uh, I'm right bloody here," B snapped.

"We're just teasing you, darling," Zander said, draping his arm over her shoulder.

"I'm not! Next time she comes home to Uskiville, you need to escort her. Not that she'd fucking behave for you, either."

"Fuck you, Tiny," B said, still frustrated by his teasing remarks.

Tiny's head jerked back with laughter. "Oh, I love how easy it is to rattle you, Dragon. You're not that bad. Anyhow, I'm gonna stick around and grab a beer with Tyr. I'll crash at the club tonight and head home tomorrow if that's cool, Prez?"

"Aye, nae bother, pal."

Tiny's engine roared to life. He saluted to Zander as he sped off in the club's direction.

"Asshole," B snapped.

"I bet you were a pain in the ass, though."

B smiled. "A little."

"That's my woman. Give them hell wherever you go."

"It's what I do best!"

"Oh. I'm aware. It's why I fell in love with you," he said, taking hold of her waist to look at her.

B smiled. "You, okay?"

"I am now you're home. Where's the laddies?"

"They're with their dad for a few days. Figured we might spend some time together. If you're not busy, that is?"

Her words took Zander back a little. "Uh, sure. I'd like that."

"Let's go for lunch from here. Noah used to take me to a great place nearby, and if you fancy it, we could have a few drinks and stay at the club tonight?" B suggested with apparent awkwardness in her voice.

The warmth returned to Zander's heart with every breath he took. "Darling, nothing would make me happier. You have no idea how relieved I am to see you. We can do whatever you want."

B, a little embarrassed, stuffed her hands in her back jeans pockets. "You know, I came home early, hoping to find you at home."

Zander narrowed his gaze in confusion. "Why didn't you say when I messaged you?"

B shrugged. "I wasn't sure if you wanted to return home. I heard you've been sleeping at the club, and I thought—"

"What?"

B turned away, forcing Zander to rotate his body to confront her. "Welsh Cake, what did you think?"

She swallowed hard before whispering, hurt in her voice, "Maybe you were done with the drama. We haven't been on the same page lately, an—"

"Let me stop you there. We may be going through a storm in a teacup, darling, but I would never—" Zander rubbed his chin. The disbelief in his eyes mirrored his vocals. "Why the hell would I want a cheap burger when I have filet steak? Christ, I've told you before, I dinnae work without you."

"I'm sorry, Scottie."

Zander squeezed her waist. "You need to understand. You're my world. All I ever want is you. You're home to me, darling. Without you, I'm lost forever."

"Even when I'm broken? Scottie, you have no idea what I'm going through."

"Then explain it to me, please?"

B closed her eyes. "I'm trying."

Zander pulled her into him, holding her as if he never wanted to let go, talking into her ear as he held her tight. "You are the best thing that's ever happened to me. I dinnae care about what's happened, and I take full responsibility for my calamitous fuck up, but I'm yours. I'm right here. Let me in."

Zander felt B's hands dig into his back, reciprocating his embrace.

"Hey, hey. I got you and dinnae ever forget it. You hear?"

B nodded into his neck, releasing an enormous sigh of relief.

Zander pulled away, pecking her on the lips as he did so. "Come on. Let's teach you how to shoot. God knows what bad habits that novice has been teaching you. We'll figure the rest out as we go?"

# CHAPTER THIRTY-ONE
## Jimmy and T

Jimmy had just finished the breakfast rush, tossing a pile of plates next to the dishwasher where T was working.

"So, you're not in charge anymore?" T sulked, dragging plates from the dishwasher.

Jimmy laughed, "No. Prez assumed leadership the moment he returned from Uskiville. He won't be so grumpy now that Dragon is home."

"And I get to meet her, right?"

"For the seventh time, yes."

"Promise?"

"How many yesses does a woman need? What's the obsession here?" he asked, as he began preparations for the lunch menu.

"Not an obsession. She's a big deal around here. I want to make the right impression if I'm going to stay."

Jimmy's jawline tightened. "Then don't mention your papers or lack thereof. Otherwise, you'll be out on your ear. There're no second chances with Dragon. You piss her off, and she'll cut you out like a disease!"

"Okay, okay. I get it! Now, when can I meet her?"

"As soon as she arrives, and I confirm she's not in 'kill mode,' T."

"What's that supposed to mean?"

Jimmy placed the knife on the chopping board and faced her. "Listen, babe. I enjoy your company and feel a special connection despite our short acquaintance. I'm not ready to lose it."

"Aww, you going soft on me, Jimmykins?"

"What if I am? I'm into you, babe. Like really into you."

T smiled a devious smile. "Enough to make me your old lady someday?"

Jimmy's eager eyes bloomed. She was becoming everything to him in the short time he'd gotten to know her. "You'd be down for that?"

"A VP to take care of my every need?" she said, licking her top lip.

Jimmy quivered, weakening at the knees. "Yeah, babe. I'd take good care of you. Knowing your position in the club is crucial. You'll have to act like my queen and follow the club charter?"

"And you'll be Prez one day, right? I mean, you practically run everything here, anyway."

Jimmy grinned. He wasn't used to having his ego stroked. "One day, yeah!"

"Count me in. Just promise you'll do anything for me?"

"Of course, babe."

"How soon can we make it official? I don't want to wait another second to be yours."

Jimmy took half a step back, scratching his head. "Uh, I'll talk to Prez when he arrives."

T huffed, showing her distaste for the club's hierarchy. "Why do you need to ask for his permission?"

Jimmy tilted his head in amusement. "I don't. It's a respect thing. He's my best friend and, like I've explained, Dragon doesn't like outsiders."

"And what if Dragon doesn't approve?"

"Club business isn't up to her. Look, she's been through a lot, and she's my friend, too: my family. I promised to look out for her, so allow me to handle this?"

T pouted, turning back to the dishwasher. "Don't make me wait too long. I get bored easily."

Jimmy turned back to his chopping board. Panic washing over him at the thought of losing his new woman. He liked T and loved the fact that a regular woman liked him back. He didn't have to play the VP card to get her into bed. T appeared to like him for who he was.

"Hey, T," he said, diverting her attention from the dishwasher. "I'll have you on your knees, making you mine before the week's end."

T displayed a seductive smile. "I can't wait!"

# CHAPTER THIRTY-TWO
## *Nice Shot!*

B studied Zander's movements as he took aim and fired his first round.

*Bloody hell! I forgot how handsome he is.*

"Now you, darling," he said, disturbing her thoughts and handing her the handgun. He had suggested B start small before building up to a rifle.

B's hand trembled as she clasped her hands around the cold weapon. Guns still terrified her, despite Mack's best efforts to teach her and ease her fear of them.

"Here, hold it like this," Zander said, adjusting her grip. "Now relax your shoulders and adjust your stance," he said, placing his hands around her waist to aid her.

B's heart skipped a beat, his gentle grasp sending shockwaves through her rigid body. She hadn't realized how much her body yearned for his touch.

Zander stood close, his breath tickling her neck as he provided the instruction.

"Loosen your grip. Handle it as if you were caressing it."

B smirked, unable to compose herself. "Caressing it?"

"Listen darling, I handle my gun like I make love to you. Now relax into it, keep your eye on the target, and squeeze the trigger."

B raised an eyebrow. "Like you squeeze me?"

Zander dropped his head in embarrassment. "Fine. You dinnae want my help. That's cool."

"Sorry. It's just, it's a gun. I'm not looking for it to take me to bed."

Zander raised his hands in defeat. "Okay, you do you. If Mack's teaching methods are better?"

B placed a hand on his chest. "No, please. I'll listen. I appreciate this. I really do, good boy."

Zander placed his hands on his hips, cocking his head back with a devilish grin. "Are you sure now?"

B took his right hand, placing it back around her waist, following his previous instruction. "I'm ready. You have my full attention."

Zander placed his chest to her back, placing his hand over her naval. "Slow your breathing. Relax," he whispered, placing his other hand over hers to steady her hand. "Good. Now aim, keep your eyes on the target, and when you're ready, squeeze the trigger."

B steadied her breathing, releasing a shallow breath as she squeezed the trigger, feeling a slight kick-back from the weapon. She turned to Zander for approval, who smirked at her, trying to hide his amusement.

"Good. Now this time, keep your eyes open and keep firing," he said, giving her a cheeky wink.

B couldn't help but chuckle. "Shit. Sorry."

"Well, at least we know why you kept missing the target. Try again," he said, holding her close once more.

This time B cleared her mind, following Zander's instructions to the letter as she relaxed in his firm hands.

"That's it. You got this, darling." His warm breath tickled her ears as he whispered encouragement.

B fired multiple shots, unleashing her magazine upon the target and once again turning to Zander for approval.

Zander grinned, and B couldn't help but flush, finding his caring demeanor attractive.

"Let's bring it in and see how you fared," he said, pushing the green button to retrieve the target.

Studying the bullet-holed card, he squeezed her into his side. "Not bad, Welsh Cake. Not bad at all."

B's eyes washed over it. One to the chest, two to the shoulder, and a few misses. "I hit it! I hit it!" she shrieked in excitement.

Zander stared at her; a huge grin flashed across his face.

"What is it?" she asked with concern in her tone.

"It's just nice to see you smile, beautiful. I've missed seeing you happy."

B flushed again, smiling. "Thank you, Scottie."

Zander shrugged it off. "That's all you, darling. Now, do you fancy another round?" he asked, replacing the target sheet.

"Please," she said, stepping into his personal space so he could wrap his arms around her.

"Remember what to do?"

B nodded before setting herself up and emptying the magazine. The excitement was almost too much as she retrieved her target for a second time.

"Nice headshot, Welsh Cake!"

"I did it," she shrieked again, jumping up in excitement to wrap her arms around him.

"Of course, you did. You had an excellent teacher," Zander said, meeting her vibrant gaze.

Mesmerized by his handsome arrogance, B's mind went into overdrive. Leaning in to kiss him, she could feel Zander's eyes burning into the depths of her soul, studying her eyes until she parted his lips with her tongue.

"Mm," he moaned.

B continued to explore the inside of his mouth as he ran his hand through her hair, pulling her closer in a steamy embrace.

B's heart raced, her chest slamming into his as if they were breathing in unison. Gripping his cut, she held him close, desperate for more.

Zander reached for the button on her skinny jeans until the sound of voices approaching startled them, making him pull away.

They stood staring at each other in silence, catching their breath as the voices entered the next booth.

B smiled. "Maybe that's enough practice for today."

Zander took her hand, planting a gentle kiss on her neck. "Aye. Let's get out of here. You must be hungry after that."

B and Zander spent the afternoon enjoying each other's company. B took Zander to Noah's favorite food spot, where they devoured their meals and reminisced about Noah's cheesy jokes.

Zander took B for a walk around the lake where B insisted on small talk, explaining she wasn't ready to talk to him about her attack, knowing the details would upset him.

Zander placed his arm around her shoulder. "Take your time, darling. I'll no' pressure you."

B's heart palpitated at a rate of knots.

"About this shooting practice. You sure you want to do this?"

B's palms became sweaty as he knocked the wind out of her sales with the unexpected comment.

"Scottie, if you're having doubts, why help me?"

"No, darling, I'm no' having doubts! Understand, I'm right there with you. Front and center. We do this together or not at all."

"No! I don't want you near this!"

Zander stopped mid-stride to face her. "You dinnae get it, woman. You're the love of my life. I'm doing this! It's you and me forever, darling, but that plan of yours is pretty shit and will get us both killed. We'll think of a better one."

B's heart jumped into her throat. "Scottie, please!"

Zander shook his head, brushing her cheek with the back of his hand. "We started this together and God knows I've let you down.

Let's make it right by going back into black together. Whatever it takes, Jericho dies."

With a heavy heart, B dropped her head.

"Hey, hey, I want this. I want to string the bastard up for looking at you, never mind hurting you."

"I don't want you hurt," she whispered.

"Darling, I've been hurting since the day that son of a bitch took you away from me. I want to make things better. Let me in and allow me to continue teaching you how to shoot."

"What if we run out of time?"

"Welsh Cake, the DA is still building the case against him. There's a string of murders and charges they have him on. It'll be a while. Let's work together and stop trying to do everything on our own. You're no' alone, you never will be. I got you!"

# CHAPTER THIRTY-THREE
## *You Get One Night*

Zander watched B step down from her truck and scan the parking lot just as she always had. Her regulars occupied their favorite spots outside the bar and bistro, and the gym was busy as usual. Nothing had changed except the red-haired, slim woman waiting tables outside the bistro.

"Who's the new waitress?" B asked.

*Shit!*

"Jimmy's new girlfriend, T."

"What? How? When?"

Zander let a nervous chuckle escape his lips. He knew B would want the specifics. Her protectiveness extended to all members, not just Zander. B was like a lioness, and Zander's brothers were her cubs.

"Just after your attack. He's smitten. Not that he'd admit it," Zander explained, guiding her away from the bistro and into the club.

"She got papers?"

*FUUCKK!*

"I assume so. Jimmy understands the rules, darling. He'd never jeopardize the club."

B nodded. "Yeah, sorry. I'm doing that trying to control everything again thing, aren't I?"

Zander sighed. "Would it rile you if I said a little?"

B smiled, "no, you're right. I'll try to let up."

Zander watched a wave of uneasiness sweeping through her as she glimpsed T.

"She looks familiar." B said.

Zander attempted to ease her concern. He'd handle the paper's situation if it meant easing B's mind. "You want to meet her? I've no' officially met her yet on account of her only leaving Jimmy's room to wait tables, but we can go say hi?"

B's hackles went up. "No!"

Zander stopped dead in front of her as she tried to hurry into the club. "Hey, you alright?"

B pursed her lips before sighing. "I just want the evening with you, Scottie. No drama, no one else. You."

Zander kissed her forehead. "Whatever you want, I'm just happy you're home."

Zander took B's hand, leading her into the club. The members flocked toward her, ensuring her welfare. He squeezed her hand, noticing how overwhelmed she was becoming. The ambient glare in her eyes was prominent, as if she was ready to blow a gasket.

"Right!" he bellowed. "Take a hike! I've missed my old lady. She's mine for the rest of the night. I'm sure Welsh Cake will catch up with you all tomorrow," he said, dragging her off to the bar.

"You okay, darling? We can leave if it's too much?"

"I'm fine. I'm just desperate for the loo," she said, leaning up to kiss his cheek.

Zander watched her head toward the restroom. It concerned him how unnerved she'd seemed at the sight of T.

Jimmy interrupted his thoughts as he snatched a couple of beers from the bar refrigerator.

Slapping Zander on the back, he smiled. "Where's Dragon? I want to introduce her to T."

"No' tonight, pal. We've had an awesome day. I dinnae want to trigger her when we're getting on so well."

Jimmy's smile vanished. "What the fuck's that supposed to mean?"

"Look. I know T doesn't have papers, and that's a conversation for tomorrow. Now please, let me have this with my old lady tonight. God knows I need it."

"She has papers!"

Zander's face went stiff. "Dinnae start lying to me now over some piece of ass you just met. We're brothers, remember. Tina Hideaway doesnae exist. I had Frankie check her out. She's no' being truthful, Jimmy and I get you've found a chick that digs you, but B and I are trying to fix things. T not having papers will send her over the edge in the current climate. We'll discuss it tomorrow. Now please keep her out of sight for tonight."

Jimmy grabbed the second bottle of beer from the bar, taking a huge gulp. "Understood," he said, walking away in a huff.

Zander grabbed another beer, snapping the cap off, handing it to B when she emerged from the restroom.

"Thanks."

"Pool?" he asked.

B licked her lips. "You remember what happened last time?"

"Beginners luck!"

"No chance, good boy!"

"Rematch then?"

"What's the wager?" B teased.

"Oh, we're betting. I like it. I'm buzzing we're spending time together, so I'll be nice and say whatever you want."

"How about the same as before?" she said, licking her top lip.

Zander laughed. "Darling, you dinnae need a wager to get me into bed. You want me, you got me," he said, leaning in to kiss her.

B stopped him, placing her hand on his chest.

"I know, but—"

"But what?"

"I need—"

"Yes?"

B blurted it out. Dropping her head in shame. "I need to feel in control again!"

Zander took her chin between his thumb and forefinger, the rasp in his voice airing his frustration. "I thought we were past that."

"We were, but what happened… took everything from me."

"And you need to feed the inner dragon, feed the chaos inside?"

"Yeah," she nodded.

"Will it help?"

"I don't know," she whispered.

Zander sighed into a smile, picking up the pool cues. "Tell me the odds."

"I win, I get to do whatever I want with you. No questions asked."

"And if I win?"

"I'll try my best to open up."

Zander closed his eyes. The hurt too much to handle. He had helped B become a better version of herself. Tamed the inner dragon and now she was asking him to feed it. He could see how desperate she was, so he agreed.

"I'll wrack them up, but you dinnae have to talk if I win. I'll wait until you're ready for that. If I win, I want to make love to my old lady. Nice and slow."

B nodded with uncertainty.

The pool game was over fast, with Zander annihilating B. He could tell her head wasn't in it. The very mention of making love put her off her stride. Zander could feel her tremble as he escorted her to his room. Stopping at the door, he gazed at her, running his fingers through her silk hair as she matched his gaze in fear.

"You get one night, darling. One night to cross me off your list. Make the most of it," he smiled. Reminding her of her own words spoken to him on the first night they spent together.

B kissed him hard, her nerves all but gone as he led her into his room. "You remember the safe word?"

Zander laughed. "I'll no' scream 'black,' darling. I'll take it like a man," he said, kissing her hard, pulling her into his room and closing the door behind them.

Removing his shirt, he watched her eyes fixate on his torso.

"Like what you see, Welsh Cake?"

"Yes," she said, helping him out of his jeans, taking his boxer briefs with them.

Zander helped B out of her clothes until they both stood naked. His anger bottled up inside him as he studied her healing body. New skin was forming where her tattoos once sat, forcing Zander to remove his gaze and fixate on her intense stare.

B took his hand, directing him to the bed, distracting his thoughts by pushing him down onto it.

Zander took his lips to her breast, desperate to feast on them, only to feel a tug on his hair.

Growling, he raised his head to meet her gaze: the familiar wildfire staring back at him as B pushed him onto his back.

"Christ," he managed as she straddled him. He hadn't noticed the belt in her hand until she raised his hands above his head.

Uncertainty crossed his lips. "Is this what you want, darling?"

B nodded; her glare was serious, as if she was ready to devour him.

Zander despised B's need to treat him like a sultry boy, only he understood how much she needed him tonight. Closing his eyes, he submitted, allowing her to fasten his wrists to the bed frame.

B's teeth nipped his ear, forcing another growl from him: her smile devilish as he did so. She moved to his neck and down onto his chest, tracing his body with her teeth and nails.

"Fuck," he seethed, the nipping of his skin making him angry. He wanted to break free and dominate her, bend her over and show her the true definition of control until her lips reached his hard cock.

"How the fuck am I so angry, yet so fucking hard for you?"

"Because you want what I can give you, good boy," she teased, licking his shaft.

Zander's eyes glazed over. They hadn't had sex like this in a while, especially since her attack. Zander had been trying to bring out B's softer side. He'd forgotten about the dark display of dominance she exerted over her prey.

Taking a firm grip, B massaged his cock, hard and fast, making him grit his teeth. The combination of pleasure and pain wreaked havoc on his trembling body.

"Dragon," he said breathlessly.

"Easy good boy. I'm not ready for you yet. If you come, I'm gonna have to start over." She commanded, before wrapping her lips around him, indulging in the full length of his shaft.

Zander moaned through gritted teeth. "Ride me!"

"Not yet," she said, returning to his hard and pulsating cock, her tongue dominating him, forcing the pressure in his erection, escalating his arousal.

"Darling, please? Ride me."

"Beg," she commanded.

Zander's mind when into overdrive as he thrusted his hip to encourage her to take him further.

B pulled away, trailing her fingers across his chest.

Zander panted; his anger overwhelming him. "Stop edging me woman and ride me or so help me God. I'll break this belt and fuck you until you can't walk."

B reveled in her control, teasing him. "Beg me and I'll allow you to come. Beg me, Scottie. You know you want to."

Zander's blood boiled. His cock was hard and desperate for her. Unable to take anymore he snapped. "Christ! Dragon please? Ride me. I beg you."

B positioned his throbbing cock at her entrance, her slickness suggesting her pleasure at his anguish. Zander shifted his hips to encourage her to take his length as B lowered herself to kiss him.

"You ready, big guy?" she asked, biting his bottom lip.

Zander allowed a whimper to escape. "Please, darling. You're killing me."

B kissed his cheek, lowering herself down onto him in one slow glide.

"Oh, thank fuck." Zander moaned as B rode him slow, until he matched her rhythm.

"You like that, good boy?"

"Yes. Dinnae stop for anything."

B increased her stride, riding a little faster. The disappointment of not being able to clasp her breasts felt like torture to him, as she pleasured herself on his cock.

"Untie me, Dragon. Unbuckle this belt so I can suck on those beautiful breasts. I want to play, too."

"Sorry, good boy," she grinned. "One night, remember?"

Zander's agonizing grunts rattled the room until B quickened.

"Scottie," she gasped, riding him hard and fast. Her hands pulling on the scruffs of his chest hair as she soaked his length.

Zander growled, thrusting his hard cock into her as he yanked on his leather belt.

B arched her back, bucking and writhing with pleasure.

"Come for me, Scottie," she commanded.

Zander lost his mind. His body responded to her command as he lost his battle with his electrifying climax.

B came hard. Her thighs clamping around him like a vise as she screamed into her orgasm, bouncing hard as he filled her.

Collapsing onto his chest, they stilled in silence. Neither of them choosing to speak first. Zander attempted to piece together the fragments of comprehension their experience provided.

*Torturous, yet mind-blowing comes to mind.*

Calm in his sweat-soaked skin, he whispered into her ear, afraid she had fallen asleep.

"Welsh Cake?"

"Yeah," she whispered.

"Would you mind removing my belt, please?"

B shot off his chest with embarrassment. "Scottie. I'm so sorry," she said, reaching for the buckle with urgency. Her face was still scarlet red with a hint of satisfied afterglow.

Releasing his hands, she climbed off him, dashing to the bathroom.

Zander dived off the bed to find her gripping onto the sink with rage.

"Hey, come on now," he said, removing her hands.

B buried her head in his chest.

"Welsh Cake. You continue to surprise me."

"By taking you like a bloody sultry boy?"

Zander grabbed her head between the palms of his hand. "No, by making my body respond to unimaginable things, my body screamed for you. I know I'm no' a fan of being controlled but showing me no mercy made me explode so hard I thought I astral projected for a moment."

"You're just trying to make me feel better. You hate me dominating you."

"As you despised me controlling you, at one point. Yet you enjoyed me making you mine."

B narrowed her eyes. "What are you saying?"

"I'm saying we need to get comfortable with each other again. There's too much pent-up rage in that strong ass body of yours and I want to help you release it."

B remained silent.

"What I'm saying is, maybe we explore control with one another. You dominate me, like you did. I'll take whatever you give me, and, in return, I get to do whatever the hell I want with you. If I want to make love to you, I will."

B studied him, considering his suggestion. "So, you're leveling the playing field?"

"Correct."

"The safe word remains?"

Zander kissed her soft lips. "Always has, always will."

B nodded, "Deal."

"Good. We start now," he said, picking her up and carrying her back to bed.

# CHAPTER THIRTY-FOUR

# Back to School

B readied herself to go back to work after spending the night with Zander at the club.

"Your nightmares scared me last night. You sure you're ready to go back to work so soon?" Zander asked, showing concern.

"I'm fine. I need to do this," she lied, kissing him goodbye and pulling out of the parking lot.

She parked in her allocated parking spot at the school, refusing to succumb to the anxiety instilling fear inside her. Walking along the wide corridor, past the English department, B made a right to reach the stairs leading down to the Phys Ed department.

Fear swept through her like a tornado, freezing her to the top step, B couldn't move. The lasting images repeating in her mind like a stuck record. Squeezing her eyelids together, she shook her head to rid herself of the images and took a deep breath.

*Man, the fuck up! Get a bloody hold of yourself. He's behind bars!*

Her feet stuttered as she forced them down the steps to her office. As she reached for the door, a voice called out to her.

"B?"

B made a three-sixty with panic and relief shocking her to her core.

"Gonzalez?"

"*Si, si,* it's good to see you safe."

B hugged him like a long-lost relative. "You're alive," she said, studying the stitches on his forehead and matching black eyes. "He hit me pretty hard with his piece. The police found me in the storage closet; I woke up in the hospital."

"I'm so glad you're okay."

"Thank you. And you?"

B shrugged, "Yeah, I'm good. Just glad to get some normality back. I just want a boring Wednesday."

"Well, I take your trash now and see you at lunch for a chat?"

B nodded. "Yes, but it's probably empty. I've been absent from work."

"I check, okay?" Gonzalez said with an endearing smile.

Entering the room, she placed her bag next to her desk as Gonzalez followed. She was about to retrieve her trash can when flashbacks of Jericho injecting her came to the forefront of her cerebral cortex.

"Empty," Gonzalez said, bidding her farewell.

B slumped in her chair.

*Five minutes in the door and I'm a bloody mess!*

The morning flew by, bringing some normality to B's Day with the usual cheek from her students and the banter from her girls' soccer team. Lunch was a little too much, with teachers providing her with sympathetic looks and offering support, only aggravating B.

*I want to forget this shit, not be reminded of it!*

Excusing herself from the lunch table, B rushed back to her office and straight into her private restroom to relieve herself of the contents of her stomach.

Sweat poured from her brow as the day became overwhelming.

Jericho had invaded her dreams the night previous, and now he was controlling her day.

After flushing the toilet and washing her hands, B filled the basin with cold water, immersing her face into the water, hoping it would short circuit the negative feedback loop wreaking havoc in her brain.

*Just a few periods left.*

The school bell rang, and B couldn't wait to leave the building. Saying a quick goodbye to Madoc and Rhys, who were spending another night at their dad's, she then rushed into her truck and sped down the road to the club.

Not making eye contact with anyone, she waltzed behind the bar and knocked on the red church door.

"Yeah." Zander barked.

B pushed the door open as Zander sat in the Prez chair looking up at her. His eyes drifted to the two tie wraps she clasped in her hands.

"Rough day?" He gestured to take her hand.

B didn't say a word, straddling him where he sat, searching for his lips with hers. Removing his hands from her waist, she placed them behind the back of his chair, attempting to tie-wrap him to his chair.

"You dinnae need to use them, darling. My hands will remain here until you want them. Remember, trust works both ways."

B dropped the tie wraps onto the carpet. "Tell me to take control, Scottie."

"You want me. Take me. I'll no' stop you. You're in charge, Dragon."

B kissed his lips before sucking on his neck. She wasted no time in unbuckling his belt and releasing his already hard cock from his pants. Slipping out of her clothes, she straddled him with urgency, consuming his shaft as if she was rushing to her orgasm.

Zander jerked his head back in pleasure as she ensured his hands remained grasping at the wooden spindles on his chair.

The man who had clouded B's thoughts returned as she took control.

Zander noticed the strain in her face and stopped her, taking hold of her head to connect with her.

"Let me take over, Dragon. I'll take your pain away. Give in and tell me to take control, darling. Trust me to give you what you need. Allow me to shut that troubled mind down long enough for you to breathe."

B nodded, the pain ripping through her, making her grit her teeth.

Zander coiled a firm hand around the back of her head, fisting her hair, driving his forceful tongue to the back of her throat, taking her breath away. Lifting her off his lap, he bent her over the table.

"Hands here," he guided. Placing her palms on the hand-crafted club badge, he dropped his pants to his thighs. Spreading her legs with his dominant foot, he gripped the back of her head with one hand and inserted his hard cock into her soaking wet pussy with one sharp thrust.

B cried out in frustration, forcing Hyde to close the door so to muffle her pleasurable screams.

Withdrawing halfway, B's body trembled as he drove into her again, repeating his rhythmical thrusts.

"Scottie," she moaned.

He slapped her ass. "It's Prez in church, Dragon. Let me hear my name on your lips.

Thrusting forcefully again, his hard cock delivered a combination of pleasure and pain. B had no idea what she needed until her Prez gave it to her, distracting her frantic mind as he became merciless with his cock.

"God."

"No' God, Prez. Say it, Dragon. Scream my name as I give you what you need."

B backed her ass into him as he traveled his left hand to her nub. His combined actions teasing her G-spot.

"Take me, Prez."

"Yes, that's it, Dragon. Take it," he moaned with delight. "Oh yes, darling," he said, his cock stiffening inside her.

"Fuck, I'm close," she cried.

Zander dragged his hand down her back to grip her hips, "Scream my name, Dragon. Tell me who you belong to."

"Prez, Prez," she cried, convulsing into her orgasm. Her legs wobbled, threatening to buckle from her debilitating pleasure, as her head reared back into a wild scream.

Zander didn't break his stride as she came. He was machine-like as he continued thrusting.

Removing himself, he pulled her in to kiss her. "I'm no' done with you yet, Dragon. You can take one more for me."

"I can't!" she cried.

Zander slapped her ass again. "Yes, you fucking can," he said, moving down to feast on her chest.

B's mind and body conspired to bend at his will, his fingers toying with her clitoris. "Dragon, I'm going to fuck you against this wall and you're going to scream my name. I see your rage, darling, and I'm no' stopping until I fuck it out of you. You got that?"

B nodded, unable to speak.

Zander growled, biting her nipple. "You got that?"

"Yes, Prez," she moaned.

Zander picked her up, pinning her to the wall beside them. Wasting no time, he buried himself inside her, filling her with brutal intent and glaring into her eyes.

"Stay with me, Dragon. I promise it'll be worth it!" he said, taking his time with her.

B gasped as his fierce cock showed no mercy. His length and girth proving too much as he filled her with every inch.

"Bite down, darling. This is going to get rough," he said as he drilled her into the wall, forcing out her yielding cry. "It feels so good to fuck you, Dragon. I've missed making you mine."

B gripped his hair, pulling his head back to suck on his neck. Her mind fixed on her next orgasm. Any images of Jericho were lost in a sea of pleasure as she relinquished control of her mind, submitting to Zander's will.

Biting his bottom lip, she forced him to look at her. His expression of celebration was clear evidence of his success, and his confidence showed through his thrusts.

B moaned as he slammed his chest against hers. His primal grunts matching his deepening thrusts, nailing her against the wall like a jack hammer.

"Prez," she cried. Trying to fight back another orgasm.

"Don't fight it, Dragon. It's mine to take," he said, delivering another mindless blow to her quivering pussy. She arched into him, unable to endure the pressure against her nub, and begged for more.

One more long, hard thrust had her screaming in ecstasy, her legs threatening to slam shut to control her body as she writhed on his cock.

Pinning her legs open with his torso, Zander jerked into his climax. Gripping her hair and moaning into her mouth until he stilled.

Delicate strokes filled her lips until he set her down.

B steadied herself against the table, still in shock from their encounter as Zander pulled up his jeans and buckled his belt.

Trembling, she watched him mop up the beads of sweat dripping down his face and chest with his flannel shirt before he sat to catch his breath.

B searched his facial expressions, taken back by the demonic scowl matching her gaze.

"Are we gonnae talk, or am I gonnae keep fucking you into oblivion, avoiding anything real?" he growled with impatience.

"Scottie—"

He steepled his fingers together. "I mean, I can go all night if you want to keep going, but I want real, darling. I need real! I gave you what you needed and now you need to give me something. Understand I'm no' your gigolo. I'm the man who loves you more than life itself. Now talk to me."

B stared down at the table in silence, forcing a frustrated sigh from Zander.

"Right. If you're done using me to make you feel better, I have work to do," he said, getting up to leave.

B reached out, grabbing his wrist.

He turned to face her with his distraught expression staring back at her. "What? You want more?" he growled. "Trust me when I tell you, you dinnae. The mood you've put me in, I'm likely to split you in two."

B swallowed hard. "Today was overwhelming and a little shit. No." she shook her head. "A lot shit," she began, biting her lip.

"How?" he asked, towering over her.

Her voice shook in fear. "Every minute there, every sound, placed me back in that warehouse, watching him remove my dignity. Cutting away my identity. And his knife at my chest right before Frankie arrived. It was too much." She pursed her lips in frustration. "I tried all day to keep it together, rushing here to take back control from you. The one person I never want to hurt. I don't mean to control you, Scottie, but when I'm with you, you take the pain away and allow me to take control. It makes me feel like I'm not the broken woman I was until I met you."

Zander pulled her into him, kissing her temple. "Darling, you're no' broken and you're still in control. That bastard is behind bars. You survived a tough day and I dinnae care if you come home feeling like that every day, as long as you talk to me."

B nodded; her face crumpled in hurt. "I'm sorry. I don't want to hurt you. I'm still learning to be open with you. I've been battling alone for as long as I can remember. The partners I had before you never cared enough about sharing my troubles. Frankie and Mackie tried their best and provided me with security but, I've always handled my shit alone. This is just so hard!"

Zander raised his head to the ceiling before returning his gaze to her. "Woman. I adore your strength and I understand this is decades of learnt behavior, but how can I get through to you? make you see you will never be alone as long as I'm breathing."

B lifted her gaze and Zander pulled her head to his chest to hold her.

"We need to disrupt these cognitive fucking behavioral patterns and create some new, healthy ones. I'll never let you face the world alone again, darling."

"I want to, I just don't know how," B said, clinging onto him, afraid to let go.

"Oh, darling. You're fucked if I know how, but we'll get there. Now, how about you get dressed before I have to go kill my brothers for ogling through the glass at your fine ass body."

"Oh, shit!" B shrieked, hiding behind Zander, forgetting the church had a large window into the bar.

Zander chuckled. "Oh, we gave them a show, alright."

B blushed.

"Welsh Cake, there is no need to be embarrassed. That was fucking beautiful. They've always wondered how I tame my Dragon. Now they know."

B shook her head before asking the question stuck in her mind. "Scottie?"

"Uh huh," he said, gathering her clothes whilst maintaining her modesty with his torso.

"Why do you call me Dragon when we fuck but Welsh Cake when you make love to me?"

Zander helped her back into her bra, throwing her gym shirt over her head. "Because your eyes are like wildfire when we fuck. You have an inner rage consuming you like you're burning inside. It's like you struggle to control yourself and your inner Dragon wants to burn everything to the ground," he stroked her cheek. "I dinnae know why Mack started calling you it because I know you've never been on the end of his cock, but baby, you're like a burning inferno. It's sexy but fucking scary and the only way I've learned to control it is to make you come until the fire's out."

B's shocked expression made Zander laugh.

"Well, I wasn't expecting that," she smiled, tilting her head in humor. "Very bloody apt, mind."

Zander helped her into her gym shorts. "I think so," he winked. "Now, we're going home tonight. I plan to stop for moving target practice to clear your head. Then, I'm gonnae make amends for standing you up at dinner. How does curry sound?"

B took his hand to lead him out of church. "Fantastic!"

# CHAPTER THIRTY-FIVE
## Betrayed

Jimmy and T were in the bar when Zander walked in with B on his arm, and before Jimmy said a word, T had invaded B's space.

"Well, Jimmy said you were pretty but dang, girl. Aren't you just the cutest thing?" T said to B.

Zander grimaced at Jimmy.

Jimmy raced to interject, watching the thunderous expression decorate B's face.

"And you are?" B clipped.

"I'm T, Jimmy's soon-to-be old lady. We're going to be like sisters, silly."

Jimmy's mouth stuttered into his speech, with B and Zander providing a death stare.

"Uh, yeah. T and I have become close in your absence, Dragon."

"You've just fucking met. I haven't been gone that long, good boy." The distaste was evident in her voice.

Jimmy shrugged, "I know, but you knew Zand was your man when you met, right?"

"Not exactly. I couldn't stand the prick," she lied.

Zander's jaw dropped. "Thanks very fucking much!"

B turned her attention back to T. Her venomous stare making T shuffle backward. "I know you from somewhere. Tell me, why have my hackles gone up every time I've laid eyes on you?"

T's mouth turned into the widest grin. Zander and Jimmy's dumfounded expressions were blatant from her reply. "I guess I have a way with people. It's my special talent."

B stared deadpan at Jimmy. "Get bloody rid. She's no good for you. You want a real woman? I have a good friend at work."

Jimmy looked at her like a wounded puppy. "Dragon, please?"

B pushed past T, making her way to the door. "No papers, no fucking chance. I'm not stupid, asshole. You want to fuck her? You do it as far away from my property as possible."

Zander put his arm around Jimmy's shoulder. "She checked the database at breakfast and, like I said, she doesnae exist, pal. Get answers and get rid. Worst-case scenario, you take out the trash. Sorry, pal. The club's safety is paramount."

"You mean Dragon's?" Jimmy said.

"Careful Jimmy."

"Oh, don't worry Jimmykins. I'm about to serve my purpose," T said, turning to B with malicious intent.

"Dragon, oh, Dragon," she said, mimicking a familiar voice. "Please, can I see my brother's artwork? He always brings me pictures for my scrapbook, but you took that away from me and I couldn't quite see it through the church window."

Jimmy's world broke into a thousand pieces as B turned on her heels to confront Jericho's sister.

"Red hair, freckles and the same malnourished appearance. Your brother sent you to piss me off, did he? You picked the wrong day, bitch." B shouted.

Zander stepped toward her.

"Wait. You're Jericho's sister?" Jimmy said, distraught.

"Well, duh! I wanted to see what my brother was fussing about. Jericho has obsessed about you being his next addition to his cut, and now I see why. See, when my brother sets his sights on his prize, it's already his. You just haven't realized it yet. The prison won't hold him, Dragon, and he'll return to finish what he started. He always does," she said, skipping around B like a psychopath.

Zander came to B's side. B stepped forward as Jimmy watched in horror. "Your brother's not long for this world, good girl. He'll die soon."

T stood a whisker from B. "Honey. Oh, ho-ney! It's cute, you think that. Now, don't keep a sister waiting. My brother is an artistic genius. Show me his work."

"You're as sadistic as he is," Zander growled.

T curtsied. "Thank you, but we prefer creative."

B stepped within an inch of T's face. "You want to see them?"

"B, don't do this!" Jimmy begged.

T turned to Jimmy. "Oh, can it, Jimmy! A woman of my caliber wouldn't consider someone as repulsive as you. She's the one I want, and I'm not leaving until I get what I came for."

"You're right," B said. "His artwork is something special." She lifted her gym shirt.

Jimmy could only watch as T's eyes lit until B blindsided her and punched her in the face, dropping her to the floor.

"Your blood will be the only artwork you'll see," B said, kicking her in the face.

T laughed a sinister laugh, spitting out her own blood-soaked tooth. "You think this is my first beat down? My brother will kill you all."

B grabbed her hair, dragging her to a nearby bar stool. The other club members watched in horror. Even Tyr stepped forward in B's defense.

B snarled. "I'm not planning on giving you a beat down bitch. I'm gonna do to you what your brother did to me. An eye for an eye, good girl."

T screamed, trying to claw her way out of B's grasp as Jimmy charged forward, provoking Zander to stand in his path.

"Step aside, Jimmy. She doesnae give a crap about you, brother."

"I know. This is my mistake, Zander." Jimmy said, fighting back the tears. "I brought her in. Please let me fix this!"

Zander stood aside as Jimmy placed his hand over B's, urging her to let go of T's hair.

"That bastard took plenty from me, Jimmy." B said. The anguish in her face tore out his heart further.

"And we'll take something precious from him. Please Dragon. He hurt you, and she cut my fucking heart out to get to you. I brought her into our home knowing she had no papers, blinded by seduction. I made a fucking fool of myself. Now allow me to make it right with you, myself, and the club, please?"

The desperation in his voice proved a catalyst to releasing B's grip.

She gripped him, embracing him with a warm hug. "I'm so sorry, Jimmy. You sure you want to do this?"

Tears rolled down his cheeks into his low hanging beard. The hurt was gut-wrenching as he took hold of B's shoulders. "This is on me, Dragon. Go home, I'll make it right."

Wiping his tears with his forearms, he gave Zander the nod to escort B from the club.

"Everybody out!" Zander bellowed, placing a hand on Jimmy's shoulder, "I love you, man," he said before leading B and the other members toward the exit.

Ensuring everyone had left, Jimmy turned to T. The blistering anger consumed every vein in his body with urgency.

"Jimmykins, you know I didn't mean that, right? I love you. Don't you get it? With B out of the way, you can remove Zander and we can ru—"

"Argh! Lies!" he said, slapping her across the face with force. "I was ready to give you the world, but you used me. You betrayed me! You're just a sick sociopath like your brother."

T laughed. "Yeah, and I'd do it again just to see those ridiculous puppy dog eyes. You're pathetic! Death is heaven compared to spending another minute with you. You slob!"

"Don't worry. It'll take less than a minute, babe," he said, choking her. "And you're not going to heaven."

Anger, despair and raw hurt erupted within him as he crushed her windpipe in one swift squeeze. "You horrible bitch. I hate you," he wailed as T went limp in his hands.

Jimmy still had hold of her when Zander placed his arm around him. "It's done, brother. You can let go now. Your brothers will take the trash out."

Jimmy's trembling hands released T, allowing her to slump to the floor in a heap. Turning away, Jimmy broke down in tears in Zander's arms.

"You're alright. Let's get you a drink." Zander reached over the bar, retrieving a bottle of whiskey. Unscrewing the cap, he placed it in Jimmy's hands. "Drink."

Jimmy drank with urgency until he couldn't drink anymore. "I'm sorry, Zand. I'll accept the punishment the club dishes out."

"Dinnae do that to yourself, Jimmy. You've been punished enough. We identified the problem, and you eradicated it. It's done!"

"Everyone warned me, and I didn't listen. T could have destroyed us," he said through clenched teeth.

"She dinnae, though!"

"Yeah, but she sucked me in, man. I would have given that bitch the world," he said, kicking a nearby stool.

"She fucking used you, brother. It was all a lie! Dinnae dare give her a second thought."

"Still fucking hurts, though."

"Aye. Women are good at that. We think it's our dicks we need to worry about until they crush our hearts."

Jimmy changed the subject. "You and Dragon alright?"

Zander took the whiskey. "Fuck, pal. It's so hard trying to console and protect someone like her. I know she's hurting. I see glimmers seep through when things get too much. She keeps everything else locked up inside. God knows what this will do to her. She's gutted for you. Typical Welsh Cake. Blames herself for everyone hurting."

"Sorry, man."

"Shit. No! I'm sorry! This is about both of you today. Welsh Cake and I will sort things."

Jimmy slammed his hands on the table before storming outside.

"Where are you going?" Zander asked, following him.

"Fellas," Zander shouted, pointing to Hyde, Eddie, and Sandy who were smoking out front. "Clean the bar and take out the trash. Oh, and Hyde, I want the same extraction as Welsh Cake received from Jericho."

The three men rushed in the bar as Zander raced to catch up with Jimmy.

"You, out. Now!" he said to B, opening her truck.

B stared at Zander.

"Don't look at him. I got something to say!"

"Jimmy, I—"

"Shut the fuck up and listen." Pointing to the bar, he continued. "That in there is on me. My shit! My cross to bear. I was thinking with my dick. She meant nothing, just a toy to play with. Ending it was easy!"

"Jimmy."

"No listen, Dragon! I brought someone in without papers and Prez will deal with that. Don't you dare let this shit get to you and don't give me your fucking sympathy? I don't fucking want it! You want to help me? Help this club? Stop letting this shit control and consume you. You have something so fucking special with my best friend. Don't let Jericho win by shutting him out."

B dropped her head in shame and Jimmy stepped forward, lifting her chin.

"Look at me, Dragon."

B's saddened eyes stared back at him, and Jimmy gripped her shoulders. "You're smart, fierce, and dangerous, but what makes you special is how much you love and care for everyone around you. Now, let us return the favor. This big, handsome bastard," he said, grabbing Zander's arm. "He loves you more than you can imagine, so let him do the same. You two have the fucking world. You would die for one another. Don't let a couple of psychos destroy something so special."

Zander pulled B to his side as Jimmy continued. "You two are endgame. We all knew it from the start. The chaos that erupted when you two got together strengthened our family. Noah was right about you two being meant for each other. Nobody said it would be easy, but you both know it's worth fighting for."

Envious of the pair and hurt by the earlier transgressions. Jimmy sought comfort knowing that B and Zander were the club's future and doing what he could to bring them closer again was the least he could do.

He made one last attempt to get through to B, hoping his words meant something.

"Dragon. Promise me you'll open up because Zand is ready to listen, and you," he turned to Zander, "I'm so damn proud of the man you've become," he said, placing his arms around them. "Now go on. I got this."

B pulled away first, climbing into her truck, leaving Jimmy and Zander alone.

"Thanks pal. You sure you're going to be okay?"

Jimmy wiped his face with the palms of his hands. "Yeah. I'll find a bunny or three to console me tonight. Now go on. Don't keep her waiting."

Zander embraced him, with Jimmy fighting back the tears once more. "Love you, Zand," he said.

"Love you too, pal."

Jimmy watched them leave; the hurt still crushing his heart as he turned back to the bar.

*Back to square one, Jimmy.*

# CHAPTER THIRTY-SIX

Zander drove B to the woods on the way home, explaining the target practice would calm her after the incident with T.

B assumed it would be clay-pigeon shooting when she hopped in her truck, allowing Zander to take the wheel.

Zander drove for half an hour before stopping and leading B into the woods.

"I thought I was shooting at moving targets?" she asked.

"You are. There's plenty of moving targets here, darling. We'll start with rabbits and deer."

B stopped in her tracks, her hand tugging Zander's back when he realized she stopped.

"What's the matter?"

"I'm not killing innocent animals for target practice."

"If you cannae shoot a rabbit or a deer, how will you take down Jericho?"

"The rabbits and deer have done nothing to me. That cunt has!" she snapped, throwing her hands in the air.

"You have to start somewhere, Welsh Cake, and this is it."

"I thought you meant clay-pigeon shooting or something."

Zander chuckled. "Different ball game. Unless Jericho is falling out of a plane when you shoot him, that is. Besides, we're surrounded by trees."

B tugged a piece of long grass from the earth. "Alright, smartass."

"Here we are, he said, setting up his rifle on top of a huge fallen tree lying in their path."

B's stomach churned as she watched Zander sprawl onto his knees and scan for prey.

"There, look," he whispered. Directing her to look through the rifle's scope.

B peered through the magnified lens to see a beautiful doe grazing in the distance.

"No. It's just an innocent doe."

"B, I cannae let you loose if I can't trust you. You need to find your nerve. Now take the damn shot."

B gulped, setting herself up to shoot the innocent animal. It seemed harmless and serene, much like B before Jericho had begun hunting her.

B's hand trembled. She couldn't breathe as images of her torture flashed through her mind again.

B sprang to her feet, hurdling the fallen tree and ran, scaring off the doe in the process. Adrenaline provoked her fight or flight response, and she kept running as if she was running away from all the feelings she'd been suppressing since the day of her attack.

Zander's voice became incoherent as B sprinted through the warm forestry, until she reached the lake. Dropping to her knees, she screamed, releasing all of her stored trauma, frightening the birds in the distance. The echoes spread far and wide until she sat clutching her terrified torso. Shuddering, her loud, uncontrollable sobs made her wretch as her world collapsed at the realization of what she'd been through.

She was unaware of how long she'd been there when Zander found her. Wrapping his muscular arms around her.

"Oh, darling. I got you. Shh, come here," he said, cradling her to his chest.

"I can't... I can't do this, Scottie, but I want him gone. He's going to keep coming for me if he lives. I keep seeing his face, and it terrifies me."

"Oh, darling, I know. I'll nail this bastard. I promise!"

B gripped onto his leather cut, crying out, the pain too much to bear, and Zander held her, allowing her to release the troubles that kept her scared for so long.

"That's it. Let it out, darling. I'm here," he said, stroking her back.

B cried until she ran out of tears. Composing herself, she turned to Zander.

"You knew I couldn't go through with it. So, why did you offer to teach me?"

Zander stroked her face. "Guided discovery, darling. You needed to see for yourself that this path wasn't yours. Your heart is too big for this."

"But I killed Blaze."

"That was different. That was survival. Totally different from being a stone-cold killer."

B sat in silence for a moment, choosing her next sentence.

"Scottie, I won't relax until I know he's gone. Every time I look at my scarred body, I'm reminded of what he did. I close my eyes and he's there, taunting me. I can't bear it. Please, help me."

Zander ran his fingers through her hair. His touch, so gentle for a man with unwavering masculinity.

"My gorgeous Welsh Cake. I'll do anything for you. That man will die, and we can move forward. You will be happy again, I promise!"

B closed her eyes. "I don't want you going to prison. I can't live without you!"

Zander's eyes widened; his appearance was numb.

"What's wrong?" B asked in a panic.

"You have no idea how much it means to hear you say that beautiful, and dinnae worry. I'm no' going anywhere. I meant what I said about growing our family. I'm growing old with you whether you like it or not."

B cupped the back of his head, kissing his soft lips.

Zander rubbed her back. "Let's get you home. we can salvage the evening with a bottle of Merlot by the pool."

# CHAPTER THIRTY-SEVEN

# Is it Done?

Zander waited for B to head to the pool before checking in with Hyde.

"Is it done?"

"Yeah Prez. We completed the extraction as you asked and took the trash out. Incinerated to ash," Hyde confirmed.

"Good. How's he doing?"

"He's putting on a brave face, but we all know that slut destroyed him."

"I'll make a call to Uskiville. Welsh Cake needs me now, and Jimmy would be pissed if I showed up after the motivational speech he gave earlier."

"Of course! How's she holding up? You know we're all worried about her, Prez. Tyr is like a lost soul wandering around here. We're all ready to help put Jericho down."

Zander observed B from the kitchen window. "Thanks, pal. She's up and down. She won't find peace until he's in the morgue."

"You want me to call it in? He'll be dead by morning."

"Thanks, but this is personal. Just take care of things until Mack and Tiny arrive, would you? Tiny's gonnae be pissed. He's only just arrived home."

"No problem. And Prez... Tiny would go to the end of the earth for you and Welsh Cake. We all would."

"I appreciate that. Right, pal. See you tomorrow."

Zander hung up the phone and dialed Mack's number.

"Hey, man. Everything cool?" Mack asked upon answering.

"Mack, we've had some shit go down here. I need you and Tiny down here asap."

Zander heard the unrest in Mack's voice as he scanned the wine rack for the perfect bottle of red wine.

"What's happened? My Dragon, alright?"

Swallowing his distaste at Mack referring to B as his. Zander continued. "She's holding up as well as expected. She'll no' be having anymore target practice. That's for sure."

"She break?"

"Hard. It damn near destroyed me, but that's no why I need you here."

"Oh?"

Zander picked out a French Merlot, checking the label on the back while grimacing at his words. "Jericho's sister infiltrated the club. Got Jimmy all whipped to fuck with Welsh Cake's head while we focused our attention on her brother."

"Holy shite! Has the threat been neutralized?"

"Jimmy took care of business. Almost had to fight Welsh Cake mind. I'm worried she's slipping from gray to black. Jimmy is a mess, pal. He needs seasoned wolves around him like you and Tiny. I cannae be there for both, so I'm asking you as my friend to share the load."

"Say no more, brother. I'll get Gnarler to hold down the fort with Bampfa. He's been an asset since he arrived from Sunnyville. Tiny and I will ride down within the hour."

"Thanks, brother, I appreciate it."

Mack was about to hang up when Zander called out to him. "Irish, wait!"

"Yeah?"

"Listen. I cannae imagine how difficult this is for you. I know you love her as much as I do and while it pains me to say this, I know she needs you, too. She's opening up to me, but I cannae help thinking she needs her best friend. So how about you help Jimmy out tonight and head over here tomorrow morning? Spend time with Welsh Cake, so I can be there for Jimmy. I cannae abandon Jimmy, and I know she adores you. I've asked her to take a sick day. She's no' ready for work yet."

"Oh, man. I appreciate that. I just about got back on her good side before she left Uskiville."

Silence loomed for a second and Mack continued. "You know she's besotted with you. Puts you on a pedestal. She only ran to me first because she didn't want to hurt you. Didn't want you near black again. I may be her best friend, but you're her entire universe, along with the boys."

Zander inhaled a sharp breath, the oxygen cutting through him like a knife through butter. "Let's just hope I dinnae let her down again."

"Not this time, brother. We'll finish this together. Bring balance to our world again and find a new fecking normal. Now, I'll drop you a text when I reach the club."

"Aye, cheers, pal."

Zander hung up the phone, staring out at B stripping naked by the pool. His knees still threatened to give way every time he laid eyes on her.

He watched her enter the water; her face relaxed from its heavy expression as the water rippled against her sun-kissed skin. Once immersed, she swam the length of the pool.

Collecting two large wine glasses and the bottle of Merlot, he exited through the nearby patio doors.

After walking the short distance to the pool, he sat everything down and stood at the end of the pool, waiting for her to emerge.

As she popped up out of the water, B's panting breath swept through him as she held onto the edge of the pool catching his mesmerized gaze. The orange and red sunset cast its last light onto the water, reflecting onto her soaked skin, enthralling him in her beauty.

Zander grinned, absorbing her naked body in all its glory. "Mind if I join you?"

B managed a somber smile. "I'd like that."

Zanders stripped naked and sat near her, the icy water cooling his legs as they dangled over the side of the pool.

"Christ, that's fresh," he gasped, lowering himself into the deep end.

Aware of B's eyes fixating on his every movement, he ducked his head under the water, flicking his floppy hair from his eyes as he came up to meet her gaze.

B giggled, floating toward him. "You did that on purpose."

"Of course, I did. You told me it turns you on. My buff chest emerging from the water and my glistening skin was too much for you last time, if I remember right."

B blushed. "It still is."

"Oh?" he teased, pinning her against the side of the pool.

B sighed, tensing beneath his touch.

"We dinnae have to—"

B shook her head. "I want to. It seems control and sex erase the dark images from my mind. Only, whenever I close my eyes and try to relax, his knife is at my chest."

Zander's eyes narrowed at the strain in her voice. Her pulse-rate quickened as panic loomed.

"How about we try to fix that?" he whispered.

B's fearful eyes hurt his breaking heart. The sorrow was almost too much for him. He was desperate to make her feel better.

*Dinnae dare break, Zander. She needs you!*

"Trust me," he whispered.

B nodded, allowing him to kiss her trembling lips. Her delicate tongue made him feel heady.

"Eyes on me, darling," he said, kissing her neck. "Keep them open and fixed on me. Every time that bastard claws his way into the forefront of your mind, you hold on to me tight, keeping your eyes locked on mine. You got that?"

B's pained face nodded in agreement as Zander lifted her up, wrapping her legs around him.

"I got you, Welsh Cake, and I'm never letting go."

"Oh, Scottie," she whimpered. Her voice was shaky as she pulled him in to kiss him.

Adjusting his stance in the cold water, he positioned himself at her entrance. His hands traveled to her ass, palms pulling her close as he penetrated her.

B moaned into his mouth as his eyes locked onto hers.

"Eyes on me," he moaned.

B opened her eyes, her mouth making "oh" sounds as he delivered slow thrusts.

Strain etched over her face as she blinked back her tears.

Zander placed his head to hers, caressing her cheek with his hand. "Stay with me, darling." The hurt in his own voice was thick and desperate.

"Don't stop," she whimpered, digging her nails into his back, holding him with all the strength she could muster.

Zander ran his hand through her wet hair, his thrusts bolder with an urgency to please her.

"Zander," she cried.

The desperate symphony in her voice transpired like music in his ears. He'd longed to hear her cry out his name in a moment of imperfect perfectness.

"Let go beautiful, I got you," he pleaded: his breathless, heavy, tone unnerving to him. His primal, innate desire taking control of his sharp and steady thrusts.

B cried out again, her tears trickling like a broken tap, and she shook her head. "I can't, please?"

"You can, darling. Eyes on me and let nothing else in. Feel, darling. Feel my arms around you, my lips on your skin. Feel every loving thrust I deliver."

B locked eyes with his, his lips caressing her almost inconsolable mouth until her misty eyes widened, as if she was mustering all her courage to release.

Shockwaves of electricity arose from deep within, his erection strained and growing. "Release," he begged. His tongue became forceful, yet full of restraint. The pool water crashed against her breasts like waves along the coast.

B's scrabbling hands gripped the back of his neck until they were raking his hair, pulling him closer.

Coming up for air, she cried out, causing immense pressure to build. Zander was ready to release. Gritting his teeth and desperate to compose himself, he thrusted harder and faster, praying he'd please her. Thrust after thrust, they cried out together as Zander gave himself to her. Their eyes remained locked on one another, not even a fleeting stray glance escaped their gaze as they became lost in one another.

B's cries became high-pitched, more desperate than ever. Her tears had stopped flowing as she quickened, crying out into her orgasm.

"Yes, Welsh Cake," he rejoiced. Placing his palm on her back, he allowed her to jerk her head back, allowing him access to her neck.

Still thrusting through her orgasm, Zander brought his mouth to her nape, sucking hard against her pulsating jugular.

B's loud screams called out to his arousal. Travelling his free hand to her wet hair, he tugged down, preparing for his imminent release.

Jerking into his climax, Zander's guttural moan ripped through his chest in a moment of instinctual passion.

His long and pleasurable release like no other as the satisfaction of helping B overcome her demons filled his body with a warm afterglow.

Zander dragged her into him, raining down elated kisses onto her lips and neck. "Oh, Welsh Cake, I'm so fucking proud of you. You're so strong, darling. That was amazing."

His chest heaved in uncontrollable pants as he set her down to look at her. A golden silence settled between them as they stared at one another in awe.

Zander felt like a God, as opposed to feeling like a failure, unable to console the woman he loved. Trying desperately to help her with her frantic mind, he'd almost lost her and all but given up hope of ever getting close to her again until he aided B in overcoming her fears today.

Removing the cluster of wet hairs from her innocent looking face, he couldn't hide his jubilation as she smiled back.

"God, I fucking love you. You dinnae have to be scared anymore, okay?"

B nodded, her tears now of relief as they poured onto his chest.

"Let it out, gorgeous lady. You're alright."

Zander held her close until she calmed.

"How about a cwtch and a glass of wine?" he asked, leading her out of the pool, wrapping her in a towel she had fetched earlier.

"Can we go to bed, please? I'm knackered."

"Sure," he said kissing her cheek and rubbing her back. "You go ahead, I'll lock-up."

Zander closed the patio doors and switched off the lights, following B up to bed. She had already fallen asleep on top of the covers when he entered the room. The exhaustion of the day weighed heavy on her shoulders as she slept. His eyes fixed on the scars where her tattoos once sat. Jericho had tainted her perfect body, yet somehow, she appeared more beautiful than ever in her vulnerable state.

Zander climbed into bed, pulling her onto his chest so he could stroke her back. He loved to feel her warm breath tickle his chest as she slept.

He closed his eyes and focused on killing the man who hurt her.

# CHAPTER THIRTY-EIGHT
## Brothers

Zander left a happy B with Mack after he surprised her at breakfast. They planned to grapple if B's healing wounds held up. Failing that, they planned on watching old British comedy.

She had woken up feeling like her old self. Smiling and laughing with Zander as he chased her around the kitchen, teasing her with his lips.

When Mack arrived, Zander felt a rush of relief at seeing how at ease she felt compared to yesterday. He left without second guessing or feeling paranoid about her spending the day with Mack, after the night they'd spent together, knowing it would be good for her and Mack to spend time together.

Zander was worried about Jimmy after Mack had informed him Jimmy had had a rough night, unleashing his anger upon a full bar upon Mack and Tiny's arrival. Fortunately, they were able to calm him, but not before he caused an immeasurable amount of damage to the bar. Upon entering the club, the broken glass crunched under his biker boots. A cracked window, three broken bar stools, and two broken pool cues were within his line of sight. Not to mention the extensive damage to the bar optics and fridge doors.

Pursing his lips, he did his best to suppress the anger building inside as he stepped into the kitchen where Tiny accompanied Jimmy, sitting with his head in his hands in the room's corner.

"Take a break, pal. I need to talk to Jimmy," Zander said to Tiny.

Tiny stood, patting Jimmy on the shoulder. "You'll be alright, brother," he said before leaving.

Zander poured them a fresh pot of coffee and lifted Jimmy up with one hand, setting him down on a dining chair.

"Rough night?" he asked, placing a coffee in front of him and sitting opposite him.

Jimmy raised his head to look at him. "Fucking awful! I'll pay for the damage and apologize to everyone as soon as I get it together."

Zander raised his hand. "Forget about it. I would have acted the same."

"I just feel so stupid. I should have seen it a mile off. Thinking someone like her could be real, ha!"

"She fooled everyone, man."

"Nah, she had me whipped and begging for her pussy. Knew exactly what to say to get close to Dragon. She could have been hurt, and I would have broken my promise to Noah."

Zander blew into his coffee. "But she wasn't hurt, and I know how hard it was for you to end T."

Jimmy shrugged. "My senses came back real quick once she revealed herself. Jeez, Zand. What makes me so damn unlovable?"

"You're no' unlovable. You've just no' met the right lassie. Look at me. I had no interest in settling down and now I'm fighting with everything to keep hold of Welsh Cake. I would rather die than be without her. Now that's whipped. Your time will come, pal."

"You reckon?"

"Aye. Now no more smashing up Noah's bar. My old lady will castrate you if she sees this."

"Sorry, Zand. I'll make it right!"

"Dinnae worry. How about a trip down to the old marina? You, me and Tiny on a ride out. Like the old days. Hyde and Tyr can handle things for a bit."

"Yeah, man. What about Welsh Cake?"

"Mack's at the house, spending some time with her. They're grappling and watching old British comedy. They laugh at some shit."

Jimmy raised his eyebrows, wrapping his hand around his coffee mug. "You're alright with them spending time together?"

Zander retrieved a pack of cigarettes from his cut pocket. Lighting one up, he took a long drag. "Aye. I think it'll do them both some good. To heal like?"

"And what do *you* need? You're running around trying to keep all of us afloat. Who's got *you*?"

Zander smiled. "Welsh Cake. I have all I need with her. She's opening up to me. She's vulnerable and raw, but this thing with Jericho has weirdly helped our relationship."

Jimmy's puzzled expression prompted an explanation.

"It's forced us to unearth and deal with all the things we used to ignore. I used to resort to rough sex to suppress her dark side during tough times until yesterday, when she opened up more than ever. The glass bottom of our relationship shattered last night, and now even I feel free."

"And you trust Mackie with her?"

"No! I trust *her*. I know now, I've nothing to worry about with him."

"Why's that?"

"Because last night it took everything to give herself to me. She'll no' go elsewhere. We've finally connected."

"That's great, man. I'm happy for you both."

"Thanks, pal. Look. I'm gonnae ask Frankie to meet us at the Marina. I have some leverage for him to rattle Jericho. It's high time we win again!"

# CHAPTER THIRTY-NINE
## Nice Touch

Frankie parked up alongside Zander's bike in his sleek government issue SUV.

Stepping out of the vehicle, he buttoned up his designer suit jacket and removed his sunglasses to greet Zander.

"Alright, pal. Thanks for meeting me."

"What's so urgent?" he asked, watching Zander retrieve a small, clear medical bag from his pocket and hand it to him.

Frankie peered down, somewhat confused, as he held the bag up to the light. "What the fuck is it, Prez?"

"Depends. Are you a cop, or a wolf?"

"You may have taken away my cut, but I'll always be a wolf. I'm in sheep's clothing until this is done."

"Correct answer. That there is Jericho's sister's dolphin tattoo. I had Hyde surgically remove it before he incinerated her corpse."

Frankie waved the medical bag, raising an eyebrow at Zander. "I'm not following."

"T infiltrated Sunnyville. Got Jimmy's cock in a tizz to get close to Welsh Cake."

Outrage consumed Frankie. Panic ripped through him like a wild tornado. "What? Is she alright? Why didn't you call sooner? Where is she?"

"Calm your nan. She's fine. Mackie is looking after her. T admitted who she was upon meeting Welsh Cake. Another sick biscuit just like her brother, that one," Zander said, resting against Frankie's SUV, retrieving his packet of cigarettes from his inside pocket. "Welsh Cake gave her a slap and Jimmy took care of business to make amends."

Zander directed Frankie's attention along the road where Jimmy and Tiny were waiting. "Cut him up though."

"Shit. I bet! Explains why I couldn't find anything on her."

Zander lit up a cigarette, offering the packet to Frankie. "Want one?"

Frankie shook his head. "Nah, I'll stick to whiskey when it comes to corrupting my temple, brother."

"Suit yourself."

"I heard they reduce your sperm count."

Zander dropped the cigarette from his mouth. "Christ. Ruin my day, why don't you?"

Frankie sniggered. "It's true!"

"Prick! Anyhow, you gonnae use the fresh evidence?"

"Too right, I am! I've been letting him stew, but now I'll taunt that sick fuck like he's taunted us."

"How about explaining that plan of yours? I want to know what's happening?"

Frankie gave him a firm stare. "Nope!"

Zander pushed himself from the SUV with his planted foot. "Christ, Frankie. Give me something. I've done my bit. Welsh Cake has downed weapons and has agreed to let us big boys handle it. She won't settle until he's dead and neither will I!"

Zander stood his ground. "Once I get a court date, we'll put the wheels in motion. Until then, the plan stays with me. No room for error, remember?"

"Fine, have it your way. I'll just tell Welsh Cake to be patient."

Frankie glared. "She good?"

"Getting there. She could do with some wise words from big brother, mind."

"I'll call her after I'm done with Jericho. I can't wait to wipe the smile off his filthy face."

"Tell me about it. I'd love to take my tools to him. I'd torture him until he begged for death and torture him some more."

Frankie slapped his back. "His day is coming, Prez, and soon. And when this is all put to bed, I'm coming home. I understand the club won't like it, but I promised B. She's, my family."

Zander gave him a curt nod. "I think that's a good idea. She misses you, pal. I'm looking for a new Sergeant at Arms if you're interested. It's no VP role, but in case you haven't noticed, security at Sunnyville is shit."

Frankie remained composed while inside, he was dancing in excitement. He thought it would be an arduous fight to get his cut back. "I'll take it. Thank you. I miss her too; you know and I'm so fucking tired of wearing a suit and playing by the rules," he said, kicking a stray soda can.

"I got your back, brother. I'll sort Mack and make arrangements. We'll vote at the next meeting. I cannae see it being an issue."

"Thanks Prez. I should head to the prison before the bag stinks out my car. The dolphin was a nice touch, though."

Zander chuckled. "I thought you'd appreciate it."

Frankie flashed his badge and signed in at the secluded Wellridge Maximum Security Prison, at the bottom of a valley, four miles outside of Sunnyville.

After Frankie left his firearm with the prison clerk, a guard escorted him through the prison with his file and evidence until he reached interview room three.

He grimaced through the security glazed window at Jericho, who remained handcuffed at his table. Directing his attention to the prison guard, he gave him a serious stare. "Did you follow my orders, soldier?"

"Sir. Yes, sir. The cameras are off. The security officers won't notice anything unusual. They will appear to be working from their end."

"Nice work, son, and call me Frankie. I'm not your sir anymore, but it's nice to know I still have friends in civvy street. Here, for your trouble," he said, handing him a roll of one-hundred-dollar bills. "And if you ever get fed up with mopping up prisoner puke, drop me a line. I could use a guy like you."

"I appreciate it, Frankie. Thank you."

The officer granted Frankie access to the interview room, where he met Jericho's disturbing grin.

"Agent. I hoped you'd stop by to see an old friend. How's Dragon settling into her scars? Pretty, don't you think? I do hope she's well. I'll be seeing her again soon."

The bile in Frankie's stomach riled up into his throat. "She's doing great! In fact, she's looking forward to seeing you again, now that she's met your sister."

Jericho tilted his head in confusion.

"Nice try, agent. My sister wouldn't be so stupid to involve herself in my business. She knows to wait until I bring her prize to her."

"Oh, I must be mistaken. Does this not belong to her?" he said, slamming the medical bag onto the table. "The unique detail on the dolphin. What do they say? An eye for an eye." Frankie looked him straight in the eyes. "You picked the wrong eye, asshole!"

Jericho peered down at the table, tracing his fingers over the bag. He foamed at the mouth with a sadistic glare. "You better be lying or everyone you love will die!"

A bitter chill swept through Frankie before he regained his composure, dragging his chair across the floor, turning it to straddle it. "You messed with our dragon, and you got burnt. Well, she did. Incinerated, in fact. Just to clarify," Frankie said. Relishing being in control for a change.

Jericho pulled on his handcuffs. "You're lying! An officer of the law.

You're not capable. That stick up your ass keeps you playing by the rules."

Frankie laughed, shaking his head. "I'm no officer of the law, dickwad. I'm a fucking wolf, and I'm done playing. T, as she called herself, came looking for Dragon, confessed who she was and pissed a lot of wolves off in doing so. She's not coming back, Jericho. The only family who stuck by you is gone. Pay back's a bitch, huh?"

"No! No!" Jericho howled, banging his head on the table.

Frankie continued. "My pack is hunting, and the only reason you're not dead yet is because I'm allowing you to breathe a little longer."

Jericho spat in Frankie's direction. "That works both ways, agent. When I'm done, Dragon, Mack and the rest of the wolves, they'll all be dead. Their blood on your hands just like Rocky's. You know he begged for his life?"

"Is that before or after he told you that you meant nothing to him? Ooh, I bet that stung. The man you loved. Your first love, and you meant nothing to him. Rocky was never yours, always mine. He screwed you in more ways than one."

"Oh, he was mine. I tainted your boy. He spent night after night inside the enemy."

Frankie rolled his eyes. "Doing his job, jackass!"

"And he did it well."

"And your sister? Did she go above and beyond? How does it feel knowing you have no one to share your trophies with? You're alone Jericho. You're done!"

Frankie stood up to leave. Swinging his chair back under the table and swiping the medical bag away from a furious Jericho.

"I wouldn't be so sure, agent."

Frankie laughed. "You're never reaching that courthouse. No one can save you now." He turned to smile at him. "And when you take your last breath, know that I'm the one who took it. Rot in hell, asshole!" Straightening his tie, he left a seething Jericho.

# CHAPTER FORTY
## Wiped Out

Mack and Tiny headed up the highway to Uskiville, following their brief trip to Sunnyville. They were three miles from Sunnyville when a gang of five Pitbulls raced to catch them.

"Heads up, Prez. We got company!" Tiny said to Mack through his motorcycle headset.

"I see them. We'll try to lose them at the underpass."

A shot was fired from behind, just missing Mack, striking the sidelight of the green pickup in front.

"Shite! Fecking dirty Pitbulls!" Mack snapped, swerving to miss the halting vehicle.

"We need to get off this highway, boss."

"Feck!" Mack said removing his firearm from his holster. "Head back into town. They're less likely to pull the trigger in a town full of folk," he added, pulling onto a slip road.

Swerving in and out of traffic, Mack and Tiny attempted to dodge the bullets fired at them. "Shit," Tiny gasped.

"Two miles from Sunnyville, Keep going, Tiny." Mack called into his Bluetooth, "Call Zander!" he instructed, welcoming the dialing tone in his earpiece.

"Yeah," Zander answered.

"Feck! We're dodging bullets a couple of miles off the highway. Cutting across Eastbrook to get to you. There's at least five Pitbulls up our asses."

"Christ. We're on our way, pal. Just keep heading toward us and make your way through Colcot Avenue. It's a graveyard there and our best chance to take them out."

"Argh! Shite!" Mack cried.

"Jeez. You alright?" Zander asked with concern in his voice.

"Feck, just a nick, man."

"Hang in there. We're on our way."

Mack bared his teeth through the pain, feeling warm blood trickle down his arm as he white-knuckled his handlebars.

A bullet ricocheted off Tiny's motorcycle frame. "Colcot Avenue," Mack said with urgency as car horns sounded around them.

Tiny followed Mack down Bradbury Lane and onto the secluded Colcot Avenue. The abandoned industrial estate with a long stretch of road, away from prying eyes.

As the men continued to avoid a vicious spray of bullets threatening their existence, the roar of motorcycle engines sounded up ahead.

"Fuck, yeah!" Tiny cheered as a team of seven strong Gray Wolves raced toward them.

Paving a safe passage for their pack, Mack and Tiny passed through to safety as the Gray Wolves opened fire on their enemies, easily picking them off with their automatic firearms. Motorcycles slid and crashed; their victims slain in the onslaught. The Gray Wolves had arrived and were taking no prisoners.

Zander and the Gray Wolves parked to check for survivors. Zander instructed Sandy and Hyde to drag the dead Pitbulls to an abandoned building nearby, to burn their bodies with gasoline.

"Thanks, brother," Mack said to Zander.

"No bother, pal. Let's just clean this shit up and keep this quiet from Welsh Cake. I want her to hear this from me."

"Sure! I see you haven't lost your killer instinct."

"Never, pal. Fuckers come after my family; I show no mercy."

Mack gulped. Zander's dark persona always made everyone fear him, even if they were on his side. Zander's unique skill set for switching to stone cold and merciless in a fraction of a second made him deadly to his enemies, and Mack was relieved to be on the same team.

"You, Tiny, Hyde, and Jimmy head back to the club? Get that arm looked at," Zander suggested. "The rest of us will stay here until we have packed their bikes up onto the trailer. We might as well salvage them. They're worth thousands, and they won't be needing them anymore. I've called an emergency church meeting."

Mack peered down at his bloodied limb. "Yeah, I'll see you back at the club."

The commotion rattled the walls of the church as chaos erupted.

"How many Pitbulls remain?" Hyde asked.

"Are we on lock down? What about our families?" Sandy panicked.

"Sit down and shut the fuck up, the lot of you," Zander said, slamming his gavel onto the oak table to bring order.

The men took their seats by order of their Prez. Their eyes were full of fear.

"Jimmy, get hold of Topher and Marcus. Determine prison chatter. I want to know everything regarding the Pitbulls. Where their base is located, how strong an army they have, their connections, everything! For now, we remain vigilant. Nobody goes out alone. I've asked Frankie to brief Tyr and bring Welsh Cake and the laddies here. We keep the club tight and guarded until we know how deep their roots are."

"What about Uskiville? My mother is there." Tiny asked.

"Already locked down," Mack said, pulling his sleeve over his dressing. "I made the call while Hyde was patching me up. We'll ride up again in twenty. They won't strike again so soon. They'll regroup to formulate another plan. We need to get home to look after our chapter, Prez."

"You sure you dinnae want to stay until we know it's safe?" Zander asked.

"Nah, the chances of them striking twice when they've lost so many is slim."

"Fair enough," Zander said, turning to his Sunnyville counterparts. "Right, while everyone is here. I have another order of business... Once we bury Jericho, Frankie will return to Sunnyville."

Gasps Surrounded church.

Zander raised his voice. "Look, I get it. He lied, but he's like a big brother to Welsh Cake. She wants him home and when all's said and done, she is still the club's finance."

"And on the end of your cock," Tiny teased.

Zander growled. "Shut the fuck up when I'm talking. You're a guest in my playground. I broke your nose before. I'll no' hesitate to kneecap you next time."

Tiny raised his hands apologetically, and Zander continued.

"Frankie has demonstrated unwavering loyalty to the club and Welsh Cake. He continues to be an asset as FBI. He wants that fucker dead more than any of us, and let's face it, we've not exactly been security conscious of late."

"Thanks man! Rub it in, why don't you?" Jimmy huffed.

"That's no' a slight on you, pal. I'm just saying. We seem to be getting sloppy when we need to be vigilant. We need to keep our wits about us. Now, I want to vote him in as my Sergeant at Arms. He'll be here every day, and my old lady will have a job waiting for him. She won't let up on that. He's here to stay, regardless. That is, unless anyone wants to change Welsh Cake's mind?"

The room went quiet.

"Ha! Dinnae fucking think so!"

Mack sighed.

"Hey, your loss is my gain. You may not see past his betrayal. but just remember, we're all gray here."

Mack nodded, "Right. You'll have no objections here."

Zander chuckled. "You're no' entitled to vote here, anyway. This is Sunnyville's vote. My club, my rules!" He clutched his gavel. "I have Tyr's proxy vote. Sunnyville, let's see a show of hands. All in favor of Frankie earning his place here. Raise your hands."

Hesitant hands raised in the air, as the members gave Mack a nod. The admiration for the founder remained despite his demotion.

"Full house." Zander said. "We'll welcome him back when Jericho meets his maker. For now, we do what's necessary for the safety of our club."

# This is on Me

Frankie had been at his desk all afternoon writing up reports when Zander called to update him on the latest Pitbull attack. He had just hung up the phone to ready himself to leave when his superior officer knocked on the door.

"Sir." Frankie said, rising to his presence.

"Sit please," the weary-looking agent encouraged.

Frankie narrowed his eyes.

"Rocky's mother, Rosa Atombottom was found dead in her apartment thirty minutes ago."

Frankie felt a sucker punch to the stomach. "What? How?"

"Murdered in cold blood. A neighbor called the local PD after hearing her scream. A Caucasian male, early thirties, blond hair and wearing a Pitbull cut was seen fleeing the scene. CCTV tracked him to Mason Street before he disappeared. No hits in IAFIS. He's unknown and in the wind."

Frankie's hand covered his mouth.

"I'm sorry, Frankie. I know how close you were."

A single tear left Frankie's eye before he swiped it away. "This is on me," he said, clearing his throat. "I went to question Jericho earlier. Thought he'd let something slip now that he's had time to stew. It turned nasty, Ray," he said, addressing his superior by his first name. "I promised her I'd find Rocky's killer. I promised a conviction, and now I've got her killed."

"This isn't on you, son. This is on the sick bastard who bludgeoned her to death. What did Jericho say to make you think it's your fault?"

Frankie shook his head. "He said he'd kill everyone I love. I wound him up. Told him his plea wouldn't work. It didn't occur to me he would go after Rosa. She was like a mother to me after Rocky died."

Ray placed a hand on his shoulder. "Sorry, son, but I'm pulling you off this case. You and whoever Jericho believes you love are in danger. We need you in protective custody. It's for your own good."

Frankie stepped closer to Ray. His bloodthirsty demeanor present and willing. "No way! This is my fucking case, and with all due respect, nobody understands Jericho like I do. You need me."

"Maybe so, but your life is at stake, and I've lost enough agents on this case."

"Ray, how long have you known me? I need to do this. Please!"

Ray sighed, raising his hand in despair. "Desk duty from here on out. Now I want a list of Jericho's potential targets."

Frankie grimaced. "No list. Just B and her boys."

"I'll have agents bring her in." Ray turned to leave.

Frankie grabbed his arm with urgency. "B won't listen or go with anyone she doesn't trust. Let me do this, please. Jericho won't come for me. He wants me alive and suffering. Please Ray. I'll ask nothing of you again."

Ray pursed his lips. "You get them to a safe house and get your ass back here."

"Negative, sir. I don't trust safe houses. Jericho is smart. He'll find her. Allow me to take them somewhere I know they'll be safe. I won't lose them to Jericho, too!"

"God damn it, Frankie," Ray said, slamming his palm into the wall. "This is not the bureau's protocol. You know this!"

"And I understand that, but they're the only family I have left. Please sir. Trust me on this."

Ray dropped his head in defeat. "Fine. You better move. If the Gray Wolves find out, there'll be war and the press will have a field day. Oh, and keep me posted and get B and her boys to safety.

Frankie's puzzled expression encouraged Ray to continue. "Five Pitbulls were discovered burned to a crisp ten minutes ago. I was enroute to inform you of Rosa when it was brought to my attention."

"How do you know they were Pitbulls?" he asked, despite knowing the truth following a phone call with Zander moments before Ray entered.

"A Pitbull cut was mounted on a pillar next to their burning bodies."

"Son of a bitch!"

"I believe this is retaliation for B's abduction."

Frankie shook his head. "No chance! The Gray Wolves are straight. It was B's condition to working with them. They break that bond; they not only lose their club, but the Prez also loses his old lady. Not to mention the promise they made to Noah."

"Even after Jericho took the Prez's old lady?"

"Yeah. I'm telling you; you're barking up the wrong tree here. Zander agreed to allow me to bring Jericho to justice with the full force of the law. He would never risk losing B. Ray, I'm telling you. That guy hangs on to her every word. If she says no, then it's fucking no!"

Ray stroked his clean-shaven chin. "What if B approves and seeks revenge? What lengths will Zander McGovan go to for his old lady? He's a dangerous man with an army of wolves, Frankie."

Frankie stared Ray down. "The sun would fall out of the sky before B sought revenge. Justice, sure. Not revenge. Besides, B has faith in me, don't you?"

"Frankie, I've never doubted your resolve. I'm just concerned you're blurring the lines here."

Frankie's temper reared its ugly head. "How fucking dare you! I've given my life to this case. Lost family, my best friend. Yes, I met an innocent woman who became family to me, but no lines were crossed. I did my fucking job, putting her in harm's way to get results and now look where we are. Jericho came after B because I was hunting him down. Not B, not the Gray Wolves, me. You want to blame someone for this shit storm? Blame me for doing my fucking job."

"Frankie," Ray said, placing a hand on his shoulder.

"No. With respect, sir, I'm done with this shit. Reprimand me, cut me loose or allow me to do my job!"

The coroner pulled back the white sheet cover with sympathetic regard.

"That's her," Frankie murmured. "You can cover her now."

He walked away, the medley of disappointment, frustration, anger, and thick hurt running rampant in his mind.

Rosa had placed her faith in him to bring Jericho to justice.

Casting his mind to the day of Jericho's arrest. Her rejoice and relief as Frankie delivered the news that Jericho would pay for his crimes a mere memory in the cold light of day.

*At least she's with Rocky now.*

After climbing into his vehicle, he revved the engine in anger and put his foot down. His priority on B and her boys.

*I can't let Jericho take them, too.*

Speeding through the town, rage consumed him, filling his veins with adrenaline. Frankie halted the engine, taking a moment to pause at the water's edge.

The low hanging sun illuminated the vibrant sky as Frankie stared across the river. Flipping a quarter through his fingers, he became lost in his thoughts, realizing he and the Gray wolves alone were not enough to keep B safe.

He retrieved his cell phone from his jacket, the lock screen displaying a portrait of himself, B, and Mack, portraying the happier times at B's cabin. Pressing his index finger to the screen, he unlocked his cell. Flicking through his phone book, his finger hovered over a particular contact, making Frankie release all residual carbon dioxide from his lungs, tipping his head to the clouds with his eyes slammed shut. This was the last number he wished to call.

*I have no choice!*

Pressing a firm finger to the call button, he gritted his teeth and waited for the call to be answered.

"Frankie?" a man called down the line, clearing his throat. "Is everything alright?"

"Yeah, look, I apologize for the unscheduled intrusion. It's ju—"

"You're in trouble!" the man said with certainty.

Frankie turned away from the river, as if avoiding the conversation. He kicked a beer can across the broken concrete. "No. Well, it's B. I'm worried I can't keep her safe. I don't want to repeat the same mistake I made with Mom."

An enormous sigh vibrated into Frankie's eardrum, rattling his troubled mind. "How many times have I told you, Frankie? It wasn't your fault!"

Frankie's face hardened. His back teeth grinding as he spoke. "I guess we'll have to agree to disagree with that."

Impatience crept into the voice on the phone. "Tell me what you need."

Frankie blew air from his cheeks. "I need to hide B and her boys for a few days so I can execute my plan."

"And you want to bring them here?"

"You're the only person on the planet I trust to keep them safe."

A pregnant pause forced Frankie to catch his breath. "You still there?"

"I'm here," said the man, clearing his throat. "A little taken aback that you trust me with them. They mean everything to you."

"That's why I came to you. Listen, you know this will risk..."

"Exposing me?"

Frankie pursed his lips. His big heart panged as it rattled against his chest. "Yeah."

"Are you sure you want that? You've already lost so much, Frankie. I mean, I'm happy to take the risk. Living off grid isn't all it's cracked up to be."

"No shit! I never wanted you to lock yourself away."

"No, that was on me. I just figured you'd lost enough."

Frankie's frantic heart calmed in his chest. "Then step out from the shadows and help me."

"What's the plan?"

"I'll bring B and the boys to you for safekeeping. I'll also require you to hack into the MC security system in Sunnyville."

"Didn't you create that?"

Frankie laughed. "Yes, but I'm back in uniform. I need to remain clean on this and you're a ghost. Besides, it's a simple hacking job. No problem for someone with your expertise."

"Security, check! What's next?"

"That's it! I'll handle things here and put an end to Jericho."

"And if shit goes south?"

Frankie walked the short distance back to his car. He had ignored the possibility of the plan failing until now.

"You mean, if I don't make it?"

"Yeah," he whispered.

Frankie gulped. "Then it'll be down to you to keep B and the boys safe!"

"You mean wipe everyone from the face of the earth? Because if anything happens to you, that's exactly what I'll do."

"That's not what I said. B's safety is your primary aim."

"Then stay alive and I won't have to adjust my course of action."

Frankie chuckled, aware of the man's abilities. "Listen. When I'm done with Jericho and B is safe, I'm turning in my badge and gun."

"I take it a move to Sunnyville is in the cards?"

"I made B a promise. The bureau isn't in alignment with me anymore. I belong with the wolves."

"That's the most sensible comment that's escaped your trap tonight."

"You approve?" Frankie asked in confusion as he adjusted his windshield wipers.

"Your damn right! The bureau was never your true calling. You walked around with a stick up your butt for years. Frankie, Uskiville undercover made you a better man. It made you see the world isn't about chasing perps and pen-pushing. Truth be told, I wish I'd learnt that lesson years ago. Maybe things may have been different now."

The hurt constricted Frankie's chest like a boa constrictor crushing its prey. "Maybe the universe has alternate plans for you?"

"We'll soon find out. When can I expect you?"

"Later on, tonight."

"Good. Bring some groceries! I'm tired of living off canned food and home-grown shit. Chicken, salmon, steak, I want it all," he joked.

Frankie chuckled. "Whatever you want. Just send me a list."

"Oh, I wouldn't know where to begin. Hey, are those dark, circular cookies with the cream inside them still a thing?"

Frankie released a roaring laugh, tapping on the car hood. "Yeah. You've only been in hiding for a few years, not decades. I'll bring you some."

The man chuckled before adopting a serious tone. "Frankie?"

"Yeah."

"I'm proud of you, and I'm glad you came to me with this. Stay safe, son."

"Thanks, Dad."

After parking on her drive, Frankie wandered around back to discover B in her kitchen, washing up dirty dishes with Tyr keeping a close eye, perched in his usual spot.

"Hey!" he called through the open window, disrupting their conversation.

"Hello, stranger! You scared the crap out of me," B said as he opened the patio door.

"To what do I owe the pleasure? I've missed you, good boy."

Frankie didn't hesitate to drag her into his embrace. He didn't care that she wrapped her soapy hands around his expensive suit.

"Everything alright?" B asked, holding him tight.

Frankie pulled away, giving Tyr a nod, straightening his suit jacket and making eye contact. "B, Rocky's mom was murdered in cold blood by a Pitbull today. I have to take you and the boys into protective custody! Keep you safe until we sort Jericho. I understand Prez wants to protect you, but you need to listen to big brother on this one."

Tyr stood in contempt as Frankie witnessed the color seep from B's face as she provided a firm stare.

"For how long."

"Just until I bury that prick. A week tops! And I'll need your cell phones so you can't be tracked." Painstakingly, Frankie studied her silence. "Please, B. It's hard for me to ask this of you."

B dried her hands in a hand towel, tossing it on the counter.

"You don't think Scottie can keep me safe?"

"I refuse to take that chance, B. You're my family. I just want you safe, please?"

"Are you asking or telling me?"

Frankie stared at her. "Asking out of respect and pleading with you as a brother. B, allow me to end this, knowing you and the boys are safe."

"And Scottie's okay with this?"

"Come on, B. You know I can't take this to him. I came to you first. Logic before love."

B turned to exit the kitchen.

"Where are you going?" he asked.

"To gather the boys and get packed. You can fight them for their phones, though, and mine is on the table."

Zander breathed a sigh of relief. "So, you'll let me take you somewhere safe?"

B stopped in her tracks. She didn't even look over her shoulder.

"Frankie, you've never given me a reason not to trust you. You want me in protective custody? I have no reason to doubt your reasoning."

"Mrs. Prez, I can't let Prez down again. He'll have my patch," Tyr said.

B backtracked to Tyr. The fear in his eyes showed his youth.

Placing her hands on the breasts of his cut, she looked him in the eye. "Listen, good boy. You're going to go to the club and explain I sent you upon Frankie's arrival. Just explain to Prez that Frankie is bringing me to the club later. You got that?"

"You're going to stop by the club first? Prez'll never let you out of his sight. He's just got you back," Tyr confirmed.

B smiled. "No, Tyr." She patted down his cut. "You may not understand this, but Frankie has never let me down. This is the right move."

"Let me come with you. Keep you safe?"

B kissed his cheek. "I don't want you in any more trouble, my lovely. Promise me you'll keep this a secret and allow Frankie to do this. I'll be home before you know it. Now stay safe, Good boy."

Tyr bowed his head, turning to the counter to collect his keys. He gave Frankie a nod and left via the patio doors.

Frankie turned to B. "Will he tattle?"

B shook her head.

"Adopted another lost soul, I see," he said, wrapping an arm around her.

She shrugged. "You know me, I'm a sucker for anyone who has a trauma story."

"You need to start filling your own cup, sis. Now get ready. I want us gone yesterday."

# CHAPTER FORTY-TWO

# Marshall

Frankie watched B ready herself and quash the boys' objections to leaving.

"What about Dad?" Madoc asked.

"Your father is safe. I have agents outside his home, bud, and you'll be home before you know it."

"Promise, Uncle Frankie," Rhys interjected.

"You have my word."

Frankie hit the road with urgency, wasting no time as he drove his family to safety, and two hours after hitting the road, he stopped at a supermarket, pulling into a parking spot and switching off the engine.

"Right, everyone out. We need supplies."

B, Madoc, and Rhys stared at him with raised eyebrows.

"Supplies?" B asked.

"You plan on eating while I'm gone, right?"

"Yeah, but..."

"Then get out of the bloody car and grab a shopping cart, woman," Frankie said, mimicking her accent again.

B and the boys exited the car, and Madoc and Rhys argued over the shopping cart.

"Knock it off!" Frankie shouted, stunning the boys to a stop. He'd never raised his voice at them as loud as that before.

Checking himself, he stared at their scared faces. "Sorry boys. I didn't mean to snap. It's been a hell of a day."

Madoc nodded, allowing Rhys to take the cart.

"You guys go on in and grab some snacks, whatever you want," B said, waving them into the store. "We'll be right in."

Turning to Frankie with a face like thunder and her hands on her hips, her silence needed no words.

Frankie raised his hands. "I know, I snapped. I'm sorry. It's just a lot of shit's gone down today, and I won't relax until you're safe."

B softened. "Are you okay, Frankie? I've never seen you like this."

Frankie draped his arm over her shoulder. "I'm alright. B, this is nothing I can't handle. I just want it sorted is all. Now, would you like to know about the shit storm surrounding us today?"

B shook her head, walking into the supermarket. "I've had all I can endure right now, Frankie. I'll happily listen if you need to get something off your chest. Otherwise, I'm going to pretend I'm a normal woman buying groceries on a regular trip to the store."

Frankie gestured to the fresh fruit and vegetable aisle. "Right this way, madam."

Catching up to the boys, Frankie began filling the cart with an array of different groceries. Just after the boys left to gather sweet treats, Frankie shared disturbing news.

"On top of Rosa's murder in cold blood by a Pitbull today, Mack and Tiny were shot at until the Sunnyville chapter rescued them."

B's eyes bulged from her head. Looking over her shoulder and turning back to Frankie, she whispered in anger. "What the actual fuck, Frankie?"

Frankie's sympathetic eyes shifted to her after dropping a bag of pasta into the cart. "I'm sorry, B. I just want no lies or deceit between us. Transparency is important. You are important to me, and I need you to understand why I've removed you from harm's way."

B took hold of the shopping cart, pretending to ram him. "You know, you could have led with that earlier. Crikey Moses. I'm sorry Frankie, no wonder you're on edge. How are you holding up?"

Frankie dumped two cartons of pasta into the cart. "I'll be happy when you're safe."

"Speaking of which, who the bloody hell am I staying with? Chicken, salmon, saffron, avocado oil, pasta. You're not expecting me to fix up a banquet, are you?"

Frankie smirked. "You'll see."

After paying for their groceries, Frankie hit the road again then exited off the freeway, twenty miles west of the grocery store. When they turned down a narrow and unmarked road almost covered by nature, a set of large, steel gates confronted them with perimeter signs that read: "Electric fence. Trespassers will be shot on sight."

Frankie wound down his window and punched a series of numbers into the electrical keypad attached to the gate pillar and drove through the gates as they opened. He continued down the winding, beaten track until he approached the wooden cabin.

A broad, gray-haired, white-bearded older man stood out front, armed with a shotgun as Frankie switched off the engine.

"Frankie, where the hell are we?" B demanded with concern in her tone.

"Off grid!"

"And who are we staying with?"

"The only person I trust besides you."

B's puzzled expression made Frankie smile.

"My father, Marshall. He'll Keep you safe."

"You said you had no family."

"I'm sorry. B, I promise this is the only lie, other than being FBI. My dad was CIA. He lives off the grid because hardly anyone knows he's alive. I'd like to keep it that way if that's cool?"

B sighed, pinching the bridge of her nose. "Then why did you bring me here? Why risk him, too?"

"Because it's the only place I know you'll be safe. Come on. He's looking forward to meeting you."

Frankie stepped out of the car, walking the short distance to the cabin steps. "Hello, sir," he said to Marshall, who peered down the steps at her.

Marshall placed his gun against a wooden beam holding up the porch.

"Frankie," he said before breaking out into a fit of laughter. "My boy," he said, opening his arms to him.

"Missed you, Dad," Frankie said, embracing him.

"It's been too long, son," Marshall said, giving him an encouraging slap to his back before pushing him aside. He greeted B with a warm embrace. "And you must be Blethen? Frankie has told me so much about you."

Frankie watched his father greet Madoc and Rhys as if they were his long-lost grandchildren, before ushering them inside, closing the door behind them.

"Your rooms are down the hall, second and third on the left. I hope you boys don't mind sharing?" Marshall shouted after them.

Frankie gave B an encouraging smile, gesturing toward the guestrooms.

"Thanks, Dad. I appreciate this."

Marshall brushed him off with a wave of his hand. "Don't mention it. Besides. It brought you here, didn't it?"

Frankie chuckled, the warmth in his heart returning along with the essence of home. Despite the cabin being a long way from their family home in Boston, Marshall always made Frankie feel at home.

"You keeping well?" Marshall asked.

"Uh. Yeah. You?" Frankie asked, filling a tea kettle.

Frankie retrieved some mugs from the cupboard. His father interrupted him. "I see it, you know. No wonder you're so protective of her."

"Don't know what you mean?"

"Cut the crap, son. You think I wouldn't see she's the double of your mother? She even has her mannerisms, albeit Welsh ones."

Frankie ripped the milk from the fridge, the truth unnerving him.

"I figured something caused you to break the rules. Don't get me wrong, I'm glad. You're far more human now. I always worried you'd never recover from your mother's passing, but you've grown, son."

"It's not like that, Dad. B has no idea about mom. Yeah, she helped me grieve, recover, and helped me feel whole again. She's like a sister to me, Dad, and I love those boys like they are my own."

"That I don't doubt. You get that from your mother."

"Funny. She said I got my lovingness from you."

"Is there anything I can help you with?" B interrupted.

"Nah, take a load off. Just milk, okay? I'm fresh out of sugar. Frankie's told me how you Brits take your tea." Marshall asked.

B's amused smile beamed at Frankie before turning her attention back to Marshall.

"Yes, thank you."

Frankie handed B a hot mug of tea. "How long were you standing there, stealthy?"

"Too long."

"I bet you have a lot of questions?"

B clasped her hands around her tea. "Not if you don't want to answer them."

Awkwardness crept in as Frankie sat on the leather recliner next to her, staring at his mug.

"When we first met. You freaked me right out. You looked like a younger version of my mother. I kept my distance. The hurt was too much to deal with. We'd only lost her ten months prior to my assignment in Uskiville."

"Frankie. It's okay—"

"No, B. Please let me explain," Frankie said, making eye contact.

B nodded, and Frankie continued. "Then I got to know you. You're tough like her. No fear, yet compassionate. B, you helped me heal, and while I know you're not her, you *are* like the sister I imagined I would have. The sister I wished I had. Is that weird?"

B sipped her tea. "Not at all. Frankie, I'm glad you found some comfort and peace meeting me. You'll always be a big brother to me. I love you, Boyoh."

"You can call me Dad, too, if you like," Marshall teased, attempting to make light of the conversation.

"Jeez, Dad. Eavesdrop much?"

Laughs echoed around the cabin and Frankie had never felt so relaxed, forgetting his troubles for a second until he remembered why he brought B there.

"B, you're safer here than anywhere else in the world. Sit tight. This will be over soon."

B smiled. "I trust you. The boys may never forgive you for unplugging them from the world, mind?"

"It'll do them a world of good," Marshall added. "I'll teach them to play chess."

"Careful, Dad, Rhys is a legend. I've never beaten him."

Marshall rubbed his hands together. "Oh, challenge accepted!"

B laughed, turning back to Frankie, handing him a small white envelope addressed to Zander. "I need you to give this to Scottie."

Frankie appeared unimpressed.

"He won't understand if I don't explain."

"B, please!"

B's endearing and desperate eyes pleaded with him. "I haven't revealed my location. Not that I know where we are. Please Frankie?"

Frankie frowned, taking the envelope. "Fine, and thank you for trusting me. I understand how hard that is for you."

"Not with you. Now promise me you'll stay safe."

"Promise," he said, nudging her chin while his stomach churned.

*I can't guarantee my safety, but she sure as hell will be safe here.*

Frankie's legs felt heavy as he left the house, stepping down from off the porch.

"Hey, Frankie." Marshall called.

"Yeah?"

"Your mother would be as proud of you as I am. Be safe, son."

Frankie nodded; his Adam's apple stuck in his throat. "You know what to do if anything happens?"

"Yeah, wipe them all out!"

Frankie shook his head. "Dad."

"Keep them safe. You have my word."

# CHAPTER FORTY-THREE

# The Letter

Zander tapped his fingers on the table with urgency, his patience wearing thin.

Frankie had promised to fetch B and the boys hours ago. He was unimpressed with Tyr for leaving B's side despite Frankie appearing at B's, ordering him straight out the door on surveillance duty. His knee jerked in a nervous disposition, awaiting B's arrival.

Jimmy handed him another whiskey, no doubt to calm his nerves.

"Just heard from Topher on the inside. The Pitbulls have dwindled since our cookout earlier. Turns out we took out the big guns. Only nine remain. They're holed up, squatting in a place in Kranktown. Just off Glebe Street."

"Have we got eyes on the building?" Zander asked.

"Yep! Say the word and we'll take them out."

"Not until B arrives. I want her and the laddies safe before we move."

Frankie strolled through the door, clinking his keys and the loose change in his pocket.

"About fucking time," Zander barked, rising to his feet and looking past Frankie.

Puffing out his chest, his face turned sour. "Where the fuck is she?"

"Safe!" Frankie said, as cool as a cucumber.

"What the fuck do you mean, safe? She's no' safe unless she's here with me."

Frankie retrieved the bottle of whiskey from the table, unscrewing the cap, he guzzled the golden firewater straight from the bottle.

"If we're going to do this. It has to be done right. Not with half your mind worrying about her. She's being protected and kept out of sight."

Zander shook his head, pushing past him. He paced the room with his hand clasped to his chin. "And she went willingly?"

"She did," Frankie confirmed.

Zander dropped, slumping in his Prez chair. "She still dinnae trust me to keep her safe."

"She does. This is on me. Not her. She asked me to give you this. Said you wouldn't understand unless she explained." Frankie handed Zander a small white envelope addressed to him.

Zander's trembling fingers snatched at the letter, studying it. His face crumpled in frustration.

"We'll go gear up and leave you until you're ready, man," Jimmy said, providing a sympathetic smile.

"Gear up for what?" Frankie asked, stopping Jimmy from leaving.

"We're taking out the last of the Pitbulls. We're no' waiting for them to come to us. They're squatting in a place on Glebe Street. Tyr has eyes on them."

"Oh yeah, about the bonfire. I had my superior up my ass about it. Nice job with the mounted cut, by the way."

"What did you tell him?" Zander asked, flipping the letter between his fingers.

"The Gray Wolves couldn't have done it because the Prez's wife would castrate him."

Zander raised his eyebrow, shrugging his shoulders. "She wants peace, Frankie and I'm gonnae give it to her."

"Am I not invited to the party? I want in on this. I have some hell I want to unleash, too."

"Stand down Frankie. We need you squeaky clean until Jericho is in a fucking body bag," Zander said.

Frankie huffed. "I need their cuts for Jericho's demise. At least 4 of them."

Zander and Jimmy shared glances.

"Why?" Zander asked.

"Jericho has his hearing on Friday. I'm not risking him being transferred to some nut house. He dies tomorrow."

"So why the cuts?" Zander asked again.

"All in good time. I'll head back to the precinct and get the ball rolling and Prez, don't go getting yourself killed."

Frankie turned to leave when Zander called out to him.

"Frankie?"

He turned, giving his Prez his full attention. "Just tell me she's no' in protective custody."

Frankie laughed, his head dancing as if he'd just heard the funniest joke. "I'm not stupid, Prez."

Zander exhaled a sigh of relief. "Right."

Frankie stepped forward, placing a hand on Zander's shoulder. "Believe me when I say there's no man alive who could hurt her right now, and the quicker we nail Jericho, the quicker she comes home."

He turned to Jimmy, handing Zander over. "Look after this big-hearted bastard, will you?"

"I always do, man!" Jimmy said, escorting Frankie out.

Zander stared down at the sealed envelope. Placing it face down on the table, he took out his Swiss army knife, slicing the envelope open. Unfolding the white sheet of paper, his heart sank as he read.

*Hey, hot stuff.*

*Please don't be mad.*

*I get this will make you believe I don't trust you. However, after Rosa's murder, Frankie requested we disappear until this is over.*

*Listen to me when I tell you I'm safe. Like really bloody safe. Nobody can get to me here.*

*I know we haven't had the easiest run. It's been hard, volatile, and downright fucked up. It's also been intense, fiery, passionate, and bloody wonderful. Through the thick and thin, I wouldn't change a thing because I have spent every minute loving you. Pointblank, period.*

*I have some requests, even though I have no right to ask.*

*1) Tear down the Pitbulls organization. Every fucking one needs to be un-alived, Sunshine.*

*2) Don't get arrested or your life won't be worth living upon my return.*

Zander couldn't help but chuckle as he continued to read.

*3) Make sure you and Jimmy take good care of Mackie and Frankie. Their emotions will cloud their judgment with Jericho.*

*4) Put a bullet between Jericho's eyes for me without getting yourself incarcerated. I'm so over white and gray. You have my full permission to go back into black when it comes to that sick and twisted animal.*

*5) Please don't spend a minute worrying about me. Focus and get this shit done.*

*6) Last, DON'T YOU DARE BLOODY DIE ON ME! I want to come home to you, not a corpse of the man I can't live without.*

*Now do what you do best, handsome, so, I can come home and show my appreciation by riding you like an old lady should ride her Prez.*

*See you real soon, good boy.*

*All my love*

*Welsh Cake*

*xxxx*

Zander's heart sank; his palpitations and anxiety crippling him as he hung onto her last words.

Unaware if he'd survive the journey, he kept his mind on Welsh Cake. Jericho and the Pitbulls had to meet their maker, even if Zander died making it so.

Folding up the letter, he kissed it and retrieved his wallet from his back pocket, taking one last look at the letter before placing it in his billfold.

*Fuck! I cannae wait for this to be over!*

# CHAPTER FORTY-FOUR

# B and Marshall

B watched Marshall enjoy his battle of wits with Rhys at the chess table, while Madoc Sat reading one of Marshall's World War II books. She could see the same facial expressions in Marshall as she saw in Frankie.

Marshall appeared menacing, yet his soft, husky tone was endearing.

Having another piece removed from the table, Marshall laughed. "You've got talent, young man," he said, smiling.

"He's reading your facial expressions. They are the same as Frankie's." B laughed.

"It's true. Your tells are the same," Rhys added. "Checkmate!"

Marshall studied the board. "Dang it. You got me again," he conceded. "All that brain exercise has made me hungry. I better fix us something to eat."

"Can I help?" B asked.

"Sure, you can chop some vegetables, if you don't mind?"

"Great."

Marshall gathered and washed the vegetables, placing them on a chopping board. Handing B a knife to chop them, he turned the oven on and readied an oven tray.

"So, how long since Frankie last visited?" B asked.

"He rode in drunk as a skunk after Rocky died. Didn't say much. Spent the night and left. Before that, his mother's funeral," Marshall said, placing chicken breasts on a tray.

"Oh, I'm sorry. I thought you guys were closer," B said, handing him the chopped mixed vegetables.

"Oh, we're close. We talk every day on the phone. He's just been so invested in his work. I think it helps him with the grief and guilt he still carries.

B glanced at Marshall as if to question him.

"He feels guilty about Rocky's death. Frankie was his handler. Blamed himself until he caught Jericho. Saving you was like his redemption."

B went quiet and Marshall continued. "He also feels responsible for his mother's passing," Marshall confided, adding the vegetables to the tray of chicken and seasoning them. "I was on an operation for the CIA and I was compromised. I left a message on Frankie's voicemail to protect her until back-up arrived. Only I hadn't realized he was in court that day. My wife was shot in cold blood in the middle of Main Street. Frankie blamed himself for not getting to her sooner."

B placed a compassionate hand on Marshall's big biceps.

"It was impossible for him to get there in time. Lilly died before he left the courtroom that day."

"I'm so sorry, Marshall. I really am."

Marshall continued. "No point dredging up what you can't change. Lilly and I were aware of the risks. I took four in the chest and fell off a catamaran."

B arched her eyebrows. "Bloody hell!"

Marshall stifled a laugh. "Yeah! Presumed dead. A trawler man rescued me. Somehow, I survived. The CIA gave me a new identity and discharged me. I arrived home a few weeks later and just in time for the funeral. Frankie thought he'd lost both of us. He was both pissed and relieved when I interrupted the service."

"Is that why you've remained off grid?" B asked.

"Yeah. The man responsible for Lilly's death is part of a mafia ring. The CIA tasked me to collect intel on an Italian Mob boss. I got made after getting close to him. The bastard shot me, and we believe he sent his brother, who heads his business stateside, to take a hit out on Lilly. I'm surprised they didn't make an attempt on Frankie's life, to be honest."

B gave Marshall a hug, attempting to hide her sorrow. "It must have been a challenge for both of you."

"It was. We both adored her. After her funeral, I returned home and packed up my things. I couldn't stay in the family home without her. So, I bought this old chunk of land and turned it into a fortress. I live a life of solitude now."

B pulled away, shooting him a look of disapproval.

"I'm not hiding!" he confirmed. "I just don't want Frankie to lose anyone else. He's lost enough."

"You're a good man, Marshall. I'm grateful for your help."

"Are you kidding? This is the most fun I've had in years. I can see how you've helped Frankie. He dotes on you, you know, and he's right. You're the sister he never had. You could have been our daughter. You're so much like Lilly!"

B smiled. "I hope it's not too painful having me here. I don't want to upset you."

"Oh, Sweetie. I only hold fond memories in my heart for my wife. Any similarities you have with her bring me joy. She would have smothered you with love," he beamed.

B laughed. "A bit like her son."

"About that? You two ever—"

With a slice of her hand through the air, B cut him off in disgust, cringing at the thought. "Nope! Definitely not. We were like siblings from the start; he's protective and never hesitates to call me out on anything."

"Figures. Has there been anyone else? I want him to be happy, B."

B placed the chopping board in the sink, proceeding to wash it. "He fancies the pants off, my friend. Only his attention has revolved around

Jericho for so long. He needs to put an end to this case to move forward."

"He gets that from me, I'm afraid." Marshall's tone lowered. "After Lilly died. I've always been a dog with a bone. I'm still pissed. I've never tracked down the true details surrounding her death. Apparently, nobody saw anything, so I got nothing. No leads, no case."

Madoc interrupted their conversation.

"Mum, will everyone be okay back home? I'm worried about Dad, Uncle Frankie, Uncle Mack, and Zander."

Marshall gave them some space as B ran her fingers through Madoc's thick mop of blond hair. "They're the toughest people I know, my boy. They're just taking precautions to make sure we're safe. Jericho has some awful connections, and Uncle Frankie wants to make sure they're all arrested before we return home."

"And if he can't find them?" Madoc asked with pain in his face.

"Oh, son. Your Uncle Mack is relentless, and Zander has connections to his old club."

"Because he used to be a criminal?"

B blew air out of her cheeks. "Sit, Madoc, please?" she said, gesturing to the dining table by the kitchen window.

Madoc took a seat, giving her his undivided attention.

"Zander and his club were criminals who did some regrettable things. Noah had a vision for the club to go straight. And they have been since I invested. When people have nothing, they become desperate, much like Jericho. He's lost his family and his club, and he blames Uncle Frankie and the wolves for that. Hurt people, hurt people, my boy."

"But you didn't hurt Jericho?"

"B shook her head. No, son. I didn't, but I helped Frankie catch a friend of his."

"But Uncle Frankie was just doing his job, right?"

"He was. Only Jericho is a vile type of criminal son. He's not bound by any laws of the land. Zander and the Wolves did what they needed to survive. They had nothing until Noah and I agreed on a deal to invest in their future. Whereas Jericho hurts people not just because he's hurting, but for sport, making him more dangerous than anyone."

"And that's why we're being protected by Marshall?"

B smiled, glimpsing Marshall re-setting the chess board with Rhys. "That's correct."

Madoc remained silent as B studied him, watching the cogs in his brain process and digest her half-truths. She hated lying to him, only he was too young and vulnerable to learn the whole truth.

"Can I ask you something?" B continued.

Madoc raised his innocent eyes to meet hers. "Sure."

"You and Rhys have grown close to Zander and the Wolves. What's your honest opinion of them?"

Madoc bit his top lip before answering. "Hyde and Jimmy are kind and funny. Jimmy always gives us whatever we want in the bistro. He's a feeder, like you."

"You, cheeky...." B poked him. "Go on."

"Zander always looks out for us. He helps with my math home-work because he knows you can't and even though it's so embarrass-ing, Rhys and I love that he gets all gooey-eyed with you."

B narrowed her eyes into an embarrassing smile. "Gooey-eyed?"

Madoc giggled. "Yeah, he's all like.... I love you, Welsh Cake, and smothers you with cwtches and stuff."

B burst into a fit of laughter. "And what if I like him smothering me?"

"Mum, that's gross."

"You just said you love that he gets gooey-eyed with me."

"Yeah, we love that he makes you happy, but can he tone down the smooching?" Madoc teased.

"Okay, okay. Point taken."

"I'm just kidding, Mum. If he makes you happy, then Rhys and I will just have to suck it up and grow a pair."

B tilted her head, her jaw dropped in shock. "Madoc!"

"What? I didn't swear and you say that to Uncle Mack all the time!"

"Alright, smart Alec! What about the rest of the Wolves while we're being honest?"

Madoc raised his eyebrows. "Tyr is so bad ass; he's twenty-four, has a motorcycle and belongs to a club. He acts like a big brother, wrestling and having a laugh with us."

"Yeah, I have a soft spot for Tyr, and I've enjoyed having him at the house. He's also extremely clever, son. Anything else you want to add about the rest of the wolves?"

Madoc pondered for a second. "Well, some of them are a bit mental, Mum. They don't scare us or anything, and they always ask if we're alright. It's just some of them seem like they belong in an institution."

B's laughter became so much she had tears running down her face. "You're not wrong."

"Mum." Madoc said. "What I know is... until the abduction, you seemed so happy. I know Uncle Mack and Ari didn't make you as happy as Zander does."

B took a deep breath, composing herself. "That's correct, son. I adore Uncle Mackie and I'll always have fond memories of Uskiville, but my place is in Sunnyville and I'm hoping you and Rhys feel the same, too."

"We do. We love our lives. it's just, we want you to be safe and for this to be over,"

B reached out to him, embracing him tight. "This is a tiny bump on a long and happy road, my boy. The tides will change, I promise. Now, what have I taught you?"

"What doesn't kill you makes you stronger? Right, Mum?"

"Good boy!"

Madoc and Rhys insisted on washing up after Marshall made a delicious evening meal. As B approached him in the sitting room, she observed him for a moment, not wanting to disrupt his concentration as he completed a crossword.

"Something on your mind, Blethen?" he asked, his eyes still fixed on number ten down.

"I'm sorry Marshall. If I've overstepped at all today. I meant no offense."

Marshall placed his puzzle on the nearby ottoman. "Don't be sorry. It's good to get things out in the open. How about wine on the porch? The sunset is amazing here. I'd offer you something stronger, but I've not stocked up on spirits in a while."

B gave Marshall a devious grin. "I can do one better than wine. Give me a second and I'll fetch it."

B returned from her room with a bottle of the good stuff.

"A girl after my own heart," Marshall said, retrieving two whiskey glasses from the cabinet. "Neat or on the rocks?"

"On the rocks, please," she said, handing him the bottle.

The boys disappeared into their guestroom whilst B and Marshall sat out on the porch, enjoying the golden silence between them as they watched the sunset behind a picturesque backdrop of forestry.

"Beautiful," B said.

Marshall gave her a cheeky wink. "Yeah, I know but I'm too old for you and Frankie sees you as a sister." His teasing tone and mischievous grin almost caused her to choke on her whiskey.

"I meant the view!" Her cheeks heated.

"Ha! I know you did. Sorry, I have a warped sense of humor. I don't get out much."

"No kidding."

"You want another?" he asked, shaking the ice in his empty glass. "I can't remember the last time I sat enjoying a good whiskey in lovely company."

"I'd love one. Thanks."

B continued to indulge in the view, reminiscing about having Zander's arms around her in their own haven. She missed their spot near Portland. Zander made it their special place, even though she still missed Uskiville's valleys.

B frowned. The hurt in her heart creeping up on her. She'd do anything to be in Zander's arms watching the sunset now. Her family was going to war with the devil and B was terrified she would lose someone.

"Oh, no getting sad on my watch," Marshall said, handing her another.

"Sorry," she said, checking herself and sitting up in her chair.

Marshall sat back in his own chair. "Don't go worrying about them. They're grown men and can handle that pissworm and his pack of savage dogs. Frankie will get things done. He always does."

"I know. I just hate feeling helpless."

"You're doing the one thing that keeps them concentrating on their task: staying safe."

"Marshall, aside from my boys, they're my world. All of them. They're the thorns in my side, but I love them all. Obviously, Zander owns my heart, but that doesn't mean I don't love the rest of the pack."

Marshall reached out for her hand and squeezed it. "Listen, kiddo. Soon, this will all be over and you'll forget what you're feeling now."

"Thank you."

"Anytime."

B knocked back her whiskey. "Can I ask you something?"

"Ask away."

"Would you ever consider reintegrating back into society?"

Marshall stopped short of his sip, removing the glass from his mouth. "You know, I've thought about it a million times. I just don't think I could risk Frankie losing me, too."

"Didn't the CIA give you a new identity?"

Marshall tilted his head at her with a bemused curl of his lips. "They did."

"And you went to the funeral, and nobody attempted to kill you there."

"Too many agents and cops there. They wouldn't risk it!"

"But they had the chance before you moved to the wilderness."

Marshall's dimples showed his attempt to humor her. "What are you getting at? I sense a sneakiness in your inquisitive tone, Blethen. Now, out with it!"

B wriggled in her chair. She didn't want to interfere or overstep with Marshall. It saddened her how the quirky and delightful man sat beside her lived his life in isolation.

"I'm just saying, the mafia hasn't tried to finish the job in all these years. So why not come out of hiding? I have an apartment above the bistro at the club where Frankie will stay once he's done with the bureau. You can have a proper relationship with him."

"Blethen..."

"Sorry Marshall, I know I'm overstepping, but I'll just tell you what someone told me not so long ago: this ain't living. It's a life sentence."

Marshall stared out into the distance. The awkward silence enabling B's anxiety until he spoke. "I'm not sure Frankie wants his old man hanging around his place of business. Hell, I bet you didn't even know I existed until he brought you here."

B threw her hands in the air, her blood pressure escalating, making her red in the face. "He wants to keep you safe! I get that. But what's the plan? Don't bloody die of boredom?" B pressed, unable to help herself.

Marshall frowned.

"Shit. I'm sorry! I care s—"

Marshall attempted to keep a straight face until he broke out into laughter.

"There she is!"

"Frankie told me they called you Dragon. I wondered when I'd see you shine!"

B narrowed her gaze.

"Used to getting your own way?"

"It's nothing to do with that! I care!"

"I see that!"

"Fine! I'll shut the fuck up and drink my whiskey!" she said, pouting in her chair as she scanned for the bottle to refill her glass.

Unable to find it, B watched Marshall retrieve the bottle of good stuff from the kitchen counter. Returning, he poured her a double. "Here, drink up and stop sulking."

"I'm not sulking!" she huffed.

"You look like you want to murder me."

"You'll do that to yourself if you remain here much longer. Jeez. Former CIA, I bet you traveled everywhere on assignment. Don't get me wrong. It's beautiful here if you want a holiday home. Some down time to collect yourself. How have you stayed sane, being so cooped up?"

Marshall sat on the porch steps. "I'll admit, it's no picnic. I manage though."

"Marshall. I think it's admirable, your sacrifice for Frankie, I mean. I would do anything to keep my boys safe."

"Thank you, but why do I anticipate a *but*?"

B laughed. "I'm paying you a compliment."

"Yes, and refraining from the backhanded comment."

"Not me."

"Liar!" Marshall grinned. "Blethen, thank you for making an old man smile again. Having you all here has been great, and I understand your concerns. Hell, I appreciate them. Who knows? Maybe I'll surprise you one day and visit."

B's insides warmed. She had enjoyed getting acquainted with Marshall. Finishing her drink, she stood, placing a hand on his shoulder. "Night, old man. Thank you for looking out for me. Even if I am a pushy bitch."

"You're alright, kiddo. I've missed having someone call me out on my shit! Now rest up. Busy day tomorrow."

"What do you mean?"

"You'll see!"

# CHAPTER FORTY-FIVE
## Blue Rinse!

Zander, Jimmy, and the rest of the Gray Wolves met Tyr at his surveillance spot, near the Pitbulls' hide out.

"One-hundred yards, two on watch. I'll take the back, Prez?" Tyr suggested.

"No. I will," Frankie said, appearing from nowhere.

Zander's clenched jaw and intense glare showed his disapproval. "What the fuck are you doing here?"

"I'm not sitting by anymore, Prez. My loyalty is with B and the club, and I can cover my ass with the Bureau. Besides, you need me."

"If you fucking die…"

"B will ruin you. Don't worry, I'm not planning to."

"Prick! Tyr, Eddie, Sandy, go with him. Jimmy, Sims, you're with me around front. Now, on my mark. Listen to your orders. Nobody dies today. You hear me?"

Grunts of acknowledgement echoed until Frankie attempted to lighten the mood.

"We go in, simultaneous, Sunshine." With his best impression of B, spreading an infectious spray of laughter among the wolves.

Zander nudged him. "She'll chop your balls off if she ever hears you talk like that."

Frankie scoffed. "Not mine, I'm big brother, fucking untouchable I am," he teased again before running off to get into position with his team in tow.

Zander eyeballed the Red Pitbull guarding the front of the building through his sniper scope. The area was desolate, nobody lived in close proximity. Nearby dock closures had caused the area to remain abandoned. Still, Zander was taking no chances, ensuring he attached his silencer. Frankie confirmed his state of readiness in his earpiece, and Zander signaled to Jimmy and Sims to be ready to move.

"On my count," Zander said, staring into his scope. "Three... two.... one."

Zander watched the front man drop from his headshot as Frankie confirmed they had secured the rear lookout, too.

"Move in!" he commanded, entering through the front with his team. Jimmy, Sims and Zander remained downstairs with Frankie, Tyr, Sandy and Eddie headed upstairs.

Clearing the Kitchen, Zander heard voices coming from the sitting room.

*Don't you dare bloody die on me.*

Welsh Cake's words ruminated in his head. Zander shook them out, stepping into a room where three Pitbulls sat watching football and drinking beers.

"Drop it!" Jimmy said to a bald guy, noticing them and reaching for his gun. Along with the others, the frightened-looking man dropped his gun. Jimmy stood, pointing his gun at the men, whilst Zander and Sims removed their weapons.

"Jackets, too," Zander demanded.

"I'd rather die," the bald man spat toward him.

Zander shrugged. "Fair enough," he said and shot him in the head.

The other two members scrambled out of their cuts, throwing them on the floor.

"Now, who's the fucking Prez?" Zander demanded.

"Fuck you!" a short, curly headed man snapped.

Zander shot him in the shoulder, laughing at the man is he wailed, "I'll ask again. Who the fuck is your Prez?"

"Jericho. Jericho recruited us. He said you killed his Prez and wiped out his club. Told us you were traitors," the wounded man said.

"And who's the VP? Somebody has to be leading shit on the outside."

"That's the scumbag." Frankie said, dragging a cut-less beaten man with a blue mohawk into the room. Tossing the cut at Sims for safe keeping.

"Who the fuck are you supposed to be? You look like a gone wrong downloadable character. I'm sure my stepson has kicked your ass multiple times on his gaming PC. Jeez, look at the state of you. You couldn't find your way out of a paper bag, let alone lead an MC!!"

"I'm the brains of the Pitbulls," he spat.

"That explains the sloppy approach to attacking my men. Now Mr. Fuck-up, what are your orders from Jericho?"

"I ain't telling you shit!"

Zander gave Jimmy a nod, watching him pull out a handgun, shooting the already injured Pitbull sitting on the sofa in the head.

"Uh-uh. Wrong answer," Zander said, watching the panic set in on the man's face. "Try again, asshole."

The man remained silent. "Oh, fellas, we got ourselves a real tough guy here," Zander said, placing his gun in his waistband and removing his Swiss army knife. "Perhaps it's my accent. You no' hearing me right, pal?" he asked, kneeling on the man's chest as he cut off his ear with one jagged slice.

The man squealed as Zander raised the bloody ear to his mouth.

"Can you hear me now, laddie?" he taunted.

The man nodded in desperation and wet himself as Zander peered down.

Shaking his head in disappointment, he continued, "I'll tell you something. If my VP pissed himself, I'd be ashamed to call him my brother. Now, tell me everything before I chop off the other ear and make you shat yourself."

Zander tossed his ear at him, watching the sweat filled blood pour down his face.

"I'm not the VP. H-he recruited us a few weeks ago. Paid us five G each to join him."

"Is that when you treated yourself to your blue rinse?" Zander mocked.

The Gray Wolves roared in laughter as Zander continued. "I dunno, boys. Five G to join a brotherhood. You all would have preferred that rather than prospecting, wouldn't you? Fuck my life, you've insulted every MC known to man. I should shoot you in the fucking face now."

"No. no. He only said we had to distract and kill you all, to bide time until Jericho escapes prison."

Zander cast a concerned look at his brothers. "That's it!"

"That's it. I swear."

"If you're lying?" Zander spat through gritted teeth.

"I'm not, Come on man. We were just a street gang until Sully, the VP, recruited us. We're not cut out for this, please. I need a doctor. You cut my fucking ear off!"

"What are Jericho's plans with the Pitbulls when he's out?" Frankie asked.

"To rebuild in Sunnyville." The man winced. "He says he has a club there."

"What else?" Frankie demanded.

The Gray Wolves glared at the man.

"What else?" Frankie repeated, kicking him between the legs.

"Argh! He's going to kill the woman, The English one."

Zander pulled his gun from his waist band, pointing it at him, before pulling the trigger and blowing the man's brains across the damp-ridden wall. "She's Welsh asshole."

"Feel better?" Frankie asked.

"Yeah! Nobody insults my old lady!" he said, turning to the surviving Pitbulls.

"Where's the VP and the rest of your club? Our intel said nine of you remained."

Zander turned to a mop-headed blond man. His grubby fingers twitched in his lap. "You." Zander grabbed him by his throat, lifting him up onto his feet. "You know something."

Tears ran down the man's face as he nodded.

"Talk!"

The man couldn't speak; instead, he pointed to the room's corner. Tyr followed his line of sight, stopping to glance over the sofa.

"Shit!" he gasped. "We got to go now, Prez!"

Jimmy hurried to his side, discovering a pipe bomb with less than three minutes remaining on the timer.

Zander dragged the blond guy toward the front door. "You're coming too, asshole."

They were met with heavy gunfire from Pitbulls at the front of the building as they rushed toward the door. Bullets ricocheted off the door and windows, embedding into the drywall.

"It's a fucking trap! Topher and Marcus set us up," Eddie said.

"No shit! Find us a route out," Jimmy snapped.

The Gray wolves returned fire, attempting to put some distance between them and the building.

Zander directed his attention to the blond man. "Tell me what's fucking going on. Right now!" he snarled, pressing a knife to his throat.

The man cowered. "Sully and Demon took a call from Jericho. I overheard them saying they had to tie up loose ends. Next thing I know, they've planted a bomb and threatened to kill me if I tried to leave. They took Jack with them. The others didn't have a clue. They're the ones firing at you!"

"Only three shooters?"

"Yes. Yes. Please don't kill me."

Zander grinned, pushing the man out the door, "Sorry pal. You're all going down tonight." Using him as a human shield, Zander and his men made their way outside. The man was shot in the chest and face, revealing the attackers' location to the wolves, then fell to the ground.

Diving behind a burnt-out pickup, Zander, Frankie, and Eddie continued to break away in different directions, attempting to draw fire away from Tyr, Sandy, Jimmy, and Sims.

Eddie took out one attacker whilst taking a hit to the shoulder, allowing Frankie to flank him and take out the second man.

Zander, who had already located the first shooter slipped past him, slicing his throat from behind. Dropping Sully's corpse to the concrete, he signaled to his pack. "Move!" he shouted, as the building blew up, casting rubble everywhere.

A dust cloud covered the area like thick smog.

Zander dragged himself to his feet. The blast had thrown him onto the hard concrete. His ears rang as he coughed up dusty debris and called out to Jimmy.

"I'm not dead!" Jimmy muttered to his right.

Zander rushed over to witness Jimmy emerging from the burnt-out pick-up. Blood trickled down his face from a cut on his forehead.

"You got in the car?" Zander asked.

"Underneath it. I had to think fast."

Zander embraced him, "Dinnae scare me like that. My last image was you, too close to the building."

"Oh, I can move when I want to."

"So, I see," Zander said, gripping onto his dusty shoulder in relief.

Zander and Jimmy called out to the other club members. Sandy and Frankie were dusting themselves down without a scratch, the Pitbull cuts in hand, whilst Eddie clutched his injured shoulder. Tyr had a bloodied nose and a gash in his left elbow.

"Where's Sims?" Zander asked.

Everyone glanced around with concerned expressions.

"Spread out. We gotta find him before the local PD arrives. That blast could be heard for miles," Zander said.

The men searched for Sims until Tyr called out.

"Prez, over here."

Zander and the others gathered around as Tyr ripped off his shirt to apply pressure to Sims' wounds.

"Shit, Sims!" Zander said, looking down at the lead pipe and shrapnel embedded in a barely conscious Sims' stomach. "Get him up. He needs a hospital, now!"

"We can't take him. It puts us at the scene of a crime. Can you hear the sirens?" Jimmy said.

"Yes, we can." Frankie said. "I'll say he's my informant, and he was leading me to the Pitbulls when the bomb went off on our arrival. Go now. I'll call it in. You get cleaned up and wait for my call from the hospital."

"Look after him," Zander said before they hurriedly left, casting glances at Sims.

Frankie retrieved his cell to call in the explosion, requesting immediate medical attention for Sims.

"Hang in there, brother."

# CHAPTER FORTY-SIX

Frankie gave his statement to the officers on duty in the hospital waiting room. He had contacted the club prior to his arrival, just as he said he would.

Upon arrival at the hospital, the doctors rushed Sims into surgery. He had lost consciousness in the ambulance en route to the hospital.

Within minutes, Chastity, Sims' wife, rushed in with Zander, Jimmy, and Hyde, who had remained at the club whilst the club had completed their mission to end the Pitbulls. He had patched up Eddie's shoulder before arriving at the hospital.

"What the fuck happened to our boy, cop?" Zander snarled in his best acting attempt.

Frankie stood to face Zander, staring him down. "Your boy was assisting me when a bomb went off near Kranktown docks."

Chastity, who stood nearby, slapped Frankie across the face, not recognizing him covered in dust. His hair had flattened, and he'd shaved since the last time she had seen him in the club's bar.

"My Sims is no grass. He would never betray the club."

"He wasn't. He was helping me with a lead to Jericho."

"Lies, he would have gone to his Prez, you filthy pig," Chastity said, beating his chest with her hands.

Frankie raised his eyebrow at Zander and Jimmy.

"Come here, doll face. Let's get you a coffee," Jimmy said, steering her away.

Zander continued to eye-ball Frankie, ensuring he put on a good show for the observing officers investigating the bombing.

"You all quite finished?" Frankie asked.

"Not even close," Zander growled.

The investigating officers intervened gingerly. "You should get checked out by a doctor, agent."

"Yeah, I'll do that," he said, pushing past a growling Zander.

Four hours later, the surgeon operating on Sims approached Chastity, who had fallen asleep in Jimmy's arms. He explained he had managed to remove the lead pipe and the shrapnel from his stomach, explaining how lucky he was that the pipe missed his internal organs and that Sims was being transferred to the ICU, where doctors would monitor his condition.

"Can I see him?" Chastity asked.

"Of course. He's sedated, but you can sit with him. We'll need his insurance details, too."

Chastity's face erupted in panic.

"I have them," Zander informed the surgeon. "He has it through his employment with the club."

Chastity appeared confused as the surgeon instructed a nurse to escort them to the ICU.

"Welsh Cake ensured everyone and their families had insurance when she assumed ownership. Did Sims not tell you this?"

Chastity shook her head. "I handle the bills. He's not good with that stuff."

"That makes sense. I'll forward you the details later."

The nurse stopped outside Sims' room. "A few minutes," she said, showing them in.

Sims laid still with tubes helping him to breathe. A distraught Chastity kissed her husband's head, taking his hand.

Zander stood in the doorway as Frankie approached, pinning him against the wall.

"Is he alright?" Frankie whispered.

Zander pretended to resist. "The surgery went well. He's stable but critical."

"Keep me updated. I'm heading to Uskiville to prep Mackie. He should be home by now. Keep tomorrow clear and bring your acting skills. Understood, Prez?"

"Understood," Zander said through gritted teeth.

# Back to Uskiville

Frankie pulled into Mack's drive. Both Mack and Tiny sat on the front porch drinking beer and smoking.

Stepping out of the car, he shook his head. "If B catches you smoking that shit…"

"She'll never find my stash," Tiny interrupted.

"Where is she? I've been trying her phone. Jimmy said you've taken her in."

"She's safe, and that's all you need to know."

Mack's face raged with fury. "What the feck is that supposed to mean?"

"It means she's staying hidden until we take out Jericho. Now quit smoking that shit, I need your heads clear for this."

Tiny glanced at Mack, who gave him the nod. Sulking, he stubbed out the joint.

"She better be safe, Frankie. That woman is—"

"Your whole fucking world." Frankie finished. "I get it, Mackie. Now here, try these on."

he said, tossing them each a Pitbull cut he had retrieved from his car.

"I ain't putting that shit anywhere near me," Mack said in disgust.

Frankie stamped his foot onto the porch step. "You want B safe, Mackie Boy?"

"Of course, I do."

"Then try on the fucking cut!" Frankie spat.

Mack pulled on the cut, growling as if it burned his skin. "This fecking stinks of beef, cheese, and dirty pussy," he said, retching.

"Sorry, I didn't have time to wash it in between killing the fucker wearing it and running from exploding pipe bombs."

"We heard, How's Sims doing?" Tiny asked.

"Critical but stable. I'm surprised he's alive with the damage sustained to his body." Frankie stated.

"He's tougher than he looks," Tiny said, trying to shrug into a cut two sizes too small for him. "Fuck. This is tight"

"Thought you liked tight?" Frankie teased. "Make it work. It's all we have."

Mack handed Frankie a beer. "We're all set for play time. Everything is ready to go. How's Sunnyville looking?"

Frankie took a large gulp of his beer. "Jimmy, Tyr, Sandy, and Eddie are prepped. Prez won't know until I arrive at the club to question him. He knows we're taking Jericho out, but I need this shit to be convincing and our alibis solid when shit goes down. You got yours sorted?"

"Up the creek fishing. And Tiny here is entertaining two honeys."

"Do you trust them?"

"They are lifers and desperate to become his own personal bunnies." Mack laughed.

"They'll do as they're told if anyone comes knocking," Tiny explained.

"Good. Keep your channel open. I'm heading back to the office to lay the groundwork.

Jericho is done boys. "Meeting his maker," Frankie said before guzzling the last of his beer, throwing the empty bottle at their feet. "Be on fucking time. I'm trusting you, Mackie Boy."

Morning came with nerves and anticipation looming. The blinding sun casting light into Frankie's office, waking him from his slumber. A weary-eyed Frankie rubbed his beard before leaving to grab a coffee.

"Heard you had a lucky escape. You didn't say anything about meeting an informant yesterday. Your orders were to retrieve B and get back to the office," Ray said, stopping Frankie at the refueling station.

Frankie retrieved a cup from the tray of stacked mugs, next to the coffee machine. "Yeah, sorry. I took a call. Sims informed me of the Pitbulls' location. I met him a block away. We went to check it out and, well, you know the rest."

Ray rubbed his chin with his piano fingers. "Do you think he lured you there?"

"No, Sims didn't have a clue. Fortunately, I was thrown and avoided the shrapnel, but Sims took a lot of it. Besides, his intel was good. It was their hideout."

"The coroner discovered three men were shot dead prior to the blast. You know anything about that?"

Frankie shrugged. "Yeah, we came under fire moments before the bomb went off. It's all in my report."

"So where does that leave us, agent?"

Frankie poured a mug of coffee, gesturing to his superior officer.

"No thanks."

He leaned against the counter. "Something is off with Zander. My familiarity with the club leads me to believe that Zander is connected to B's abduction. I haven't found the link yet, but I just know he's behind it, Ray."

"You said he worships her? Why backtrack now after giving me that spiel about him staying straight?" Ray's puzzled expression was undeniable.

"He worships her alright, but I've been thinking about what you said regarding the Gray Wolves. B owns all the keys to his castle. She doesn't want a one-percenter club. She's warned him about becoming black to her white, as she calls it. Zander wants the bragging rights to becoming the biggest MC in the country. He's like a dog with a bone and won't stop until he gets that. He's tried to do that the legit way, but something Sims said yesterday about making the other one-percenters fear him didn't add up. B is the only one preventing him from taking the club to the next level."

"I don't understand, Frankie."

Frankie turned, giving his most convincing stare. "Look. He'd never hurt B but scare a woman enough. Make her feel insecure and frightened. She'll turn to him for protection. In fact, she almost did before I placed her into protective custody."

"Interesting," Ray pondered. "About that. Where is she?"

"She's safe and I'm not disclosing the location. I understand that displeases you, but I don't know how deep Zander's or Jericho's' pockets are. They both have people everywhere. You could be in cahoots with either of them, for all I know."

Ray grimaced. "You're skating on thin ice, agent."

Frankie tipped his coffee cup to him. "She's our key to nailing Jericho. Her testimony will see him get the chair. I'm not letting anything jeopardize that."

"Frankie, I understand what this means to you, but you need to bring her into protective custody so we can process this correctly. Do you really want Jericho walking free on a technicality?"

Frankie sighed. "Promise me you'll keep her safe if I do."

"Don't doubt my resolve, son. I want him just as much as you."

Frankie nodded, placing his mug down on the counter. "I want a crack at Zander before I bring B in. See if I can shake something loose. I know he's hiding something. If he gets B on board, there will be no stopping the Gray Wolves. Do you want the DEA or the ATF crawling up your ass when war breaks out because of his doing?"

Ray kicked the cabinet before stepping into Frankie's personal space. "Fine. Just be careful. I don't want to find you on the precinct steps next."

Frankie gulped. The flashback to discovering Rocky on that fateful night stabbing him in the heart. "I'll head down after I've showered. I want to get what I can, ahead of Jericho's plea tomorrow."

"Come and find me as soon as you return with B. I want to question her myself."

"Understood, sir," Frankie said.

*Bait taken!*

# CHAPTER FORTY-EIGHT
## *Show Time*

Frankie parked his car outside the Gray Wolves' bistro. Picking up his burner phone, he sent a message to Mack.

*At the club. It's go time.*

Mack responded instantly.

*See you on the other side, brother.*

Frankie smiled.

*See you soon Mackie Boy, and thanks for this.*

His phone vibrated once more.

*You may be a pig, but you're still my brother, asshole.*

Frankie sent him a flipping the bird emoji, chuckling to himself as he stepped out of the car.

The parking lot bustled with gym-goers and diners. Zander, Jimmy, Eddie, and Hyde were sitting outside drinking coffee among the customers.

"What do you want, officer?" Zander said, showing his distaste for the intrusion.

"You in cuffs will do nicely," Frankie said, removing them from his belt.

Zander laughed in his chair, his sarcastic grin gleaming. "For drinking coffee?"

"How about for the abduction and the attempted murder of Blethen Jones?"

Zander's eyes became malicious, his glare frightening as onlookers gasped. "What did you say?"

Frankie stepped forward, looking down at Zander. "You heard me, Prez. I have reason to believe you orchestrated the abduction of Blethen Jones, colluding with Jericho Walters to frighten her into allowing you to become one-percenters again. I have it on good authority you're trying to take the top spot in the US hierarchy."

Zander rose in anger, flipping the table over. The fear in the air forcing customers to exit the premises in haste. "You're costing me business, pal. Now choose your next words wisely or you'll lose your tongue."

Frankie stared him down. "Alexander McGovan, I'm arresting you for conspiring to abduct and the attempted murder of Blethen Jones. You do not have to—"

"Argh! I'll fucking kill you!" The rage inside Zander erupted as he lunged for Frankie. Jimmy, Eddie, and Hyde held him back as Frankie slapped the cuffs on his wrists, whispering into his ear. "Oscar worthy, Prez."

Zander foamed at the mouth. "I'm no' acting, you prick. That was low, even for you. How fucking dare you suggest—"

"We're gonna have a chat in the bistro," Frankie interrupted, pushing him toward the entrance.

"FBI! Everyone out," Frankie snapped, sending the remaining patrons scrambling for the door.

He sat Zander down in an empty booth away from the window, placing his cell on the table as if he was ready to record him for questioning. Instead, he pressed the dial button.

"Yeah," Marshall answered.

"You in yet?"

"Almost."

"What the fuck do you mean? Almost."

"You didn't tell me how much security you installed."

"You wanted to help, old man; I wasn't gonna make it easy."

Marshall chuckled, "I'm in! The cameras are on a loop. You're free to move."

"Thanks, Dad. Is B there with you?"

Zander's expression appeared thunderstruck.

"I'm here, Frankie. Your dad has been an absolute gentleman."

Frankie smiled. "I don't doubt it. Now give this Scottish prick a pep talk so he can get going."

"Scottie?"

Zander cleared his throat. "Welsh Cake, I miss you, darling."

"Yeah, I know, handsome. End this so I can come home, please?"

Zander puffed out his chest. "Consider it done, beautiful. I'll have you home by sundown.

"Promise?"

"Aww, I promise, darling. No more drama after I end that bastard. I love you and I'll see you real soon."

Frankie uncuffed him. "Go take out Jericho. Jimmy's waiting out back."

"You're no' coming?"

"How can I? I'm here questioning you," Frankie said, as a prospect wearing a prosthetic mask of Zander's face entered.

Zander jumped. "That's just fucking creepy! I thought the Doppelgänger had returned for a second."

"Doppelgänger?" Frankie quizzed. "You can explain later. This is your stunt double. Now go on. Time is precious here."

Frankie placed the cuffs on the prospect's wrists, watching Zander leave. "These questions are rhetorical. You don't say shit, prospect. You understand?"

The prospect nodded, watching Frankie retrieve a small Dictaphone from his pocket.

"Right Dad, ready to resume," he said, preparing his phone for the interview.

A minute later, Marshall gave Frankie the go ahead to begin his line of questioning.

"This is Agent Frankie Johnson interviewing Alexander McGovan on May twelfth twenty-twenty-three. State your name for the purposes of the interview, please. He pushed the button on his Dictaphone.

"Alexander McGovan," the Dictaphone relayed.

"Where were you when Blethen Jones was abducted?"

"Here at the club." Zander's voice played again.

The prospect stared at Frankie as if he was a genius, despite Jimmy already explaining to they took the audio from old video clips from Jimmy's cell phone.

# CHAPTER FORTY-NINE

# Snipers

Zander stepped outback to discover a ladder up against the high wall of the club's perimeter.

"Over you go, man. We gotta make tracks!" Jimmy said, climbing the ladder.

Once Zander climbed over the wall, Eddie removed both ladders, while Jimmy handed Zander a Pitbull cut, balaclava and helmet. Jimmy was sitting on a bike retrieved on the day of the Pitbull burner. A sleek black and red custom-made bike awaited Zander. Both bikes had fake plates.

"Ready? We got ten minutes to get to the valley next to the high-max. That fucker meets his maker this morning. He gets his hour of solitary exercise at ten, and you're all set up to put a bullet in his head."

Zander's surprised 'kid in a sweet shop' expression made Jimmy chuckle.

"Frankie knows how much you need to be her hero. He doesn't care who does it. He just wants him dead, man."

Zander donned the cut and balaclava and climbed onto the bike, adjusting his helmet to his level of comfort. "What are we waiting for? It's a lovely day to shoot a psychopath!"

Zander and Jimmy parked at the foot of the valley, stashing their bikes and helmets in a nearby bush where Tiny had been waiting.

"What the fuck do you look like?" Jimmy teased, showing to the cut threatening to cut off Tiny's circulation.

"It was the only one Frankie had left," he moaned.

Zander and Jimmy sniggered like schoolgirls.

"Pricks!" Tiny said, pointing. "Top of the valley. I have adjusted your scope to suit you. Mack is on the end of the radio in the opposing valley. You'll need these earpieces and microphones to communicate," Tiny said, handing one to each of them.

"Mack's here?" Zander questioned.

"You didn't think you were getting all the fun, did you, Prez?" Tiny snorted. "Frankie thought you both deserved a win. Redemption with simultaneous shots from either side of the valley."

"The crime lab has their work cut out for them," Jimmy joked.

Zander growled, "The headshot is mine."

"He knows," Tiny said.

Walking up the valley with frustration eating away at him, Zander turned to Jimmy. "How long have you known about this?"

Jimmy gave him a sympathetic glance. "Frankie came to me after the T incident. He asked whether to involve you or not until it was time."

"And you kept me in the dark? What the fuck, Jimmy? I'm your brother. You're fucking Prez!"

Jimmy stopped in his tracks, panting because of his lack of fitness. "You're better when you're jacked up on adrenaline. You couldn't have acted like that if you knew, and I understand how you worry about Dragon."

Zander's palpitations returned. The sight of B's torment in his mind's eye made his heart want to leap from his chest. "There shouldn't be secrets between us. Look what happened when Noah kept us in the dark?"

Jimmy looked away. "Yeah, and the club's current standing is a reflection of keeping secrets sometimes. I get you feel betrayed, man, but this is bigger than you right now. This is your club, your woman, your family and your freedom, all at stake with one squeeze on that trigger. Now, all you gotta do is hit your target."

"Hmph. I never fucking miss," Zander said, encouraging them to continue to the top of the valley.

"Don't make today your first time. Finish him and we'll ride out. Dragon will be home by supper."

Zander peered over the brow of the valley, careful not to give away his location. Their balaclavas still concealed their identities as they got into position.

Zander sprawled uphill onto the grass in front of his sniper rifle, lining up his shot.

"Hey! Are you feckers here yet? Two minutes until he's out," Mack called out through their earpieces.

"Aye, you impatient fucker. I'm lined up. Remember to take your fucking safety off, asshole," Zander barked, Mack's voice proving enough to put him in fight-or-flight mode.

"Feck you, Jock. I'll have three in his back before you've pulled the trigger!" Mack spat back.

"Will you both shut the fuck up and concentrate?" Jimmy snapped.

"Somebody's nervous," Tiny teased from the foot of the valley.

"Fuck you, Tiny!" Jimmy barked back.

"Definitely nervous," Mack added.

"Aye," Zander said, looking through his scope.

"Fuck the lot of you! Maybe I know how cocky you dickheads are. Tease me after you've put bullets in him," Jimmy said.

"Show time," Mack said as the doors opened to the exercise yard.

"Wait until he's facing me. I wanna watch my bullet take his fucking head right off his shoulders," Zander growled.

"What are you shooting him with? A fucking rocket launcher?" Mack teased.

"I'd use my bare hands on the cunt if I could. No weapons required."

Mack became serious as Jericho walked the confines of the prison yard. "On my count. We go on three."

Zander took a deep breath. The adrenaline coursing through his brains threatening to stop his heart. Like a drug, it heightened his senses, numbing the base of his brain.

"One."

Zander took another deep breath, resetting his grip on his rifle, his trigger finger hovering over the trigger.

"Two."

Beads of sweat dripped down his forehead as he peered into his scope. His sight fixated on one thing: his target. The man who had tainted his old lady by torturing her. The man who had instilled fear into the eyes of his fiery Dragon, causing her sleepless nights. Jericho did not know his time on earth was short-lived as he waltzed around the prison yard as if it was his own personal playground.

Zander grinned. Jericho's smile was about to vanish, and he didn't see it coming.

"Three."

Zander squeezed the trigger, just as he had taught B. It took a fraction of a second to impact Jericho's forehead. The shattered expression on his face as his life ended filled Zander with satisfaction. Three more bullets struck Jericho's back in simultaneous succession, showing Mack's love for the automatic setting and his flair for overkill.

Jimmy grabbed Zander's cut. "You beautiful bastard!"

Panic swept the prison, with guards taking cover, providing the wolves time to escape. After reaching the bottom of the valley, Tiny ensured they left behind no evidence as he followed Zander and Jimmy to their bikes.

"Go!" he demanded, tossing the rifle and its stand into the van before jumping into a stolen truck and speeding in the opposite direction.

After retrieving their bikes and helmet, Zander and Jimmy pelted down to the docks wearing Pitbull jackets. They rode to the same spot where they had burnt the Pitbulls who attacked them.

Tyr greeted them with a gasoline can. He burned the cuts and bala-clavas, then torched the custom-made motorcycles with gasoline, destroying any evidence of their involvement.

The sound of sirens rallied in the distance.

"We gotta go, now!" Jimmy panicked.

Tyr drove an unmarked truck with Jimmy in the passenger seat and Zander hidden in the back. They had almost made it back to the club when they saw an entourage of emergency vehicles speeding past them.

Tyr breathed a sigh of relief before turning into the alley behind the club, where Eddie waited with the ladders. Zander and Jimmy climbed the ladder, making their way back into the bistro via the kitchen door, whilst Tyr parked out front, and Eddie took care of the ladders again.

Zander waited for Sandy to give him the all-clear to enter the bistro, enabling him to swap places with the prospect.

# CHAPTER FIFTY

# Is it Done?

"Is it done?" Frankie asked, cuffing Zander and quaffing his now scruffy, salt-and-pepper-looking hair, showing the stress endured these past few months.

"Aye, it's done," Zander said.

An elated breath escaped Frankie's lungs. "Good. Now play along. We're not home and dry yet. If I know Ray, he'll be up my ass any minute."

Frankie resumed the tape after Marshall adjusted the security footage once more, ensuring any footage appeared seamless should law enforcement intervene.

"I'll ask you again. Why did you have B abducted? What's the endgame here?"

"Fuck you, traitor!" Zander barked.

Frankie delivered a blow to his jaw. "Tell me!"

Zander laughed, spitting blood at him. "Is that all you got?"

Frankie was about to strike him again when Ray burst through the door, armed and wearing his FBI jacket.

"Frankie!"

Frankie's gaping gaze cast to his superior officer before turning to grab Zander by the scruff of his cut. "This asshole is going to talk!"

Ray grabbed him, dragging him away. "Stop! He's not our man!"

"We'll see," Frankie said, pushing past Ray to get to Zander again.

Ray blurted out the words he wanted to hear. "Jericho was shot dead at the prison thirty minutes ago. I hurried to ensure…"

Frankie allowed his gob-smacking expression to bore into his superior officer. "Ensure what, exactly?"

"You didn't take matters into your own hands."

"What! And how would I manage that? Stroll into the prison with my badge and standard issue piece? How fucking dare you? I've been wanting justice more than anyone, and now this prick is going to give it to me." He turned to Zander. "Who's your guy on the inside?"

Zander laughed. "How many times do I have to tell you? You got the wrong guy, asshole."

"For goodness' sake, Frankie! Jericho was assassinated by snipers. All the details aren't in yet, but we know two Pitbulls were seen fleeing the scene of the crime." Ray grabbed Frankie's shoulder. "I know you want him for this. I understand B is family to you, and this bastard is trying to corrupt her, but he's not your guy. The Gray Wolves aren't responsible for Jericho's murder."

Frankie stopped in his tracks as Ray continued. "Just look at them. This is beyond their mental capacity. Why do you think B owns everything? Think about it, son."

"You cheeky twat! I've got more brains in my pinky finger than you have in that fat head of yours, and let me get this straight," Zander bellowed. "You accuse me of colluding with the monster who traumatized my old lady, but he was killed by one of his own? Oh, you two pricks have sentenced yourselves to death for stealing my fucking revenge!"

"Shut the fuck up!" Frankie yelled, casting Zander an evil glare, but Zander continued.

"Fuck you! That wee cunt was mine. He was supposed to die by my hands. Find and deliver the person responsible. Otherwise, I'll take my revenge out on you two."

Frankie disgorged a river of temper, kicking a dining chair across the room. "How the fuck did this happen? This isn't fucking justice!"

"I understand your frustrations, Frankie."

"No offense Ray, but you don't understand shit! It wasn't your best friend who got murdered in cold blood, or his mother. It wasn't your sister getting abducted and tortured because you live and breathe."

"Well, B isn't your family, Frankie. This connection you have with her isn't good for your career. Look who she lays with, for goodness' sake," he said, gesturing to Zander. "Maybe it's time you come home where you belong and allow the wolves to look after her." Ray said curtly.

Frankie couldn't believe what he was hearing. "Without B, you wouldn't have had a case. I'd be still in Uskiville, wasting my time and FBI resources gathering intel. I compelled her to get Blaze to talk: to testify against Jericho, and that almost got her killed."

Ray raised his voice. "You were aware that it was part of the job! I'll let your cowboy antics slide given the circumstances, but it's time to let things go. Let her go!"

Frankie's temper boiled. Taking every ounce of his strength to keep his cool, he bit back at Ray. "B would have remained clueless and safe if I hadn't brought her in. God knows that even these pricks, as criminal as they are, tried their best to keep her from knowing anything until I intervened, and now you expect me to hang her out to dry and let the vultures get her?"

"She's expendable. Just like any informant. Jericho is dead, Blaze is dead. There's no case to answer now. Any trouble B finds herself in from here on out is her problem."

Zander got up from his chair to approach Ray. Still bound by handcuffs, the rage in his face showing his indignation as he stood an inch from Ray's. "Expendable, you say? How about I fucking make you and this traitor expendable by un-aliving you? You think these cuffs will hold me? Try me? Say it again how expendable my old lady is and see what happens."

"I-I, it's—"

Frankie grabbed Zander's arm. "Sit the fuck down!"

Zander turned, head-butting Frankie in the nose. "That's for putting her in danger, traitor, and you—" He turned to Ray. "Anything happens to my old lady from here on out. I'll hold you responsible. Now release me and get the fuck off my property. You got nothing on me because we've no' done anything!"

Frankie pinched his nose to stem the blood pouring from it, grabbing a napkin from the countertop to catch the gushing blood.

"Remove the cuffs," Ray instructed.

Frankie wiped his nose, tossing the bloodied napkin into the bin. Removing his belongings from his person, he slammed his badge and gun into Ray's chest. "Do it your fucking self. I don't work for you anymore!"

"Come now, son." Ray tried, watching him head toward the bistro's exit.

"I'm not your fucking son. You won't protect my sister; you and the bureau are dead to me."

# CHAPTER FIFTY-ONE

# The Doppelgänger

It was early evening, and the news of Jericho's demise swept through the prison.

While Topher and Marcus showered, the majority of inmates were in the mess hall.

Hearing the news about Jericho had instilled both relief and terror into the two Pitbulls, making them sick to their stomachs.

They had sworn their allegiance to the Gray Wolves, only to falter at the first test of commitment.

"Do you think they know we set them up?" Topher asked Marcus.

"Nah. Jericho wanted us on the inside, long term. He wouldn't have done us like that."

"Shh! Keep it down. Besides, it's not like we can ask him. Snipers, Topher? This has Mack and the Prez written all over it. Nobody else could have taken those shots."

"We don't know that. We don't know shit. They've kept us in the dark since they transitioned into the Gray Wolves. Prove our loyalty? Fuck them! We owe them shit for leaving us to rot!"

They fell silent, changing the subject and discussing the obscenity of their prison vocation when a tall, snake-hipped, brown-haired male in his early forties stepped in, along with two menacing, well-built characters.

The tall man, who had more tattoos than untattooed skin, took the shower closest them, minding his own business, whilst the two others, one bald stumpy man and a long- haired, bearded obese man showered next to one another near the shower's exit.

Marcus glanced at Topher. "You know who that is?"

"Should I?"

"The tall guy," he whispered. "He's the Doppelgänger, a prospect from the old days. I heard he was dead. Prez busted him up when he was the Mauler's Sergeant-at-Arms. Broke his jaw. Word is, Mauler set him up, fearing he would lose Zander if he didn't. It happened like a year before we prospected."

Panic wielded in Topher's eyes. "Why call him the Doppelgänger, and what the fuck is he doing here?"

Marcus stifled a laugh. "He's not here for us, you dumb fuck. Prez hates him because he used to look just like him, only fatter. He's lost a fair bit of weight on the inside. He died his hair and mimicked everything Prez did until one day, Prez lost his shit. Told him he was a sick, creepy cunt after he stole Prez's clothes and tried to jump into bed with Prez's latest piece of ass.

Topher's eyes went wide. "For real?"

"Truth, man. Jimmy once told me he thought Prez was the imposter, and he was the real deal. They transferred him last week. He has years left of his sentence. The word is, he found God on the inside and he's been trying to repent for his sins since he got banged up."

"Poor schmuck. Everyone needs faith in something, I suppose. It's the only thing keeping us alive in here. Pass the soap, would you?" Topher asked, extending his hand.

Ignoring the unusual circumstance, Marcus and Topher finished showering and attempted to leave, but were blocked by two men near the exit.

"Problem, jerkoff?" Marcus said, shoving the bald man. "Do you fucking know who we are?"

"Yes," said the Doppelganger in a delicate tone. "Dead men walking. Never betray a wolf!" He jabbed his shiv into Topher's neck, allowing Marcus to watch his friend die.

Panic consumed Marcus, incapacitating him. "I'm sorry! Tell Prez we had no choice. Please?"

Marcus was restrained while the Doppelgänger removed the shiv from Topher's neck and dragged it down his torso.

"I am the fucking Prez and there's always a choice!" he said, driving the shiv into his stomach. "Burn in hell," he continued, grabbing his neck and breaking it with one fatal snap.

Dragging the men into the shower, they allowed the water to run, whilst the snake-hipped man removed his shiv, washing it under the shower. He casually wrapped himself in a towel to conceal his weapon at his hip before leaving.

"You must have one hell of a reason to risk your parole, Aiden?"

The Doppelganger grinned. "I do! I was leaving for nothing. Now I have a motorcycle club, a family, and some unfinished business to go home to!"

# CHAPTER FIFTY-TWO

# Cold Steak

Jimmy brought a cold steak and a couple of beers from the fridge, joining Zander at a nearby table outside the bistro.

"Here, he's got one hell of a punch on him."

"Prick! Why do you think I head-butted him?" Zander said, unscrewing the beer cap and placing the steak onto his cheek. "He can explain it to Welsh Cake. She hates my face being messed up. I'm looking forward to watching him squirm."

"What about his nose?"

"She won't say shit about his nose. I'm the one whose face pleases her every night. If I cannae perform, he'll know about it."

"Nice touch with the threats. I thought that agent was going to crap himself, the way he ran out of the bistro," Jimmy laughed.

"He made my piss boil, talking about her like she dinnae matter. Did you see how quick he ran to his car?"

"Not so big without Frankie defending him."

Zander adjusted the steak on his face to help with his swollen eye, changing the subject. "And now we wait for confirmation."

Jimmy scratched his head. "Uh. I think it's safe to presume Jericho's dead, Prez."

"No, you fuckwit! That it's over and the Pitbulls are finished."

"Oh, they're done. I took the liberty as VP to make arrangements. No survivors were left outside, and I called in a favor inside. Got rid of Topher and Marcus. We couldn't overlook their betrayal. I hope you don't mind? You were a little busy, and I figured you wouldn't want to deal with it once Dragon arrives home."

"It was a club decision, but you made the right call. Who'd you assign? Blowbacks aren't an option here."

Jimmy grinned, appearing pleased with himself. "I called in The Doppelgänger. Topher and Marcus never saw it coming. He was before their time."

Zander dropped his bottle of beer. "You better be pulling my fucking leg, Jimmy."

"Chill, Zand. He's got years left. I told him if he helped us out, I'd talk to you about allowing him home as a new prospect if he's ever released. You know he fucking loved you until Uncle Mauler had him take the fall for that armed robbery."

"He imitated me, asshole. Right down to my boots. Why do you think I broke his jaw? That creepy cunt is dangerous. Besides, he never reached out from the inside. I think he knew Uncle Mauler stitched him up to make me stay at the club."

"Nah, he went back to church to turn his life around. His father is a pastor, you know. He's spent his years repenting for his crimes."

"That makes perfect sense. How did you get him to forgo his commitment to the church?"

"I told him our church was better!"

"And he went for that?"

"After I told him we went white and there's plenty of clean pussy. He's a good-looking fella when he's not mimicking you. Imagine not getting any for eight years? He was practically jerking off down the phone."

Zander shook his head in sheer disbelief. "Ooh, you're a cruel prick, VP. He turned his life around in prison by the sound of it. I know I despise the guy, but you should have left him be. The man has fucking mental health issues!"

"I may be cruel, but I get results!"

"Yeah, you do. Let's be clear. If he ever gets parole, he's no' coming near my club. I'm no' creeped out by much, but that guy gives me the heebie-jeebies," he said as a shiver rippled down his spine.

Jimmy belly laughed, spilling his beer all over himself. "In other news, Sims woke up this morning. Chastity has updated him and you sent a beautiful care package to the hospital. It'll be a while before he's home, though."

"Thanks Jimmy. You think of everything, don't you? Damn, we've been lucky, pal!"

"Luck has nothing to do with it and you know it! It's our brother-hood that keeps us alive!"

Zander gripped him by the collar. "Thank you, brother. This shit has been long and fucking arduous. We've hurt and some are still hurt-ing, but I'm so damn lucky to have had you by my side."

Jimmy pulled Zander into his grasp. "I love you, man. Brothers until the end."

"Fucking right, pal!"

# CHAPTER FIFTY-THREE

# Dancing Inside

Frankie stood over Jericho's corpse in the morgue with relief escaping from every fiber of his being. Jericho's stillness provided peace to the agent who'd hunted him for years.

The coroner indicated the fatal wound on what remained of his forehead. "The shot to the head was enough. Did they have to put so many in his back, making my job harder? Overkill, if you ask me."

"Or they were sending a message. Nothing says, 'don't fuck with me,' like assassinating a high-profile serial killer in a high-max prison."

"True! I can't tell you any more than you already know, agent."

"Thanks, anyway, Steve," Frankie said.

Frankie left the morgue, stepping into the cold light of day, dragging in his first refreshing breath. Filling his lungs, he could breathe for the first time since Rocky's murder. Jericho was dead, with only one job remaining.

Strolling into the precinct like the devil walking through hell, Frankie's unsavory expression appeared demonic, watching his co-workers cower and evert their eyes. Frankie could sense the disappointment they experienced for him. The man who had spent years gathering intel and tracking down his best friend's killer, only to be disarmed by the justice he deserved.

*If only they knew, I'm fucking dancing inside.*

Frankie played along, throwing his weight around by pushing past co-workers in the corridor until he reached his office, slamming the door behind him.

Stifling his laughter, he retrieved a white empty box file from his cupboard. There'd be no filing cases anymore. He cleared his desk of his framed photographs of B and the boys, along with the black-framed photograph of his father, and gathered his belongings, before turning off the light to leave.

"Please, Frankie," Ray pleaded. "I understand you're hurting. We both said things we're not proud of. Take a leave of absence, don't quit the bureau. You'll be throwing a well-decorated career away."

Frankie's stony face unnerved Ray, who took a step back.

"You may have said stuff you didn't mean, but I meant every God damn word. Years of my life gone. My best friend dead and those pricks at the high-max couldn't keep him alive for one more day?" he roared. "No, that fucker planned this! Jericho knew he would get the chair and still denied me justice! I'm done."

Ray attempted to console him, placing a hand on his shoulder. "I'll give you some time to rest and digest. You'll be back once you've calmed down."

Frankie shrugged out of his hand, walking to the exit. "That won't be necessary. I don't belong here anymore."

The office fell silent, and a cold eeriness swept through the building as they watched their hero leave for the last time. Frankie exited the building with his head held high, climbing into his car. The elation consumed him and excitement filled his soul, thinking of a new beginning with the Gray Wolves. No more hiding his authentic self. He was free to become a Gray Wolf in all its glory.

# Going Home

B watched Tiny and Mack drive down the track to Marshall's home, after Frankie swore them to secrecy regarding his father's location. They had returned to the creek when they received the all-clear from Frankie, explaining he needed them to collect B and her boys from Marshall's while he tied up loose ends back at the Bureau.

Marshall opened the gates, allowing Mack to park his truck and run straight into B's waiting arms, giving her a bear hug.

"Oh, are you okay, Dragon?" Mack asked, checking her over. "Hey boys!" he said, hugging them both.

"We're alright. Marshall has taken good care of us," B said, approaching Tiny to embrace him.

A little surprised, Tiny hesitated before hugging her back. "You've been away too long, Dragon. You've not gone soft on me, have you?" he said, kissing her forehead.

B pulled away, smiling at him. "Just showing my appreciation. I'm sure you'll piss me off before we reach Sunnyville."

Tiny bellowed a raspy chuckle.

"Are you sure you want to return to Sunnyville, Dragon?" Mack asked. "You could always return home to Uskiville?"

Marshall stepped in front of B. "Your orders are to return Blethen home. If you can't follow a simple directive, son, I'll do it my God damn self!"

B placed a hand on Marshall, stepping forward to talk to Mack.

"Mackie, Sunnyville is my home now. Uskiville holds a special place in my heart, but I'm returning to Zander and the Sunnyville Chapter. Please don't worry about me."

Mack stared at the ground. "How can I do that, given everything that's happened? I worry they can't keep you safe there and your place is in Uskiville. It should be you and I taking on the world."

B put her forehead to his. "Mackie. I love Zander. Now say the words and let me go."

"I'm scared, Dragon. We won the battle, but what if there's a full-scale war someday?"

"Then I know I have my best friends and the biggest army of wolves to keep me safe. Please Mackie, I just want to go home."

Mackie took her head in his hands, placing his forehead to hers. "You'll call me the minute that changes?"

B nodded. "Of course I will. Now stop being a pussy and take me home!"

Mack sighed. "Best friends never quit!" he said before pulling away. Wiping his nose on the back of his hand, he nodded to Tiny, who stepped onto the porch to retrieve their luggage.

"Thank you for looking after them, sir," Tiny said to Marshall.

"That's what family is for," he said, giving B a wink.

Mack held out his hand to Marshall, who hesitated to take it at first. "Thank you, sir. Your son is my brother in arms, my best friend. You should be proud of him. Nobody could have orchestrated the events of today better than him."

Marshall took his hand, shaking it. "I don't doubt it. Now get Blethen and the boys home safe. I'm counting on you and, like my son, I take fuck-ups personally."

Mack gave Marshall a nod and made way to the truck, leaving B to say her goodbyes.

B gave Marshall a long hug. "Please think about my offer.

Sunnyville is a great place to live, start living there. The club protects its own, and like it or not, you're part of it now. Besides, Frankie is tougher than he looks."

"Oh, that, I don't doubt. Now go on. Get those boys home, and you take good care of my son for me."

B nodded into her sigh. "I will. See you, Marshall."

Opening the car door, Tiny stood at the driver's side. "You good?"

B smiled. "Yes, Sunshine. Take me home."

The drive home was longer than anticipated for B, who couldn't wait to see Zander again. After dropping the boys off at their father's house, B asked Tiny to put his foot down as her impatience got the better of her.

The twenty-seven-minute journey back to the club was over-whelming due to her anxiety. Her stomach churned in anticipation.

"So, neither of you will explain what happened?" she said.

"Not our information to divulge, Dragon. We're respecting the chain of command here."

"Was anyone hurt?"

"Sims! He's alive, but in a bad way!" Tiny said.

Mack glowered at Tiny.

"What?"

"Chain of command, asshole?" Mack snapped.

Tiny snorted. "Like you've ever given a shit about that?"

"Funny, I thought your loyalties were to your Dragon. Well fuck you, Mackie! I have the right to know."

"Dragon."

"Don't 'Dragon' me. If you're too pussy to tell me. Tiny can carry on. Now I know who the real man is."

Tiny laughed. "See, Dragon understands. I'm the fucking daddy!"

Mack turned to face her, reaching around his seat to tap her knee. "You really want to fucking know? Right! A bomb detonated during the pack's attack on the Pitbulls. Sims got hurt in the explosion. They're all dead, and Zander and I took Jericho out this morning: splattered his brains and body across the prison playground. There. You fecking happy?"

B's face dropped. The shock stunned her, accounting for her loss of words as Mack continued with a stern gaze.

"Don't ever question where my loyalties lie, Dragon. They remain with you always. I'm trying to do right by Frankie and Zander for you, for feck's sake!"

B's face softened as she regained her composure. "Everyone is alive, though?"

"Yes, Dragon. Alive and accounted for," Mack snapped, sitting back in his seat.

B wrapped her arms around Mack's seat, reaching around his neck, "Thank you, Mackie."

Mack grunted into a smile. "You're welcome. Now save the questions until you see Prez."

B sat back, sighing into the familiar surroundings. The gratitude she held for those who kept her safe overwhelmed her. The thought of her loved one's placing themselves in harm's way for her burdened her soul. B would never forgive herself if Sims lost his life.

"Mackie," she whispered.

"Yes!"

Mack's impatient tone made her stomach tie in knots. "Sim's will be okay, right?"

Tiny stared at Mack.

"He'll be fine, Now stop."

"Fine. No more questions."

"No, I mean stop blaming yourself. I know where your head's at, so cut that shite out."

B went quiet.

"You are not responsible for what happened to Sims, nor anything else. You got dragged into club shite, my shite. You don't get to feel guilty about anything. Got it?"

B remained silent.

Mack climbed up onto his seat to face her once more. "Hey. I'm fecking talking to you, Dragon."

"Got it, Mackie."

"Good!"

Tiny pulled into the packed MC parking lot with swarms of bikers and their families obscuring B's view as she scanned the perimeter for Zander.

Her patience wore thin with worry consuming her, causing B to race out of the truck as soon as Tiny switched the engine off.

*Why isn't he waiting out front? Is there something Mackie isn't telling me?*

B pushed through the members attempting to greet her until she stopped short of Zander, who was exiting the club. His swollen, black eye and split lip were evidence of the battle he'd won as he stood before her.

He flashed her a smile, his deep breath of relief evident as he cleared his throat. "Hey, darling."

B pursed her lips, concealing her own relief. Stepping forward, she inspected him for injuries, ensuring he was okay.

Zander wrapped her arms around her, allowing her to soften into his embrace. "Frankie's handiwork. He had to appear convincing to the Bureau."

B swallowed hard against the lump in her throat, her face sad and remorseful.

Zander cupped her trembling face in his hands.

"I'm fine, darling. Promise."

"It's over?" she whispered.

"Aye. No more Jericho. No more Pitbulls, no more drama. Just you and me, darling."

B burst into tears. The confirmation of Jericho's demise filled her with relief.

"Come here," he said, tightening his hold on her.

B held him tight, scared to let go as he scooped her up to carry her to his room.

Setting her down on his bed, he knelt to kiss her. "God, I've missed you so much, Welsh Cake."

B batted away her tears. "Missed you, too. Did you…"

"Right between his eyes. Just like you wanted. Mack put some in his back for good measure."

"And the Pitbulls?"

"Like I said, all gone. It's over."

B pressed her mouth to his, her anxiety falling away as she parted his lips with her tongue.

Zander raked his hand through her hair, cupping the back of her neck to draw her closer, moaning into her mouth.

B removed his cut, as Zander lifted her yellow summer dress over her head, tossing it onto the hardwood floor.

"Allow me to show my appreciation to my hero," B said, unbuttoning his shirt.

"I'd like that," he said. His hands reached for her bra strap, freeing her plump breasts as B removed his shirt.

Zander's mouth traveled from her neck to her breast, sucking down onto her hard nipple. B had noticed his obsession with her breasts of late.

B whimpered, pleasure surging through her whilst she tugged on his belt buckle, freeing his erection.

Zander eased her back onto the bed, hovering over her as she gazed up at him, desperate for his touch.

He bared his teeth in a devilish smile. His hands and lips caressing her body from her collarbone to her bikini line.

B's pulse rate quickened with every stroke, every kiss as his firm hands removed her panties. Bringing his mouth to her nub, his tongue stroked the length of her entrance, inducing soft "oh," sounds.

"Christ. So wet for me. I've missed making you moan, darling."

"Scottie," she whimpered as he inserted two fingers into her.

"Oh, darling, I cannae wait to be inside you."

"Let me ride you."

Zander licked his way up to meet her gaze. "Need to feel in control again, darling?" he quizzed.

"No," she panted. "I want to thank you. Please you. Please Scottie," she begged.

Zander stopped. His astounded expression soothing her. "How can I say no to your alluring tone? I'm so happy you want to ride me without controlling me, my love. But first, I'd like another taste of you."

B nodded, unable to speak. Zander enjoyed pleasing her as much as being pleased.

"That's my woman," he whispered, nibbling on her ear, before covering every inch of her quivering body with his lips, as if to study her for the first time.

He settled between her legs once more, spreading them with his firm hands.

B arched her back, watching a familiar grin dance across his face before he stroked the length of her opening with his tongue.

Moaning into her quivering mound, vibrations careened through her sex, as he enjoyed edging her with slick blows of his delving tongue.

B cried out, unable to contain her immeasurable pleasure. Dragging her hands through his hair, B raised her hips, inviting him in further.

Zander cupped her ass with his hands. "God damn it, woman. I cannae get enough of you."

"Scottie." B twitched.

"Not yet. You save it for me," he said, watching her pant. Grinning in satisfaction, Zander blew warm air onto her nub. "Are you ready to ride me, Welsh Cake?"

B nodded in desperation. "Yes!"

Zander met her lips. "In my chair, I want to look into your eyes as you ride me," he said, taking her hand and leading her to the red leather chair in the room's corner.

He sat down, his erection standing tall, pulling her on top of him. "I've been waiting to test out the new leather," he teased, referring to the chair B had gifted him a month before her attack.

Every synapse in B's body intensified as she straddled him with urgency. His hard cock sat at her entrance as she panted through her impatience.

"Ride me slow. I want to savor this moment with you," he said, threading his fingers through her hair.

B adjusted her hips, taking an inch of him inside her, Zander's eyes fixed on hers, with his hand still grasping her hair as she consumed another inch.

Zander moaned into her breasts. "Oh, Christ. I love you, Blethen."

B's eyes widened. "Oh, God. Say it again."

"Ride me, Blethen, please," he begged.

His name on her lips heightened her senses and her excitement drove her toward her climax as she accepted his length.

Zander's hands moved to cup her breasts, his hips increasing momentum as he stretched her sex.

"Scottie," she cried, gripping onto the back of the leather armchair. The extreme sensation of fullness transcending her into a climatic shower of pleasure.

Zander bit her lip, distracting her from her impending orgasm. "Zander, when we make love. Prez when we fuck, Blethen."

B accepted his demands as he continued. "Ride me Blethen. Ride me hard and scream my name when you come."

B palmed his big, tattooed chest. Her hands grasping his pecs to steady herself as she rode him with pace.

Zander's hips matched her rhythm, his hard cock forcing her to arch her back to accept him in all his glory.

As he caressed her chest with his firm hands, Zander's tone became desperate.

"You look incredible riding my cock. I can feel how ready you are. Can you take a little more?"

"Yes." she cried, taking hold of the back of the chair, riding him hard and fast.

"Oh, Christ!"

B grabbed his head, devouring his mouth with hers, crying out into his mouth as her orgasm struck her like a freight train. She arched backwards, and her hair draped down her back as she continued screaming his name while contracting around him. His teeth on her nipples, and pulsating cock overloaded her senses as she bucked and writhed.

Zander gripped her hips, driving into her with force until his manly cries made way for his own climax. "Blethen!"

B's shattered body rode Zander through his wave of pleasure until he reached completion. She had never experienced such powerful emotional fulfillment with him.

Zander tugged her head to his, kissing her like a man possessed.

"Blethen, darling. You continue to surprise the fuck out of me. Every time with you is like the first time: fucking perfect!"

B smiled into his mouth. "I've never heard anyone say my name like you. It did things to me!"

"I'll be shouting your name day and night after this."

B recognized the heat in her face. "Maybe we should contain my name to the bedroom. We'd get nothing done if I heard it elsewhere. It drove me wild as it left your lips."

Zander laughed, "Blethen Jones. I fucking love you, I do!"

B chuckled. "Your Welsh accent is improving, Boyoh."

Zander's happiness shined from his bright eyes and curled lips. "I dinnae think I can allow you to leave. I need some time alone with you."

B stroked his face. "Fine by me, handsome."

Zander beamed, seducing her with his lips. Every kiss, creating heat between her legs.

"Oh, I've missed these perky breasts," he said before easing her off his lap and bending her over the bed to study her curves. "Oh, and that ass," he said, grabbing it.

B whimpered. His every touch created pleasure throughout every cell in her body.

Grasping her hips, Zander pushed her onto her knees.

B pressed her back against his chest as he reached around to stroke her nub. Sliding his hand down her back, he eased her onto all fours. B could feel his hard cock twitch against her. "You're hard again, already?"

"I'm making up for lost time, and now I'm gonnae show you how much I appreciate you."

# CHAPTER FIFTY-FIVE

# Frankie's Home

Frankie drove into the parking lot accompanied by a clapped-out estate car that followed.

The celebrations were well underway as he stepped out of his vehicle. "Wait here a sec," he said to the other driver before heading toward the club.

He hadn't gotten far when B came from nowhere, wrapping her arms around him.

"Hello to you, too," he said, hugging her back.

B kissed his cheek.

"What's that for?" he asked.

"For not breaking your promise. You are home now, right?"

B's smile warmed his heart. She was safe and Frankie was home to keep it that way. "Head of security at your service."

"Good. I've cleared out my room at the office. I'll stay with Scottie in the dorms at the weekend."

"You sure? You love that panic room."

"I'm sure. You can furnish it as you like, good boy."

"I may buy a new mattress."

B lugged him in the arm.

"Hey! That hurt!"

"Pussy."

Frankie dipped his head. "There's something else." Embarrassment made his cheeks flush.

"Oh?"

"I brought someone. I'm hoping it's alright if he stays. He's been isolated for too long. I have much to catch up on."

He watched B glance past him toward the car where Marshall sat, his belongings crammed into the back of the vehicle.

"Oh, my days, Marshall! Frankie, this is amazing! He can have the apartment next to Jimmy. Would that do?" she gushed.

"That would be great. Thank you, B. He'll help me with security around here. It needs an upgrade."

"Whatever you need. I'll go get your dad while you get your surprise."

Frankie raised an eyebrow. B's elated demeanor pleased him, but he hated surprises.

"Don't worry. You'll love this one," B said, directing his attention to the bistro where Tiffany stood, wearing a short, black, mini dress. Her long, thick black curls swishing over her shoulder as she waved at him.

"I've hired her to manage the front desk in the gym, whilst I put her through a hair and beauty course. Can you look after her?"

"I'll do one better. I'll make her mine tonight. She's waited long enough."

"Not without this!" Zander intervened, handing him his Sergeant at Arms cut.

"I'll get your dad," B said, leaving the men to talk.

"You ready to wear this for good?" Zander asked.

"Absolutely, Prez."

Zander helped him into his old cut, and Frankie gushed with pride.

"I've missed this," he said, examining it. "Thanks Prez, I mean it."

Zander gripped him, placing him in a bear hug. "No. Thank you, pal. You'll never know how much you've helped Blethen and me. I owe you a debt of gratitude."

Frankie smirked. "Blethen?"

"Shit! Dinnae tell her I called her that in public. We confined her name to the bedroom only, and boy, does she like her name on my lips," Zander said, shaking his head with glee.

"Jeez, Prez. Remember, B's my sister. I don't want to hear that shit, if you don't mind."

"Well, at least I can trust you not to fuck her."

Frankie felt queasy. "Please, stop talking. I'm going to my woman now." Frankie extended his hand to Zander. "Thanks, man."

"Right back at you, brother. Dinnae forget, the pack will insist on making things official. You better hit that and get some beers in you before they pounce. This pack is the toughest I've ever known. In fact, maybe wear a vest. It might save your ribs when you wrestle with Tyr. He's a young buck with plenty to prove."

Frankie chuckled. "Understood."

Frankie walked across the parking lot to Tiffany as excitement flurried within him. He'd missed their regular hook-ups in Uskiville. Tiffany had always wanted more from their relationship, only Frankie's priorities had remained elsewhere. After he had left Uskiville, they stayed in contact, but he never wanted to impose by asking her to wait for him.

"To what do I owe the pleasure?" he teased, taking her hand.

Tiffany stepped into his personal space, sliding her hand down his chest.

"Heard you were putting your cut back on."

"You waited for me, then?"

"To be honest, I'd almost given up hope until B explained you had some important business to wrap up." Tiffany laughed. "She damn near threatened me. I had no choice but to wait. That bitch is crazy when she wants to be."

Frankie removed her hand. "Don't call her that. Joking or otherwise. I've killed men for calling B less, so I'll only tell you once. You got that? I don't want a half-hearted woman who almost gave up on me. You either want me or you don't."

Frankie's harsh tone took Tiffany aback.

"Frankie, I meant nothing to it. B's my friend and for the record, I moved here to be with you. I want you."

Frankie had grown tired of games. His body wanted her as much as his mind. "Enough to allow me to make you mine tonight?"

Tiffany gasped. "You mean it?"

Frankie pulled her close, slamming her into his chest. "You're top of my priority list, honey bug. Let's escape to my office and make it off—"

Zander's roar diverted everyone's attention. "Shut the fuck up. I have something to say!"

# CHAPTER FIFTY-SIX

# Let's Fucking Party!

B stood next to Zander, admiring him as he gave his speech.

"I want to thank you all and express my gratitude for your effort these past months."

"Months? Feels like fucking years!" Jimmy teased.

"Alright, alright. What I'm trying to say is, every one of you, pack, old ladies, bunnies, everyone. You held us together through the hard fucking times and I'm proud to be your Prez."

B listened. The raw honesty in his voice touched her as he continued.

"Noah. God rest his soul, is probably dancing up there now, proud as punch. If he hadn't gained the trust of a fiery dragon, the club wouldn't have succeeded. Welsh Cake, I am honored to call you my old lady."

B blushed, aware of the eyes upon her as Zander called, "Come here, darling."

B's nerves got the better of her as she took his hand. She despised being the center of attention.

Zander gave her an encouraging smile. "Welsh Cake, we've been through a lot in a short time. Any normal person would have thrown in the towel and fucked us all off. You dinnae."

B stared at her feet, and Zander lifted her chin.

"You've been through hell because of us. You could have walked away. Instead, you embraced us when nobody would give us the time of day."

"Scottie," she whispered.

"The day of our first argument? We fell out, and I went out to buy some bedding, so everything was ready for your return from the UK. Do you remember?"

B nodded. Her words escaping her.

"Well, darling, that was the day I knew I'd spend the rest of my life with you and before I bought the bedding, I blew my savings on the engagement ring you're wearing."

B's heart pounded in her chest as she stared him down.

"Blethen Aryanwen Jones, I love you and I understand you want the perfect wedding, only I dinnae want to wait to marry you anymore. Will you do me the honor of becoming my wife in Uskiville next month?"

B choked back her tears. "I don't want to wait anymore, either. Yes! Let's do it!"

Zander kissed her lips. Smiling from ear to ear, he addressed the crowd, who had erupted in cheers of celebration. "The Sunnyville chapter will stay the weekend of the thirtieth. I've booked the place courtesy of Mack. Don't forget to confirm your places before the weekend ends. Now where's Luna?"

Hyde carried Luna through the crowd and placed her in Zander's arms.

"Hey Luna, I wanted to ask you a big favor?"

Luna's eyes sparkled. The smile on her pale face made her rosy cheeks stand out.

"I think Aunt B may need a flower girl. Do you think you could help her pick out a pretty dress and walk down the aisle with some pretty flowers?"

Luna's face lit up like a firework. "I can do that, Uncle Zandie."

Reaching into his back pocket, he retrieved a small rectangular jewelry box. "I was hoping you would say that. Here, every flower girl needs a special gift."

Setting her down, he knelt to open the box for her. Inside the box sat a delicate gold chain with a daisy pendant attached to it.

Luna beamed, smiling at her parents, as proud as punch as Zander placed it around her neck. "Thank you. Uncle Zandie. Thank you, Aunt B. I'm gonna be the bestest flower girl ever," she said, hugging them both.

Zander handed Luna back to Hyde, who thanked them, then Zander addressed the crowd once more. "Right, let's fucking party!"

Tears of joy rippled down B's face as her emotions overtook her trembling body. Zander had never looked so attractive to her as she stood, shaking her head in surprise.

He swiped away her tears with the pads of his thumbs. "They better be tears of joy."

B choked back the tears: her happiness irrefutable. "I bloody love you, good boy!"

"I bloody love you, too, good girl!"

# Epilogue
## UNSPOKEN TRUTHS

Mack and Tiny sat on the wall of the parking lot's corner smoking a joint. Mack couldn't take his eyes off B, who sat in Zander's lap. She appeared happy in Zander's arms as she laughed the night away. Occasionally, she would steal a glance toward him, smiling. He watched as she ran her fingers through her hair, tussling it into place while sipping her drink.

"That must be hard for you, watching her all loved up with him?" Tiny asked as he puffed away on his joint.

Mack sighed. "It is what it is."

"You're better off. I like Dragon, but she's nuts. Way too much woman for me."

"Ha-ha, I love her and all her crazy," Mack said, snatching the joint and dragging in the hit.

"What are you gonna do about it?"

"Nothing yet. She chose him for now. She'll come around."

Tiny shook his head. "No offense Prez, but you're deluded. She was desperate to get to him earlier."

"Maybe so, but I know she loves me, too. Even if she won't admit it to herself yet. Something changed in her at the cabin. I know it did. She'll be mine one day! I can feel it!"

Tiny chuckled, taking back the joint. "Just don't cause a war to make it happen."

"Tiny, I'd burn the world to be with her. I'll do whatever it takes to make her mine."

Stealing another glance, he found that B had disappeared from Zander's lap.

Scanning the beer garden, he wondered where she had gone until she perched herself on the wall beside him.

"What are you up to, trouble? You know that shit will mince your brain?" she teased.

"There she is. Decided to grace us with your presence, huh, Dragon?" Tiny said.

B narrowed her gaze. "What's that supposed to mean?"

"Nothing. He's winding you up?" Mack said, scowling at him.

"No, I'm not. Prez is on a pedestal over there. He didn't work alone, Dragon."

"Okay. We all know what happened and I'm grateful to you all. What is it you think I should do to show you my appreciation, Tiny?"

Tiny shook his head. "Not me, Dragon, your best friend," he said, climbing off the wall and walking away.

B sat dumbfounded until Mackie spoke.

"He's Team Mack," he joked.

"Yeah, I got that. What's this about, Mackie? You know how much I appreciate what you did for me today, right?"

Mack grabbed her knee. "Of course, I do. Forget about it, Dragon. He's winding you up."

"So we're good?"

Mack laughed. "Aren't we always? Unless I go cliff diving, that is."

B scowled.

"Easy, Dragon. Here, have a beer," he said, handing her an icy can from the cooler box.

B cracked it open, taking a large gulp.

They sat in silence as Mack caught Zander watching them. Swallowing his nerves, he turned to her, stopping her from taking another sip.

"I need to ask you something."

B pursed her lips, placing her can down next to her to provide him with her full attention.

"Okay," she said in a concerned tone.

"Tell me why you came home to Uskiville and don't give me 'that teach me to shoot bullshite.' You came home to me for a reason."

B broke her gaze, turning to face Zander.

"Don't look at him. Deep down, you returned to me knowing you wanted me to protect you. We both know it, Dragon. Something changed, and I know he doesn't make you feel whole. He'll never understand you. If you're too much for him, he can find less because I'm right here and accepting of all of you, Dragon!"

B's face saddened. "Mackie, please," she whispered.

"Dragon, we've survived so many thunderous storms. Let's not get bothered by raindrops. You owe me an explanation, at least."

B fiddled her fingers in her lap. "Mackie, my head was all over the shop..."

"But why did you leave? Did I make you uncomfortable?"

"Yes, I mean, no. Mackie. It's complicated!"

Mack reached for her hand. "Then uncomplicate it by telling me you feel nothing for me, and you'll have my blessing to marry Prez."

B's face pained. "Okay, you're right!" She inhaled a sharp breath. "You make me feel safe. When you're around, I'm fearless because I know you believe in me and would die for me."

She shook her head as her voice wobbled. "Mackie, a lot's changed and when I arrived in Uskiville, I wanted to be honest and tell you how much I—"

"Who fucking died here? You're no' upsetting my lady, are you, Irish?" Zander interrupted, appearing from nowhere.

Relief washed over B's face as she pulled her hand away.

Mack swallowed his hurt, faking a smile, jumping down off the wall. He kissed her cheek. "Why would I do that? She's my best friend, and I love her to death. I'll leave you both to it. Catch you later, love birds."

Mack walked a few steps, composing himself, before B called out. He turned to find her embracing him. "Thank you for everything. I'll never forget what you did for me today, Mackie."

Mack hugged her back, whispering in her ear. "I'll always love you, Dragon. My heart will always belong to you, even if you don't want it. It's here whenever you're ready."

"Thank you."

B kissed his cheek before stepping backward into Zander's arms.

The hurt killed him as he faked another smile. "I love you both, and I'm thrilled for you."

B and the Gray Wolves will return with

# THE RED WEDDING

Coming Soon!

www.ingramcontent.com/pod-product-compliance
Lightning Source LLC
Chambersburg PA
CBHW061650190726
48289CB00006B/1810